The Crimson Edge

The Crimson Edge

Older Women Writing

Edited by Sondra Zeidenstein

Chicory Blue Press, Goshen, Connecticut

A Crimson Edge Chapbook

Chicory Blue Press
Goshen, Connecticut 06756
© 1996 Sondra Zeidenstein. All rights reserved.
Printed in the United States of America

Book Designer: Virginia Anstett

Cover painting, *The Eclipse*, 1970, by Alma Woodsey Thomas is
reproduced by permission of National Museum of American Art,
Washington DC/Art Resource, NY. (Thomas was in her eighth
decade of life when she produced her most important works,
including *The Eclipse*.)

Library of Congress Cataloging-in-Publication Data

The crimson edge : older women writing / edited by Sondra Zeidenstein.
      p.   cm. – (A crimson edge chapbook)
    ISBN 1-887344-01-2
    1. Aged, Writings of the, American. 2. Aged women – United
States – Literary collections. 3. Aged women – United States –
Biography. 4. American literature – Women authors. I. Zeidenstein,
Sondra. II. Series.
PS508.A44C75   1996
810.8'09285 082 – dc20   95-36364
                                                     CIP

Table of Contents

Acknowledgements

Rita Kiefer

Some of these poems originally appeared in: *The Bloomsbury Review, Grolier Poetry Prize Anthology 1991, International Poetry Review, Ploughshares* and *Southern Poetry Review.*

Carrie Allen McCray

Some of these poems first appeared in *The South Carolina Collection,* an anthology of the South Carolina Writers Workshop, and in *Point,* an alternative South Carolina newspaper.

Tema Nason

"Dance Steps" appeared first in the *Brooklyn Literary Review,* Number Six (1984); "A Stranger Here, Myself" in *A Stranger Here, Myself* by Tema Nason, (Puckerbrush Press, Orono, ME) 1977; "Short Takes" in *North,* Spring, 1989, Vol. 1, #2, Bowdoin College, Brunswick, ME; "Full Moon" in *Puckerbrush Review,* Winter, 1989.

Anneliese Wagner

"God's Scout," "Salt," "Saturday," "Alchemy," "Bunker" were published in *West Branch*; "Instrument" in *Yarrow*; "A Direction in Life" in *Lullwater Review*; "Return to Heinsheim: Ancestral House" in *Prairie Schooner*; "Requiem for Oma Berta" in *Lilith.*

Sondra Zeidenstein

Some of these poems first appeared in *A Wider Giving: Women Writing after a Long Silence, Embers* and *Yellow Silk.*

Introduction

The Crimson Edge: Older Women Writing is an anthology of
fiction, memoir and poetry by seven women writers past the
age of sixty. The authors in this volume range in age from
63 to 87, their average age about 70. They come from
Connecticut, Colorado, Massachusetts, New York, Pennsylvania and South Carolina. Three of them have been writing, on and off, for much of their lives, but have made a
serious commitment to writing only after retirement or their
children were grown; the other four are, more strictly, late-
bloomers. Three of the writers have never been published in
book form. What they all have in common is accomplished,
impassioned writing on strong themes.

The subject matter of these writers includes: flight from
Nazi Germany to refugee life in the United States; an
African-American woman's experience of life in the North
and South over a period of eighty years; life in a convent
and the impetus to leave it after eighteen years; the relationship of a mother and her schizophrenic daughter; the split
psyche of a closeted lesbian; a fifty-years-long friendship
between women that had included adolescent sexual attrac-
tion; celebration of sex in a long marriage.

Of course it is not only the age of these writers or their
subject matter that attracted me, as editor, to choose to publish these works, including my own, out of hundreds of
manuscripts. What literary qualities was I looking for? From
these seven, my biases can be deduced. They include: an
authentic voice; organic and resonant shaping of material;
energy, as if the writing has been a matter of urgency;
accessibility that is not simpleness, but an expression of the
writer's imperative to be understood, to share deep feeling.
What Tema Nason says in her Afterword about what she
wants her own work to accomplish holds true for me as

editor: "There's a lot of fiction [and poetry] that's very good and very skillful, entertaining, interesting, but it doesn't move you. I want my work to move people, to touch them where they live, to connect with them."

Each author's creative writing is followed by an Afterword in which the author talks about what is currently on her mind as an artist: an examination of her path as a writer; what pressures to remain silent she's had to overcome; what remains to be done, including current obsessions; what sources and processes particular poems and stories arise from.

For example, Alvia Golden speaks of having been a closeted lesbian during her career in advertising and as a corporation executive. Though she studied for an MFA in poetry during those years, she did not make a sustainable commitment to writing until retirement, when the split she had maintained between her emotional truth and her daily professional life began to dissolve.

Rita Kiefer talks about how long she avoided writing about life in the convent where she had spent eighteen years. "My husband and friends began to ask, 'Why don't you write about the convent?' My answer, 'Oh that's all in the past.' Could anyone be that naive! When the *Sister Mailee Sequence* finally came, it was an easy labor, it slipped out fast…I felt no censors."

Estelle Leontief tells about the ways she was silenced, especially during the many years of serving others as faculty wife, and how, poignantly, the death of loved ones has stirred "an exhilarating sense of freedom" in her writing.

Carrie Allen McCray, whose commitment to writing deepened at seventy-three, with the help of younger writers, says "I feel free to write on any subject now, even subjects I may have had trouble expressing openly before." She is aware of the ways her life, as granddaughter of an ex-slave and a Confederate general, has been touched by history and that what she knows needs to be shared.

Anneliese Wagner, whose life was also influenced by powerful historical forces, didn't make poetry out of them for a long time. For one thing, she had lost all memory of her childhood in Nazi Germany. Then, for many years, she felt an unspoken prohibition against "talking about the Holocaust among relatives and friends...For decades, I didn't talk about my life as a refugee." Working on the poems collected here has been "an uncovering; it brings to light what was meant to be lost."

Tema Nason speaks about taking risks in her fiction. "I am always pushing myself for the truth, to go behind and behind what seems to be, not to mistake appearances for reality." Currently she feels compelled to probe the "sanctified" role of the mother in our society and the harm it can do, when unexamined, to mothers and daughters. She believes her generation of mothers needs to tell their stories.

I am one who has felt that bondage. "I cannot bear to part with Mother. Nor can I bear to fulfill her curse that I be silent." I speak primarily about the fierce battle I have had to engage in to unstopper my voice. "The possibility of making language my own...has come to me very late...My real struggle, I think, has been to fight off the voices in my head that want me not to say anything. Or if I must, to say it nicely."

Individually, each Afterword sheds light on the writer's creative work. Cumulatively, they reveal what these older women writers have in common: an unapologetic commitment to the authority of their work; a generous movement toward community, as part of the drive to write; and, at the same time, a wresting of herself from community, to be separate, risk-taking. The Afterwords offer connection to other artists and writers, in the way support groups or conversations with sister writers do, in a lonely, often isolated profession.

Why an anthology of women writers past sixty? For many of us, literature has been our most trustworthy mentor. We have learned about how to live our lives from novels and poems, have been stirred by literature to a deeper understanding of life. We know what a difference the increase in women's writing in the last thirty years has made in the quality of our lives, how Alice Walker, Toni Morrison, Amy Tan, Adrienne

Rich, Louise Erdrich, to name a few, have extended the territory we live in. Ironically, it is the very richness and diversity of women's writing after years of scarcity that highlight the frustrating dearth of older women writers.

I am sure I am not alone in my thirst for the work of older women writers, not necessarily for what they write *about* age in poems or stories, but because they write *from* age, with the longer, wider perspective that comes from the experience of years, along with a very deep appreciation of the present. I read whatever I can find by women in their seventies and eighties. Find me a woman writer in her nineties – I want to see through her eyes! "Do you know Florida Scott-Maxwell's journals?" I asked an older woman writer friend, about a book by an English woman in her eighties published at least ten years ago. "I've read it three times," my friend answered.

I'm not alone in looking for company, for guidance in age. When a friend's companion for life dies and he goes on trying to make a life, I watch him carefully to see how he does it. I listen closely to my friends in their eighties. But there is much we don't tell each other over coffee: about our own children in trouble, about old love affairs or love affairs of the old. A poet friend, well past menopause, sat with me over lunch recently, tired, relieved at her husband's successful surgery. "He'll recover, that's the most important thing." Then, with tears in her eyes, her hand on my arm, she tells me how terribly she felt at the possibility of his impotence from the surgery, and how she had to keep her fear to herself. She couldn't acknowledge until now, even to herself, that sadness, except…"I was wet all the time, I was overcome with longing and desire." "Write a poem about it," I say. "It will be a gift to all of us."

There are, in fact, many older women writing. I can testify to that from the number of their manuscripts I read. In print, however, their numbers are few. When I count, in an anthology, journal, issue of *Publishers Weekly* or *Poets and Writers* the older women writers, including the famous ones like Grumbach, Kumin, Sarton, Levertov, Paley, Van Duyn, Stone, Gordimer, Lessing and other dear names, I usually come up with one or two or three being published, reviewed, winning a prize. I am delighted that *No More Masks,* the revised anthology of well-published American women poets edited by Florence Howe, is a wonderful exception. Perhaps because it proceeds chronologically through this century, it includes about thirty contemporary women poets past the age of sixty.

Naturally, there is a great imbalance between numbers of people writing and numbers in print, but older women writers face particular obstacles in getting published. One barrier is that by far the majority of publishers, editors, judges and reviewers who evaluate their writing are young women and young and old men who are likely to have different visions. Another is that publishers, when investing in a new writer, often require longevity in the writing life that older women writers may not promise.

But part of the problem, I believe, lies with older women writers ourselves. From the manuscripts I read, I find that many of us, in our stories and poems, are keeping ourselves safe, holding back – that few of us are daring. I have come to think of inhibition or self-censoring as our biggest obstacle in sustaining strong writing, second only to being able to find time and courage to keep on writing when health needs of loved ones and our own become imperative.

I believe, like women I consider my mentors, including Rukeyser, Moore, Larkin, Olds, that writing what we have never dared to say, even to ourselves, finding language for the unspoken, carries an energy and freshness with it in its birthing that is compelling in itself and liberating to further strong work. I have conducted several workshops to help women writers who feel they are self-censoring in their work. I ask them to identify feelings and material, important to them as writers, that they are afraid to write from, and to look at reasons why.

What comes up clearly, in our responses, is how much of what belongs to us as older women, how much of life experienced, felt, observed, we are afraid to draw from for our fiction and poetry. Some of the subjects participants mention include: feelings of anger toward loved ones, failure in relationships, the promiscuity of sexual desire, injustice from mother, husband, daughter, institutions, experienced and never confronted. The reasons have included, over and over: I will betray my mother, husband, child; what will my community think of me; I will expose myself to others, to myself; I will be hurt. And finally, why would anyone want to hear what I have to say? It seems that we who have lived so long in compromise with community or family are not available to our writing selves as separate beings.

It is a realistic problem. But what about forty years of life in marriage, what about life as parent, grandparent, sister, friend? If experiences are not available to us, in which our mettle has been tested, our humanity, our will to survive, where our courage, lust, viciousness have been displayed, many of us will not be able to write from great depth of feeling.

Carol Gilligan and Lyn Mikel Brown write convincingly, in *Meeting at the Crossroads,* about how young girls are silenced, giving up their authentic voices as early as twelve or thirteen, to conform to what they assume is wanted of them by those with whom they seek relationships. I believe there are other such crossroads in our lives when an opportunity for authenticity, once lost, seems to be offered again – for example, times of crisis such as illness, jealousy, loss. Age, I believe, is one of the crossroads.

Obviously, there are land mines in choosing to be open to our most risky material. But as Lucille Clifton said to Bill Moyers, "You can't play it safe and make art." The rewards are significant, not only for the writer. Strong writing by older women makes the contemporary world a new and richer place, as a blaze of intense color lighting the horizon – *the crimson edge* – reconfigures the sky.

Sondra Zeidenstein

Alvia Golden

Brother-Sister Act

He looks up from the hospital bed and says, "Lee-Lee." My baby name. Way he said Lily when I was born. It's his code for, "This is about the bad old days. The days only you and I understand." Being older, he understands best.

"Lee-Lee," he says looking into a corner of the off-white ceiling.

I hate hospitals. They are supposed to be so antiseptic. Up close, they're disgusting. Filthy floors, shit sticking to the tiles and the toilet-bowls in the patients' little bathrooms, wastebaskets full of stuff you could puke at never getting emptied. Sign, "Do not enter this room without washing hands;" cleaning people swilling buckets of sour grey water under the bed. Mean places to heal, worse to die.

"Lee-Lee," he turns to face me, the little plastic things in his nostrils are almost invisible. "Our father was a psychotic."

"I'm sure you're right."

I don't argue anything psychological with Maurice. He has been seeing a therapist for almost fifty years. Since he got out of the navy. Therapists, plural. The two before this one died. Almost since the beginning, used their techniques to get into my head. I didn't know how to keep him out back then. Doesn't seem so scary now, but I want to get off the subject of Daddy. Maurice hates him and can't stop talking about how much even though Daddy's been dead two years. Which is what makes me feel so especially angry about Maurice's cancer. It could have waited.

"Don't answer so fast, Lee-Lee. Do you *know* how you tell a psychotic?"

"Tell a psychotic what?" I can't resist.

"Could you be serious?"

"Dunno," I admit. "Not that this place isn't fun, but anyway, I'm sure you know how. If you say Daddy was a psychotic…"

Maurice interrupts. "Wouldn't you like to know how yourself?"

Right there, Maurice reminds me exactly of Daddy.

"You bet! After all," I kid him, "I could be surrounded by psychotics and not even know how to tell."

Pedantic, "They have no feelings. No emotions. None at all."

"Isn't anger an emotion?"

Patient, "Yes, normally."

"Well Daddy certainly got angry."

"No," forbearing. "He pretended to get angry, but he was lying. Every emotion a psychotic displays is a lie."

"Sometimes he was funny. Can being funny be a lie?"

"With him, it was. Being funny, being charming, serious, angry, all lies. He had no emotions whatsoever. None."

"So how *will* I know a psychotic? If they can pretend emotions, how do I know they don't have them?"

Pityingly, "Because *you* can't feel them."

"Oh."

"Never mind." Now there, he's not like Daddy. Daddy never gave up, even when I cried. "Doesn't matter. How long can you stay?"

Daddy and mother used to ask that and no matter what I answered, they were annoyed that it wasn't longer. "You just got here," mother would accuse after an eight-hour shift. "Off to see your *friends*?" Daddy would squeeze his mouth, as if friends were a dirty word.

"As long as you like. Just say if you're tired."

"No, no. I'd like you to stay. I'd like to talk but I want to take a little nap. Few minutes. OK?"

I turn my chair to the window, part the curtains about six inches. Straight ahead, New Jersey. To my right, the George Washington Bridge. Maurice doesn't want to look out. He reads or plays the console TV at the foot of his bed. When he looks at the screen, he stares as if he doesn't know the language being spoken. Shame there's no VCR. Lately, he's into videos. Been renting the shelves off those places. Same way he used to eat books. Mother was proud of Maurice. "My cultural gourmand," she said.

He must have fallen asleep. His breathing is steady but wheezy. The words, "death rattle," come to mind. I don't trust myself thinking about Maurice dying. Too much like the thought I haven't been able to shake since both mother and Daddy died, "Which of us is gonna go first?" Does Maurice think about it? About his being older and all? Of course now, with the cancer...I've never been this close to feeling last. Left. Nobody to talk with about all those years. I'm doing it again, burying Maurice before his time. "Quit," I warn myself.

The sun over New Jersey enflames the high-rise apartments in Fort Lee, mines diamonds in the Hudson. A paint-by-number view. Door bangs open. The nurses are overworked, peevish.

"Mr. Conklin?" Loud.

"Yes. He's napping. Worn out from the chemotherapy."

"Mr. Conklin?" Louder. "Hold out your arm." Consults her clipboard, "Maurice? I have to take your pressure."

Maurice sighs hard, sits up. His shoulders are bony outcroppings. It's starting. I smile fast to cover any worried look he might catch. When we're alone again, he slumps back, closes his eyes.

"Lee-Lee?"

"Yes?"

"Our mother should never have had children."

I grin. "Not more than one, anyway."

"Come on, Lee-Lee, I'm not joking. She should never have had any children."

"Probably not."

"Would you like to know why?"

I nod a lie. I am here to comfort Maurice.

"Because she had no idea how to raise children. She wanted toys, not children. Her children, you and I, we were toys to her."

I don't agree and since Maurice knows I don't, why upset him by arguing?

"She was very beautiful of course – which was terribly misleading – but totally unprepared and completely disinterested."

Amazingly beautiful. Told stories about all the men who had wanted to marry her. Believable. Maurice will talk about her for a while. I can tune out. This is a new building. Ten years ago, mother died in the same hospital, different building. Daddy kept her at home for two days after the stroke. Our old family doctor, Uncle Frank, said, "Nothing can be done."

"Frank is eighty-five years old!" Maurice screamed at Daddy. "He isn't even Board Certified any more, for Christ's sake."

Daddy was very wounded by what he said Maurice was "implying by walking in and taking over. But go ahead," he said and left the bedroom. Mother was unconscious on her side of their twin beds connected to the one, big, tufted-silk headboard. Maurice called his own doctor, made Daddy bring mother here. She was in a coma for three weeks till she died. Daddy sat beside her the whole time, talking to her twelve, eighteen hours a day. Even so, he looked his usual dapper self. Manly mustache, neatly combed white hair he never lost, sun-tan, the family blue eyes that match whatever blue we wear – navy, sky, royal. Nurses said he was a saint. If anyone could talk her back, it'd be he. He charmed them. His manners were lovely.

"You want me to order some lunch?" Maurice asks.
"Up to you. Fine with me."
He phones a restaurant for take-out.
"They let you?"
"Looks like."
"Oh brave new world."
"Will you hand me the urinal and give me a minute?"

Maurice's room is on the hospital's "Star" floor – carpeting, a respectable ratio of nurses-to-patients, a famous rock star dying in the room to his left, a celebrity languishing in a coma in the one on his right. At each end of his hall, a Guernica-size window frames the city. He says it's the one thing he learned from Daddy, "Give yourself the best." He's right, in a way. It probably is the "best," for a hospital. The building where mother died has since been abandoned. Even then, the linoleum floors were rotting. Her room looked east. I drove in a couple of times to see her, but I didn't want to interrupt Daddy.

"I love you, Sheila. You know I'm here. Won't you say something to me, Sheel? Tell me you love me, Sheel."

He held her hand, kissed it. IV's swelled it so her rings had to be cut off. Wouldn't let them stop treating her, just in case.

"Don't leave me Sheila. You know I'll be lost without you. I don't even know where the dishes are. You can't leave me alone, Sheel. If you don't care for yourself, think of me. Don't do this to me, Sheel."

One day he was in the bathroom. I said goodbye to her. Told her I was sorry, that I loved her. Later, I asked the doctors, "Where is she?" They said, "Nobody knows."

I tap on Maurice's door tentatively, "You OK?"

"Thanks. C'mon in. Sit down."

He's pale, has trouble breathing. Worn out taking a leak. I wish I didn't know his future. Or could talk about it. He won't. It's like when we were little and used to say, "Mine!"

"She was infantile, but he was a pig." Maurice was the locus of their desires.

"Daddy was difficult."

"He was evil and," pause for emphasis, "he was a pig."

"And, he's dead. And, he's not coming back."

"Lee-Lee, don't you see yet," wearily, "that the damage he did lives after him?"

"I know that talking about it won't hasten its demise."

"Lee-Lee, try to understand." I'm taxing his patience. "You have to remember before you can forget. Have you and I ever discussed therapy?"

"Yes." I want to change the subject, but how if there's no future and the present is unspeakable?

"Now, Lee-Lee," I know this tape by heart, "you can't run away from facts, and the fact is, we're destroyed, you and I."

His vision of us. This tack used to be so threatening. His standard preface to probing. Did I have any idea how sadistic our childhood was? Did I remember the time Father...? The time Mother...? What *did* I remember? In response to my silence, he closes his eyes again. Is the tape running on automatic? Or is he girding? Too bad if he is, it's too late. He can't trick or torment me into telling what I know. Knew.

About Daddy, that he loved the women, maybe a little too much. About the women, how long it took me to figure out who. Then, all at once – split-second images, overheard anger, mother without her weekly bridge game – a zillion irrelevancies fell in place, made a picture. That once I saw it, it was always there for the looking.

What took me so long? What the hell was I thinking when Trudy Maxwell gave me all those beautiful presents. Fine, her best friends' daughter, but one after another silk, sterling, little bracelets and rings? Answer: I wasn't thinking. Greedily grabbing. Fair enough, I was a kid. What were they thinking? Her husband the optometrist? My mother the cuckold? Assuming Trudy was blind with desire, what about Daddy?

Can't remember them all, probably didn't know all of them. Ones that come to mind, Tami Akito, the Japanese anesthetist, Mary Rose – even then, right in the midst, Daddy made us laugh calling her an "inferior" decorator, Cee Fine the multi-married, Neetra Josephs, briefly our housekeeper, and so on and so forth he rode wielding his lance. Mother made us be nice to them. Apologized for my manners later on when I truly hated some of them. Did she know? Didn't Maurice? He was mad at Daddy. Showed it. He's the tallest member of the family. Over six foot. "Too big to discipline." They took turns threatening him. Couldn't do a thing. Let him know he wasn't meeting their goals "one little bit!" "But," as Daddy used to say, "I digress." He had certain favorite phrases like that. "But," pause, inhale cigar smoke, exhale, "I digress." Since he's so interested in "facts," the fact I'd like to know is, where was Maurice when Daddy beat me, put me in bed for five days.

Some neighbor boys tied me to a tree and pulled down my underpants. That was it but Daddy didn't believe me. They looked their fill and left me there. Didn't even unzip. I was screaming, crying. Scared to death what they were gonna do, then worse scared how I'd get loose when they went away. Next thing I remember, Daddy was beating my behind raw, his big Masonic ring gouging. Hard-on, the whole nine yards. Not that I cared. More like one of those background awarenesses that get bucked to insignificance by the foreground action – the raw rear end. Background changed places with fore, over the years. Thought I'd bury it in the rubbed-mahogany, silver-handled box with Daddy. Turns out it's a phoenix. Back then, I focused on my ass, mother cried, called the doctor. She was upset for me.

I was always a joker, ("Kid with Daddy. Go on, make him laugh."). Dr. Parmenter ("Call me Uncle Frank," squeeze cheeks, wet kiss on the mouth) looked serious wondering, "This isn't one of your jokes, is it young lady?"

Daddy, "Check if she's been raped."

Uncle Frank threw in a rectal probe for free. Mother ran out of the room. She empathized with me. Daddy watched to make sure Uncle Frank behaved. Put a dressing over the wound. Suggested I stay in bed till it healed. Queen-size four-poster that had always been mother's dream when she was a little girl. Sweet William climbing the walls. Antique wash-stand, antique music cabinet, antique chairs. My clothes stuffed onto shelves too narrow, inaccessible, chair too rick-ety, desk too fragile. But so pretty.

What was I? Nine? Ten? Not eleven. Not more than a year after we moved out of the city, where the neighborhood was changing. Like it had when we moved in. First Them, then

Us, then Them.... It couldn't have been more than a year or two after we moved to our house in the "safe" suburbs, so say I was ten, at the outside. Looking back? It's a laugh what those cream-jeaned adolescent pissants must've seen with my ten-year-old pants down. No wonder I don't remember them whacking off. Or who cut me loose. None of it. As mother always said, if I forgot, it must have been "meaningless in the great scheme of things."

The great scheme included Daddy feeling guilty as the week progressed. What a softy. Sat on the bed beside me to tell me the bad things that could have happened to me.

Did those boys touch me?

No.

Well they could have. They could have tied my legs apart and touched me there and put their fingers inside me.

But they didn't.

But they could have. And they could have touched my titties.

They didn't.

But they could have put their hands inside my shirt and touched my nipples.... Rocking back and forth on the bed then grabbing me and hugging me real tight and rocking us both back and forth faster and faster then putting my hand in his mouth and biting my fingers till I yelled. Then, "Sorry, sorry, nothing happened, Daddy loves his little girl," over his shoulder and walking out fast. Later I overhear mother ask him did he make it up with me.

"Don't you think," he says, sounding offended, "it's she who should 'make it up'," as if the words taste bad, "with me?"

Not once in all that do I remember seeing Maurice.

A male attendant backs in, pushing the door with his rump, "You the VIP steak luncheon?"

Maurice nods. I shake my head, awed. He lifts the steel covers to show me – steak, green beans, chocolate cake – same meal mother always made for him when we were kids. "Only things I can get him to eat without a fight," she used to say.

"Thought you were having trouble chewing steak these days?"

"Purely aesthetic reasons. It's better to look at than anything else on the menu. Not much appetite anyway. Want some?"

"I'm off meat. Cholesterol. Thanks anyway."

Maurice cuts a piece of steak. It's tough. I can see by how the knife rips. He starts on the beans. My food arrives. He insists on paying.

"Yee-Yee?" mouth full of double-dense chocolate fudge, his favorite.

"Mm-hm?"

Swallows, "Mind if I ask you a question?"

"Ask away."

Falls back, worn out, leaves most of his food untouched, "What do you remember about our childhood?"

"Mind if I ask you one?"

"Answer mine first," child-like.

"Not much."

"Really?" He closes his eyes.

"My turn. What do the experts say is the value of memories?"

Silence.

I was his born enemy. Spoiled it for him is his story. "It," being the first and only child. He'd had it for four years. Four years more than I. I can see his point, though. It's like what they tell you about having savings deducted from your paycheck: If you don't get it, you can't miss it. I didn't, he did. He could have made better use of it is my only cavil. All those years getting all there was, why wasn't he nicer to me? He says now I snitched on him. Likely I did, that's what kid sisters do, but that's not why. He's always been jealous of me is what I think. Not much reason to be. Not much, but some, I guess.

I had to go to private school before we moved to the suburbs. Too delicate for the roughhousing of a big city public
school. Maurice walked to PS 85 for elementary school,
PS 120 for junior high. A private car came for me. Pretty in
her nightgown, mother watched me into it from the living
room window six floors up. Always somebody to open the
apartment door to me when I came back. Early on we called
her "the maid." Later, "the housekeeper," when mother said
it wasn't polite to say maid. Daddy's family was from Missis-
sippi. Always said, "Our nigras were happier down south.
We treated them well and they knew it. They appreciated it.
Northerners are too damned mean. Wouldn't want to be
a nigra up here myself." Mother taught us not to blame the
black housekeeper first thing when something was missing.
"Chances are, you've lost it yourselves." When the neighborhood got so we had to move, "It's not about being a
bigot," Daddy said. "If Marian Anderson moved next door,
I wouldn't mind." Maurice always wanted to see where I got
something he didn't. For years he said I wasn't "too delicate." Maybe I wasn't. I don't know. Can't necessarily believe
him. We weren't friends.

Maurice coughs. Clutches his groin with one hand, grips
the crib-like rail of his bed with the other. He never says it
hurts. It hurts to see.
    "What do you remember?" He breathes in gasps, eyes
closed. As if he can't spare the energy to look out.
    "All right, let's see. I remember the apartment with the
dumb waiter we used to ride," regardless of the grease and
garbage.
    "I mean about us. Remember about us?"
    "Like I said, not much."

After I told Neetra, our housekeeper, that Maurice didn't
go to school some days, hid under the cellar door then
sneaked back in the house and spied around, Daddy sent
him to military academy. He got a uniform and a fake

wooden rifle. Must have been fourteen. Broad shoulders, brass buttons. Cap had a patent-leather visor. Came home holidays, special weekends. Like Daddy, he was attractive to girls. Dark wavy hair, big blue eyes, heavy lids made him look sexy. Pouty lips like Elvis. Never a time girls weren't giving me things for him. Man's hanky covered with lipstick kisses, "Would you tell Maurice he must have forgotten this at my house?" Sealed envelopes with upside-down stamps, SWAK in nail polish, "Oh would you mind delivering this to Maurice, please?" Scared my folks would intercept it. Couldn't tell me enough how much they liked me. Older girls I didn't have a thing to say to. Embarrassing.

"Lily, would you like to join our Club?"

In high school, "Lily, I'm putting your name up to pledge my sorority."

"You want to try out for cheerleader, Lily?"

Didn't. No thank you. Shy. Mortified. Maurice? He's angry to this day. All he can see is he got sent away because "they privileged" me. It would mean an argument if I said I envied him. New school, no problems with teachers, new friends, nobody knowing enough of your history to hurt you, away from home and always being yelled at for something, plus the uniform. I'm tall, too. For a girl. I tried on his jacket and his patent-leather, visored cap. I would have made a good cadet. Now, maybe I could. Then? Hah! Maurice hated it. Complained about the food, about how he had to make his bed a special "stupid" way, about there being no girls, teachers worse than Hitler, almost. They never believed him if he was sick, made him run "on the double" or something. Mother worried he would get a heart murmur.

Daddy said, "Give them a chance. Remember their motto, 'We build men'."

Mother said, "They're gonna run him around when he's sick, it oughta be, 'We kill boys'."

Daddy laughed and hugged her. Maurice slammed out of the living room, pushed past me so hard I banged into the bookcase, cracked my head.

Daddy laughed. "They've got a lotta construction ahead of 'em."

Mother said, "You all right sweetheart?"

Daddy scowled after Maurice, "She better be all right."

"I'm fine."

Upstairs, door slammed. Things crashed.

Mother said, "Maybe he's hurt. I'll go see."

Daddy laughed, "You go on and go. I am going for a ride." Walked to the coat closet laughing, called enticingly, "Now who's coming on a grand adventure with me?"

To get hot dogs, donuts at Daddy's favorite place where they made them while you watched. They knew Daddy there. One of those places always told me how lucky I was to have such a fine-looking Daddy, such a good Daddy buying me hot dogs and donuts. Can't begin to count the number of people who've told me how lucky I was to have Daddy for my father. "Yazzuh, sho nuff," as Daddy used to say. The three of us went. While Daddy was backing the car out of the garage, mother called up to Maurice, "I wish you would be nice to Daddy. He's doing his best for you." She felt bad for Maurice.

Home, Daddy would yell in at Maurice how he'd missed out on hot dogs and donuts. Maurice pretending to be asleep. Daddy standing outside his room shouting, "Your mother and I are going out. You want any dinner, I guess you can figure out how to get it yourself after being rude to your mother. We'll be back late. You behave yourself. You hear me, Maurice?" Making it sound like, Moe-REES. Silence. Daddy turns the door handle so quietly I can't hear it from my room just across the hall. Locked.

"If your sister tells me one thing I don't want to hear...."

It's on me to tattle.

"You hear me, Maurice?" Daddy doesn't wait. Turns away, winks at me, skip-runs downstairs.

I would like Maurice to come out. Tell me all about military academy. Show me how to do whatever he's learned to do with that fake rifle. We could march. Sing. They must have songs. In the movies, soldiers always march to something jingle-y. "Left-right-left-right left my wife and forty-eight kids by the old grey mill with the chimney sweep did I do right, right, right...." Tell me about his new friends. His dormitory. What's it like to live as if you were in a hotel every day, meals served, fresh towels, and sleep in a room with your buddies?

I tell him through the door, "They're gone."

Silence. Is he still in there or did he get out while I was reading in my room? Is he on the other side of the door hanging, dead, like in a story or is he crouching waiting for me to fall asleep so he can kill me for getting him in trouble? I decide to wait up for mother and Daddy. When I can't stay awake any longer, I get scared they will want to know why I am asleep in the living room so I go to bed.

I close my door. There's no lock or I would lock it. Daddy says I am a scaredy-cat. I open the closet door and change into my nightgown with the door between me and the window. "It's nonsense" to think anyone can see into my room through the glass curtains on my windows, mother says, and besides, "there's no one close enough to see in if they could." I want to leave the light on but Daddy says, "We are not the sole support and succor of the electric company." The sheets are freezing, but I lie flat on my back because that's how I like to sleep. One minute I have goose-bumps, the next I'm asleep.

I am awakened by the sound of my door knob turning. I don't open my eyes because I love the smell and feel of mother's fur coat when she bends over to see if I'm asleep. I wait happily for the perfume-scented fur to graze my face before mother, reassured, stands, drapes it around her and I can open my eyes in time to watch her sweep out like a queen. I wait until I think I have to move because she's taking too long. Something must have distracted her. She can't be too near because I should smell her perfume *some*, and I don't. Then, just when I'm about to open my eyes and give up and look, I feel her.

She is straightening my sheets. She usually never does this unless I'm sick and the bedclothes are all sweaty and twisted. But I can feel her hands fooling around with the sheets so I wait, eyes closed, pretending to be asleep, for my kiss. Then I feel her hand accidentally brush against my leg and I almost jump but I don't. I manage to not move at all only it's really hard to keep from giggling. Except she doesn't stop. The hand feels around as if it's trying to be sure what it has found. I sense it decide, "Yes, a leg," before it slowly wraps itself around my shin and starts to slip up my right leg – the leg nearest the door when I'm lying on my back as I am. The hand is on my thigh and I know it's not going to stop. It's going to move all the way up there. It isn't mother's hand. I want it to go away. Maybe I am dreaming it and if I wake up it will be gone. It is touching me there. I want to see who it belongs to but I am pretending to be asleep because if he thinks I am awake, he will kill me. It is a man. Touching me there. I am going to wet myself. I am going to cry. He is....

The hand is gone. My door opens and closes. I hear mother and Daddy downstairs. They sound like they always do, not upset or yelling about the stranger. That means he must still be upstairs, hiding, ready to jump out, surprise them, kill them. I roll over onto my stomach and move to the other side of the bed and pull the top sheet out of the mattress and roll myself in it. Daddy and mother are coming upstairs. I press my face into the mattress so I won't see the gun flash like it does in the Saturday movie serials. My door opens. I smell mother. She bends down but I am scrunched up on the other side of the bed. She can't find me so she turns the light on.

"Lily, what on earth have you done with yourself? Look at this bed. Is this your idea of a game?"

I pretend I am sleeping and can't hear her being annoyed with me. Then I pretend to wake up.

"I had a nightmare. I don't want you to leave me alone any-more. Please. I'm scared." I am. I start to cry and can't stop.

She sits on the bed and raises me, puts her arms around me, pressing me to her, my head against her shoulder.

"My poor baby," she croons. "Tell me your bad dream and I'll take it away with me."

"I can't," I say. "Someone was in here," I tell her. I am ashamed to say what happened. I know I should have yelled, jumped up and run away. She will be mad at me for letting him do it.

She rocks me back and forth and pats my back and soothes her hand over my hair, "Nobody's here, baby. You had a bad dream, is all."

"How do you know?" I demand still crying.

"Sweetie, the house is just the way we left it."

"Did you look?" I am frightened and angry. He'll kill them and have me all to himself as soon as they go to sleep.

"I'll go look right now, if that will make you feel better."

Mother pats me again and goes out. She thinks I'm too dumb to realize she isn't going downstairs. That I don't hear her open the door to her bedroom and say something to Daddy, or hear them both laugh. I keep my eyes wide open, this time. If he tries anything, I will see him and scream. In a few minutes, mother comes back. She has changed into her nightie and her chiffon robe. She straightens my bed, tucks the top sheet in at the bottom again, makes hospital-corners on the sides and tucks the sheet and blanket in together. She makes a big, overlapping sheet-border at the top, just the way I like it so the blanket doesn't touch me. She bends down to kiss me.

"There's nobody here, Lily. You had a bad dream. Now just close your eyes and think of sweet things and you won't have nasty dreams."

"You didn't look," I whine.

"Lily," mother is annoyed that I caught her lie, "there is nobody in this house besides Daddy and mother and you and Maurice. Now go to sleep this minute before I get angry."

"Kiss me goodnight again, please?"

"That's my best girl." Mother kisses me.

"Will you leave your door open? Just for tonight?"

"I think you're being silly, but I will. Just this one night," she warns.

I tried to stay awake and didn't realize I'd failed until the sun woke me. The house was too quiet. Maybe it was still early. On Sunday, mother and Daddy didn't come downstairs until eleven o'clock, or noon. Maurice and I were supposed to get our own breakfast, get dressed and go to Sunday School. I knew he wouldn't be up. He always waited for me to wake him at least three times. Then he'd growl and throw something at me. I didn't want to get up. Maybe they were all dead. There would be blood everywhere. I lay still. Tried to fall back to sleep so time would pass but I had to go to the bathroom. I waited until I had to go bad before I crept out of my room. Daddy and mother's door was open a crack like I had asked. I listened. I could hear Daddy's snores. Mother ordered, "An-selm, turn over," in her annoyed, half-asleep voice. They were alive. I was so happy, I started to cry and pee myself. I ran into the bathroom, locked the door, sat and thought how I didn't want to think about it. Thought how I'd known all along anyway. Wondered if mother would understand if I just said I didn't want to stay home without her.

"Lee-Lee?"

It's all I can do not to jump, I've been so far away.

"Yes?"

"Where were you?"

"I don't know. Must've drifted off. Sorry."

"So, what's going to happen to me, Lee-Lee?"

"Meaning?"

"Come on." Irritated. "Meaning do you think I'm going to die?"

"We're all…"

"No kidding?" Caustic. "Please, Lee-Lee," suppliant, "you work for a big drug company, do you know anything I don't?"

"Short and honest? No. Stuff's all departmentalized,

compartmentalized. I've never worked on an oncology product."

I've asked friends in the Company who do. They give you "nine months to five years, not discussing QOL," the quality of the rest of your life.

"Worked on psychotropics." The best lies stay closest to the truth. "You want answers from me, you have to go crazy."

"You really don't know?" Relieved.

"I could get answers if you have questions." The acid test. Will he believe I care about him and really haven't asked on my own? Yes, if he really doesn't want to know.

"Nah, I can ask the doctors."

My big brother is dying. I try it on. Nothing yet. When? With Daddy, it was never, but he was 96. By then, I was more waiting than caring, God forgive me.

"I'm gonna have to go pretty soon. Make dinner, some office stuff, early meeting, blah, blah. The usual."

"Take a taxi."

"Subway doesn't scare me, and it's the most efficient."

"Why are you so difficult? Don't you know I worry about you?" The protest lifts him onto an elbow. He's mortally-wounded fragile. Limbs too heavy to support. His head, balanced like an iron ball on the tip of Chaplin's cane, sways back and forth on his ropey neck.

"Lee-Lee? Next time, can we talk?"

"Of course."

Through the window, the nighttime Bridge reminds me of Benny Goodman's old theme song, "String of Pearls." I pull my sweater over my head, wind the scarf around my neck, hang my coat over my arm.

"I hate winter. I always feel like the Michelin Man."

"I love you," he says and is caught by a body-wracking cough.

I wait till it subsides. He's chemo-bald, ashen. My big, six-foot brother. The next cough will burst through his brittle rib cage, the stressed cables of his throat, his malignant lungs and spill his metastatic life onto the rancid-puddled floor.

"I love you, too." I kiss his cheek.

"Do you?" Urgent.

"What do you think? I'm here for the high life?"

"You really want to hear what I think?"

The door bangs open. I reflex backward in time to miss a massive shoulder thrusting into the room. "You the VIP filet mignon?"

I grin and blow a kiss on my way out. I know what he thinks. Next time, I promise myself, I will find a way to assure him it's not his fault I'm a lesbian. Maurice returns my air-kiss, smiles, his teeth huge in his diminishing face.

Acting Out

When She retires in thirty-five months, I will discover it cost me dearly to spend all these years in the closet so She could stride the corridors of corporate power respected, successful, "normal." I was so proud of our ability to perform elective schizophrenia – severing me from Her whenever it seemed safer to do so, it never occurred to me to bite the bullet and "come out." Was I afraid I might bite down too hard and blow our head off? Or was I hooked by the thought that as long as I played dead, we could play in the big league. The big bucks, league. Either way, until She retires, we will continue to coexist in one skin-suit with me admiring Her, and She feeling hopelessly distanced from, and frequently embarrassed by, me.

Today, for example, She's determinedly excising me to ensure there's no "accidental" mention of Emma – our lover of thirteen years – during Her business trip to sunny southern California. Her navy-blue garment bag sits crisply in a corner of Her office. Her navy-blue suit jacket hangs smartly over the back of Her chair. In the next room, at a desk facing Her door, Her secretary types last-minute changes to Her itinerary, and the stainless steel MOMA clock counts digitally down to the moment when a taxi will take Her to the airport. As alter-egos, it's understood that we never speak in each other's space. Insofar as it's possible, we never even think anyplace where the other's thoughts have preeminence. Only the knowledge that She's about to drag me off on another endless round of stultifying dinners, meetings, fun and games among the savage heterosexuals, emboldens me to break the rules and battle for one more pyrrhic victory.

While She fiercely focuses our right brain on business, I co-opt our left. I use it to threaten Her with remembrances of times past when the office "gang" has gone out on the town and She's been kidded into drinking, dancing and generally playing the organ grinder's monkey. I suggest irresistible alternatives, sugar-plum visions of rooms full of our truly high-powered, genuinely famous friends all of whom know we're a dyke and some of whom, yes! even some of the famous whoms, are queer themselves. I win – at least a reprieve – when She finally picks up the phone and dials Margo for me.

Our college roommate Margo is just one of our class-mates who's become famous on Broadway, in Hollywood or both. Margo's had a renaissance of her career since she maneuvered the despondent slough between leading lady and character parts, that temporal ravine where experience increases and muscle-tone doesn't.

"Hello-oh," her familiar voice sings to me.

I have a theory that actors are made by their voices. Nobody who sounds like Cleveland on a dull day has a shot in hell at stardom. Margo's a perfect example. Even saying 'Hello' she sounds like what she plays – warm, maternal, funny, nice. I can almost see her twinkling green eyes and mop of red curls, dyed to their original color. Over the years, Margo's loaded more than a few extra pounds onto her modest five feet three inch frame but hell, if it works don't fix it, and the added bulk gives her a comfy, everybody's-fantasy-mom look that casting directors love.

"Hey, hi, Margo!" Getting her in person flusters me into overdrive and I'm rattling a mile a minute. "It's me. Andy. How the hell are you? God, you sound great! I loved you in *Good Girls Don't Cry*. How's Tim? How're your kids? Are you working?"

She's laughing. In character. It's cozy and chuckley.

"So, nu?" She was our *ur*-WASP in the old days; now all my famous friends talk Yiddish. "What's all the excitement?"

I tell her I'm under a four-day corporate sentence and beg, unabashedly, for a commutation if, by any wild chance, she's going to be free.

No, she's doing "a thing at the Taper, Too" but it closes

on Friday and she'd "be really offended" if I didn't stay with them.

There were twenty-six of us at graduation forty years ago, all madly in love with ourselves and each other. The passion has never abated. "A useless degree," my mother warned. Bachelor of Fine Arts in Acting? When all the world's a stage? Say not so, my Lady Mother.

Margo's enthusiasm shifts into high-gear. "Your visit'll be the perfect excuse for a reunion. I can't wait!"

A reunion! The sugar-plums are ripening already. My head fills with visions of peasants – Synge's Irish and Chekhov's Russian, of Shavian sophisticates, of twenty-six characters in search of a future, my nascently famous classmates. I haven't seen most of them since we flung our mortar boards heavenward. I can't wait, too.

"Fantastic! Tell me how I can help. I'll call, write, whatever...." Margo is laughing again.

"Down, girl. All you have to do is show up. Everyone'll be thrilled to see you. Is Emma coming?"

I let Her answer that one. She used to be what's called a "practiced" liar. She's graduated to "accomplished." She glibly delivers Her usual story – about how Emma's schedule at the University makes it impossible for her to get away at this time. Margo doesn't know any better so she accepts the explanation and sends affectionate greetings to Emma. I do know better.

"One of these days," I warn Her, "I'll tell them the truth."

Not only that Emma'd love to come along if that weren't considered a world-class CLM, career limiting move, by you know who. But also about how She'll end up sitting in some deluxe hotel room with king-sized beds feeling sorry for Herself, or calling Emma to tell her wistfully – gag me with a garden hose – how sad it is not to be able to share the experiences She's having.

Marina del Rey is Her kind of town. For four days, She attends meetings in basement-level rooms the Company favors to help minimize the danger of diversion. Four evenings, She dresses in corporate drag to eat bad dinners in tourist-trap restaurants sitting too long over too much bad wine. When they get drunk, the guys cry on Her shoulder about their unfaithful wives, their unmotivated kids, their "plateau'd" careers. She worries every moment that one of them will make a pass at Her. Usually, they close the restaurants, and return to the hotel reluctantly. As a result, She calls Emma so late they're both semi-comatose, and She puts herself to sleep by jerking off to some of my better fantasies. This is my chance to see the late-night girlie movies Emma refuses to pay for at home, but naturally Miss Corporate-America is afraid somebody in accounting will see the bill when She puts in Her expense account and demand to know what movie She watched. So we unwind to one of my good old, never fail, Lady Cop reveries. Bad as they are, they're too good for Her but I need my beauty rest, so She gets a free pass.

After four dank underground days, She tells her crowd that She's using some of her vacation days, and, "Free at last!" gives me the keys to Her rented car. I jump into the hot-pink shorts, the "A-woman-without-a-man-is-like-a-fish-without-a-bicycle" T-shirt, and the Reeboks She's had crushed in the bottom of Her dress bag, toss Her navy-blue world in the trunk, and follow Margo's directions towards the hidden hideaways of the am's and the would-be's.

I read the scrap of paper, Route 1 towards Santa Monica, and try to remember who I've seen when. My ill-starred wedding. Three days after graduation, three years before Phil and I split, five years before I discovered – admitted? – I was hanging around queers out of interest, not liberalism. East on Route 10. Jesus, it really has been almost forty years since I've seen most of them. At the wedding. Those dresses! Of course, I've talked almost nonstop with Margo across the years, and I've slunk backstage at several Broadway shows, scared, but always very handsomely received. North on 405 to Route 101.

I can tell I've reached wealth-world when the drought-dead grass metamorphoses into shimmering emerald lawns whose discreet little signs don't have names, only warnings. From here, it's ten minutes to Malibu where Margo, in character bless her, greets me with motherly warmth.

We hug and "How are you?" while we schlep my bags inside. Margo's home is impressive. It's a Frank Lloyd Wright knock-off. Or maybe it isn't. Wood, glass, vast open stone fireplaces – an organic unit that she's decorated in glowing colors of sunrise and sunset. Margo installs us in a princessly chamber. In shades of blue – "To match your eyes," Margo compliments – complete with a view of the glistening, pacific Pacific.

"Do you want to rest before lunch?" Margo offers.

"I want to move in. I'll trade you even up for my two-bedroom apartment overlooking a dumpster in beautiful downtown Baltimore. But you'd better act fast. This offer is for a limited time only. My lifetime."

It doesn't take long to get accustomed to luxury. By the time Margo's aide-de-cuisine serves us lunch under the aqua umbrella beside the azure pool, I feel pretty certain I was born to this and rudely switched at birth. We eat California food, sprouts piled on a variety of green leaves enlivened by the ubiquitous sun-dried tomatoes. We drink Perrier with a slice of lime and, for dessert, the aide presents a platter of artistically arranged orange slices.

While we "take lunch" poolside, She answers Margo's polite inquiries about Her brilliant career. When it's my turn, I ask about the juicy stuff.

Margo dishes the inside trash on the stars she's worked with. Like any good actor, she's a sincere flatterer but her true metier is slash and burn. I'm drooling over her every word when she suddenly changes the subject.

"Did I mention that the reunion's been moved to Dannie's?" That's Dannielle Dickart, our famous producer classmate with the castle in Beverly Hills. "I was all set to have it here," she waves a hand airily to indicate about four million dollars worth of flower-beds, shrubs, blooming trees and subtle, solar-activated footlights blooming along the paths. "But Dannie thought it'd be easier for everyone to get to her place, so that's what we decided."

I figure the moral of that story is, a producer ranks an actor no matter how long they've known each other.

"Of course," Margo reassures me, "I'm still providing the food."

Of course. Even I know what producers produce. And it ain't dinner. I ask about the only item unaccounted for, the guest list.

"You will love it," Margo trills, "l-o-v-e, love it. I still can't believe everyone's free and in town. Listen – Ray Stein and Paul Peters..."

She's named two of the most talented boys in our class. Ray was a wizard with costumes, Paul a genius designing sets. It seemed only fitting that they were lovers. Cooing and collaborating from freshman orientation right on through the senior play which they set and costumed. I've been seeing their names on Broadway shows, TV specials and movies for decades. "My world, my world," I sing happily in my head.

"...and their wives. I called...."

"Can you believe they're still married? I mean, to women?"

Pay no attention to that sudden increase in background noise, it's only Her. "Leave it alone!" She's hissing.

"I don't know," Margo's thoughtful, "in some ways, you're the odd one out. Most people did it like Paul and Ray. Ye olde marriage de convenience – Lenny, Danny, Larry, Kit, Kate, Kim.... Only you, Dick Daring, felt the need to send out birth announcements."

Before She can unleash the howl She's been stifling, I tell Margo, "Hey, except for you guys, I'm so deep in the closet I'm screwing with moths."

Still, the news about Ray and Paul – given today's more permissive etc., given the accepting world of theater etc. – is unsettling. With all their success and money, Damn! how I wish they'd had the courage. When She hears it, She immediately starts to review the contents of the navy-blue garment bag with a view to proposing some "traditional" dress options for tonight's party.

I'm wondering if I want to hear the rest of the guest list when the matter gets mooted by Tim's arrival. The few remaining afternoon hours are devoted to his business interests and a long boring dialogue in which She shines by displaying Her knowledge of the American healthcare crisis.

I barely have time to zip into my jumpsuit and apply purple eyeshadow, someone once told me I looked like Elizabeth Taylor, before we're piling food into the Jag and leather-scentedly drifting towards Bethlehem.

Half an hour later, we pull 'round the circular drive to the broad stairs leading up to Dannie's immense front door. I look up to find her looking down. Forty years older but easily identifiable as the same short, wide, sandy-haired, shrewd-eyed, smart-mouth I envied every day of the two years we were roommates 'til she dropped out of school and into the brave new world of television. I'm so outrageously happy to see her I forgive her for using my soap, my towels, my dungarees, my toothpaste. For losing my pearl brooch. For being smarter. I'm delighted we're both still alive, still holding each other's memories in our still sentient brains.

"Dannie!" I yell, bolting up the stairs, tears threatening to bolt down my face.

"Andy!" she holds out her arms. Then we're hugging and she's hissing in my ear, "You asshole, if you were going to be queer, why'd you wait 'til you graduated?" Then she somehow manages to bite a chunk out of my earlobe without eating half of Emma's real lapis, "they do great things for your eyes," real gold earrings.

Naturally, I'm titillated, but lady-in-blue is having an anxiety attack. It commences with a wild-eyed, though covert canvass of the crowd to discover if anyone's seen Dannie hit on me, continues with a series of warnings about not making a fool of myself and culminates in a high-handed reminder about the importance of Her reputation. It's all too familiar to bother getting into. Anyway, I have some concerns of my own. Dannie might be a fun-night-stand, but it's a lesbian article of faith, straight women are trouble! Besides, I've given all that up for Lent, or rather, for Emma.

So I'm just as pleased that Dannie's turned to the driveway again and is holding out her seigniorial arms to another classmate I haven't seen in forty years, Mick Wicks. *The* Mick Wicks, special material writer to the mega-stars. He's on first note basis with Streisand and Midler, Grey and Crystal, you name 'em Mick's written music and lyrics for them.

Mick walks upstairs at a leisurely pace. I get time to note that he still has a beard and hair, but they're both chalk-white. When he reaches us, he kisses the air beside Dannie's cheek and grabs me in a bear hug.

"You haven't changed, Andy, you look great."

"You have, Mick, you look even better than I remember, and I'm remembering the good old days."

"Let's cut to the chase," Mick rivets me with steel-blue eyes. "Who're you voting for?" Mick will turn out to be the only one of our famous friends to mention the imminent national election, though I figure it'll be the topic of the night, and She's prepared a disquisition on the subject. Mick escorts me into Dannie's where most of my classmates are already involved in serious conversation – eyebrows, hands, arms, heads bobbing and waving emphatically. I'm surrounded by a roomful of furniture, rugs, paintings, pots, baskets, chandeliers, that are gems of southwestern American art. I'm staring at everyone and everything when I hear a duet howl of my name.

"Andy!" It's Ray Stein and Paul Peters, together again. Ray is, as usual, doing the screaming. "My God! You look gorgeous, you bitch!"

"Pay him no mind," Paul soothes. "He's jealous of every pound you haven't gained. You look wonderful."

I'm positively thrilled to discover nothing's really changed. Except Ray's bigger. Even his expensively-tailored suit cannot entirely compensate for the increased girth around the middle of his six-three frame. And Paul's smaller, an effect that may be increased by his casual, almost boyish jeans and turtleneck outfit. Ray is shamelessly direct and in fine voice.

"So, where is she you devil-woman?" he thunders. "Produce her or I'll put you down as merely another crass opportunist."

It's not surprising that Ray's performance trips Her alarm, but it's sad that She hears only the noise, not his words. Because the fact is, Ray believes what he says, that Queer is an enviable state, a desirable country whose gates must be guarded against false claims of citizenship. She'd like him to pipe down. I'd like him to be King.

"Emma's at home, she's a real worker, not like you para-sites on the body politic. And not to change the subject, did I really hear you have four kids, Paul?"

The mini-man smiles impishly and raises his eyebrows in mock amazement. "They're even mine," then soberly, "I think."

Ray gestures the topic aside. "Later," he announces imperiously. "First tell me one fascinating thing about your life. Mine is dazzling. We," he throws a massive armlock around Paul's shoulders, "spend it travelling around the world teaching the indigenes the art of theatrical costuming and scenic design. Japan, China, the bloody East Bloc. You should have seen our "Butterfly" in China. They loved it. They despise the Japanese so utterly. Paul's sets were lah-vish, darling, lah-vish!

"In the bleeding ruins of Mogadishu we mounted *The Iceman Cometh,* there wasn't a dry eye in the house. Even I wept. I shame myself in the telling but it's true. Despite the fact that I couldn't understand a word they were saying. Paul's sets were merely a miracle. He didn't have a piece of canvas or wood to work with. The boy quite simply wrought a miracle."

The grappled "boy" listens with a beatific smile. Doubt-less, he learned decades ago not to try to interrupt the maestro under full canvas.

"And, of course, they demand we return every year to,"

his tone drips revulsion, "Atlantic City to do the Miss Trans-
vestite Contest. One cannot even see the beach for the
beer bottles," he shudders. "How you can live your beloved
little life back there, among 'les fauves,' is beyond me."
He pauses dramatically, then demands, "Is that all you have
to say for yourself, you ageless creature, you?"

"That's barely the beginning," I laugh and they do too.
But they're spared the details by Dannie who's bearing down
on us signalling me enthusiastically.

"I'd say you haven't changed," Dannie announces, "but
you have. You look pretty fucking good for an old bag." She
waves a hand in front of herself in a head-to-toe motion.
"This is the result of beating the system at its own game.
There isn't another woman my age in this whole fucking
town who's got the power I have." She pauses while her
expression changes from fierce pride to resignation. "But it
doesn't come cheap." Again she waves her hand from head
to toe. "Ravaged!"

"A little rumpled maybe, but ravaged?" I demur.

"Lie down with mother-fuckers," Dannie announces,
"wake up with flab."

I know enough about flab. "What are you working on?"

Dannie's black eyes light. She launches and it's wonderful. Starting anecdotally, she's a positive Baedeker to the
niceties, and not-so-niceties of the more nuanced areas of
Hollywood bloodletting. For example, according to Dannie,
whose name goes where in a movie's credits is second only
to the seating plan for the Last Supper. Imperceptibly, she
slides into a rote recitation of her own credits. An "and then
I produced…" list of her feature films.

I notice that the more bored I am with Dannie's self-
aggrandizement, the more alluring it is to my corporate
shade. She understands the uses of catalogues. In Her world,
assessments are made and rewards are assigned on the
basis of lists like Dannie's. "Producer" is the kind of hard-
currency title She feels comfortable with. I can't let that go
by unchallenged.

"I remember a phone conversation we had just before you left New York," I remind Dannie. "You thought you were too old to make it out here. That must seem pretty funny to you now."

Dannie shakes her head. "I remember, all right. That was before I realized what a break it was to be a short, dumpy forty-year-old. Almost as good as being a short, dumpy sixty-year-old. There's no limit to how far being nobody's competition will take a girl, provided she has a modicum of talent and a couple brain cells."

I make the usual reassuring noises – "oh no," "c'mon," but Dannie ignores me.

"It was pretty fucking lonely at first. You know how guys are. Even Quasimodo wanted a bimbo. The first coupla years, I could've won Olympic gold in bed-diving. Then I almost got lucky. I fell in love. Isn't it amazing," she demands, "how we thought we knew so much about love? And we didn't know shit?"

"It was true for me," I confirm. "I put a lot of miles on that word before Emma defined it."

Now She's overtly annoyed, wants to know why I always have to drag my personal life into these conversations?

Meanwhile, Dannie is shaking her head. "You sure fooled the hell out of everyone. You were a fucking Rotcy queen. Married. Three kids. When'd you turn queer?"

What a memory. I'd completely forgotten about the R.O.T.C.

"I don't think I turned. I think I always was. Didn't seem like a smart thing to be. I figured I could act my way through a marriage, but Phil was an asshole."

She'd like me to be more politic. No need to say anything unpleasant about Phil. After all, these are straight women. I tell Her they're, for Christ's sake, my friends.

Dannie shrugs. "You were the only one who didn't seem to know what a stinker Phil was. We all thought you were nuts to go through with that wedding your mother created. Speaking of which, do you remember us as bridesmaids in those pastel tulle faggot fantasies?" Half-way into the laugh she looks stricken. "Oh, shit. Sorry, Andy."

I could tell Dannie I know at least four faggots right now who'd die for those gowns. Instead I say, "Not wanting to sound like one of those queers who think everyone's queer, but where's your gold band?"

"Right where it always was, on his wife's hand. He died trying to pry it off. Collapsed in her lawyer's office in Boston. She buried him a day later then phoned an obit to the papers. Which is when I found out."

I'm nodding compassion when Dannie rears back. "Now isn't this perfect? The hostess palling her own fucking party!" She heads for the kitchen. "When I get maudlin, I know it's time to serve the food."

I watch Dannie go. I promise myself from now on I'll remember, lists are lifelines. Mine starts with Emma, my kids....

I jump about two feet off the ground when a vise-tight hand suddenly grips my shoulder. Startled, I turn, half-angry. I'm looking into the velvet brown eyes of the classmate I've most wanted to see, and been most afraid I would. The great love of my college years, Todd Baxter, ne Jason Birkowitz, star of TV's longest running sitcom.

I've been following his career for years. When my kids were little, I'd point him out to them and tell them he was "a special friend of Mommy's." Lately, I've begun to feel increasingly fraudulent about that identification. Forty years is a long-time-no-see to call myself a friend, let alone, "special." Now we're looking into each other's blue and brown eyes, and unless he's wearing contacts, we're both too close to see anything except blurry colors and vague outlines.

"Jase!" I exclaim to his outline with as much warmth as I can freight onto one word, and turn into his arms for a mangling hug.

He whispers in my ear in the same urgent voice I've heard him use in dozens of love scenes.

"I knew it would be like this, you as slender and lovely as ever, not fat and sloppy like most women your age."

He's breathing in my ear, a trick from the old days which I'm fascinated, and She is mortified, to discover may still be working. In another familiar gesture, I feel him kneading my ass. I try to pull away. This transaction's moving altogether too fast for Her comfort, and there're a couple of things I want to say. Like, "*My* age? I'm two years younger than you, buster?" Or simply, "Get stuffed, Mr. Birkowitz!"

I don't say anything. At first, I'm too busy trying to figure out what I really feel. At last, I'm struck dumb by the thought that the reason we're zipping along on the bed-bound express is, Jase doesn't know about me being queer.

He uses lines with such whiskers I'm tempted to laugh. He literally " supposes" he's "not the first man to tell" me "what an adorable creature" I am.

She's tempted to murder. "What kind of 'creature'," She'd like me to ask, "a rabbit? a roach?"

She wants me to know that he may be a fool but he could be serious trouble. From my point of view, they're both fools.

"I had no idea it'd be like this," I laugh and continue to try to extricate myself. "But I should have guessed, it's how it is in every show I've ever seen you in."

He finally lets me loose and stands back so he can get the full effect of my wrinkled neck and what I euphemistically call my 'laugh' lines, and I can appreciate the blinding dash of his capped teeth and faux hairline.

"You've been watching me," he says with satisfaction in which there is no surprise. "I thought I felt something coming back through the cameras. Let's go out on the deck." This invitation is accompanied by a slightly less forceful grasp of my arm, and a physical urging towards the door that leads out to Dannie's dimly lit pool area.

When I'd thought of seeing Jason again, I'd fantasized several appealing scenarios. I'd daydreamed jumping discreetly into bed with him for old time's sake, or, alternatively, his begging me to jump into bed with him because my being gay turned him on and me acquiescing for old time's sake. The one thing I'd never considered was, he wouldn't know. Nor how tough it'd be telling him.

She isn't making it any easier. Her daydreams are nightmares that run heavily to violence. "Tell" isn't in Her vocabulary. She doesn't trust many people, including at the moment, Jase and me. She wants "to leave the party. Now." But it's not Her party. Jason's pulling me. I hold him back.

"There's something I want to tell you first," I start.

"Jesus!" He stares at me in disbelief. "Some things never change. Give you one scant moment of erotic arousal, and stand back for hours of discursive analysis." He shakes his head. His tone of annoyance has carried. People turn to look at us. She is decidedly displeased. I need this like another nose.

"So let's go," I push him towards the door.

On the deck, he doesn't waste any time. Encouraged by what must seem like my enthusiasm, he wraps one arm around my waist and the other around my shoulder. He holds the back of my head immobile in his hand and kisses me. It's what we used to call a "French" kiss. I'm thinking I should feel violated, but what I really feel is stupid.

"How did I let myself get into this," I think, "and how the hell do I get out?"

She's thinking, "Why me, God?" and, "If You really exist, Help!"

I manage to pull my head back out of tongue range.

"How's your wife?" I ask.

"Between wives," he manages to get out before pressing my head forward so our lips meet and part once more.

Now, his desire takes over, leaving his brains in the lurch. The once-familiar stiffening of the male sex muscle prods my thigh through the thin layer of silk slacks. My brain is sending "I'm outa here!" messages to limbs that are immobilized by Jase's passionate embrace. He is blindly groping towards a bench, talking at and kissing me to obscure the fact that he's also half dragging me with him when She starts to scream. It's a terrible shriek, as much rage as fear. I'm almost amazed Jason can't hear it. It works. I pull myself away so unexpectedly he doesn't even try to hold onto me.

"I'm not," I tell him, breathlessly.

"Not what," he asks suspiciously.

"I'm not between wives. I'm married. Sort of." I've reverted to an old trick, trying to get him to say the words. It's been so long since I've been in this situation, I've forgotten how scary it is.

Jason's plainly annoyed. "How the hell can you be 'sort of' married? You mean you're having an affair with someone? Hell, Andy, who isn't? Cross my heart and hope to die if he ever hears about this from me." Then he laughs and comes at me again.

She's stopped screaming, but She's talking a mile-a-minute. She wants me to shut up and make a run for it. For Her, She makes sense. She doesn't want to be known. If I run from here, I'll never stop running.

"I'm queer. I'm gay. I live with a woman. Her name is Emma." I can't bring myself to say the "L" word. I'm afraid of his reaction to it. She closes shop. Just disappears. Can't say it. Can't hear it. Jason takes a split-second pause, then roars with laughter.

"Christ, Andy, have you ever thought of simply saying 'No'?"

"OK. Simply no, Jase."

"Why? We're not getting any younger, and you're not going to tell me you're still worried about getting pregnant."

We both laugh. "No. I'm going to tell you I live with a woman named Emma. I've lived with her for twelve years, but I've had affairs with a number of other women since I was divorced thirty-two years ago."

He squints as if he's trying to see something too small for the naked eye. "You're a lesbian."

This is the moment She's tried to avoid forever. The one we've conspired to pretend wouldn't happen if each of us was careful where we went and who we were when we got there.

Suddenly, Jason seems to deflate. His shoulders collapse, his stomach contracts and he exhales an explosive "Hunh!"

"I don't know what to say, Andy," he sounds confused and uncomfortable. "I mean, it's OK and all that. Not that you need me to tell you it's OK…"

"Vouldn't hoit," I joke.

"Yeah, well. The thing is, I just don't have anything to say." He points a thumb towards the party, loudly gala a few steps away. "Does anyone else know about this? About you?"

I hate having to tell him. "I think practically everyone. I'm sure they all think you do, too."

"Oh yeah?" Suddenly, he's pissed. "Then what do they think I'm doing out here with you."

Despite, or maybe even because of Her, I let myself get angry.

"They think you're talking to an old friend, Jase. They don't think a woman has to be a 'fuck' for you to have a conversation with her. They think you're a nice guy. That we're old friends. What're you scared of, Jase? It isn't contagious."

"Don't get Freudian on me, OK? I'm just…well, it's a surprise, isn't it?" Now he wants to be justifiably pissed. "You do understand that, right? That it's a surprise?"

"Yes, I understand it's a surprise. I wish you'd known. I wish I'd told you. But I was scared you wouldn't like me. Crazy, isn't it? Because if all you want me for is to get in my pants, why should I care? And if we mean anything else to each other, that hasn't changed. You do understand that, right?"

"Yeah, sure. I understand. Only, it's a surprise." He's backing towards the door. "Give me a few minutes, OK? To get used to the idea. OK?"

Exit Jason Baxter upstage center.

I find the bench he was groping for and sit watching the water admire itself in the mirrored tiles of Dannie's grotto-pool. I'm shaking and I feel like hell, but the fight isn't over. Now it's with Her. Before She pushes me back into the comforting shadows of self-abnegation, I grab hold of the joy I've had all day and, yes damn it, almost all of this evening, too. The unfettered joy of being whole.

Not that She rolls over and plays dead! She pulls out all the stops – I'm a fool. That was a close call. I never give a moment's thought to Her career. Do I have any idea how frightened She was?

"Yeah," I tell Her bitterly, "I have some idea."

Then, out of deference to Her fear, I think about the office. About how I'll showcase this "Evening With My Famous Friends." I have some terrific ideas for the memorable sex-scene with Todd Baxter. But, damn it! I'll have to cut that sexy bit with Dannie. Unless…Yes! All She has to do is change Dannie to Dan….

Afterword

At age twenty, I began to write for a living. Starting as a copy-writer for a small radio station in McKeesport, Pa. (WEDO-AM. We Do – get it?), I moved to a small ad agency in Abington, Pa., then a larger agency in Philadelphia, and finally capped my career with fifteen years as partner/creative director of Lane. Golden. Phillips, a consumer ad agency in Philadelphia, Pa. I was a high earning, respected, female executive – a rara avis in '60's and '70's Philadelphia, and not then considered a game bird.

For eight or so of those fifteen years, I enjoyed the unexpected (women still considered "big-ticket" jobs serendipitous in those days) delights of success, creative achievement and power. Then one morning I woke up aging and angry. The young woman who had wanted to be "a writer," had become one. A convincing manipulator of other people's emotions. I had journeyed forth and discovered the mountain of loot, but along the way I'd lost my mind. I was forty-eight. For twenty-eight years I had been abusing a fine tool of my trade and finally, it rebelled. Giving me one more chance, my short-shrifted talent rose up and said, "This sucks." (You can dress my talent up in three-syllable words, but you can't take it into polite society. Thank heavens.) "Can you be more specific?" I asked. "Exactly which sucks, the opera, the theater, the caviar, the vacations in Europe?"

"I'm bored," my talent whined.

"Go play with yourself," I snapped

"Come play with me." It wheedled.

"What do you want to play, and can I be Captain?"

"I want to write poetry."

Adapted from a taped interview.

Who could resist such a civilized desire. I called my friends to ask how to become a poet, and a friend of a friend reported, "Adrienne Rich says you should study with Audre Lorde at the 92nd Street Y in New York City."

* * * *

I signed up for class with Audre, a glorious poet, a magnificent woman. Next, I submitted poems to Jean Valentine, funny, kind, master poet who was also teaching at the Y. I commuted one night a week from Philadelphia – where, as they say, I kept my day job. About midway through her course, Jean Valentine suggested I matriculate at Sarah Lawrence College where she also taught. SLC kindly permitted me to commute to classes one day a week, and brain-feeding, imagination-rocking teachers like Jane Cooper, Grace Paley, Suzanne Hoover, Jane Rose, Tom Lux and Jean, herself, agreed to work with me despite my attenuated schedule. During the following three joyous years, I made friends with poets who were my classmates, I read poetry, researched poetry, wrote poetry, graduated with an MFA in poetry – did every bright and thrilling thing except become a poet.

After graduation ("Another useless degree," my mother shrugged. She and my father had financed my BFA in acting), I returned full-time to Lane. Golden. Phillips. I still wrote sporadically. I spent one three-week summer vacation doing nothing but sending out poems. One of them was published in the *Croton Review*. I received the acceptance notice on my birthday! It wasn't enough. I was spending all day writing ad copy, going home and asking myself to do the same kind of work on a different plane, in a different way, as a totally different person. I tormented and tortured myself for years, but it absolutely never worked. Then, my agency went west, or is it south? I jumped out of the frying pan into corporate America as an entry-level product writer at Smith-Kline & French, a "Fortune 500" pharmaceutical company.

The corporate setting is dull, dreary, one-dimensional and shot through with the sadness and disappointment of people who expect LIFE to happen where only work happens. There I was, a 52-year-old fugitive from the glamorous world of consumer advertising, refugee from my lost dreams as a poet, surrounded by many attractive, intelligent people talking unintelligible biz-speak, stifled by the fear that any lapse from the "Yes, but does it drop to the bottom line" devotion to the cause – could be a career-limiting-move. (Familiarly known as "a CLM.")

By virtue of my advanced age, I was put to work as writer to the stars. I wrote speeches, sales meeting scripts, letters, position papers for the president and a select few senior vice presidents. After three years, when the by now familiar national pattern of corporate "downsizing" began at Smith-Kline, I was offered an opportunity to create a new position, director of marketing for the pharmaceutical industry's first managed care sales department. By the time I took "early" retirement from SmithKline at sixty-two, I was the oldest person in the Philadelphia headquarters of the company.

Surprisingly, my declaration of independence was not greeted with ringing bells. The people I was leaving could not believe that anybody would voluntarily walk away from the money and perks. I could not explain my attitude without (as they say in corpse-speak) *demotivating* those left behind. I settled for repeating, "I want to write. Now." I was unprepared for the startling discovery of *what* I wanted to write, "Now."

Throughout all my careers, I'd been "in the closet." After my divorce I had a brief, long-delayed lesbian adolescence prior to settling down again. For twenty-two years, I lived, raised my three children, started my business while in the same supportive, if difficult, lesbian relationship. The next fifteen years have been deliriously happy with my current partner, the brilliant, beautiful and loving scholar, Carroll Smith-Rosenberg. Throughout those years, only a small group of close friends knew from me that I was a lesbian. My career-woman alter-ego, She, and I led totally separate lives. It was incredibly easy – I never had qualms.

When I'd had my own Agency, in the '70's in Philadelphia, I was the first noticeable-on-the-landscape businesswoman there. It was very appealing, magnetic. Men who ran businesses like Sears, Roebuck, formidable local bankers and realtors liked the idea of having a Hollywood version of a smart, funny, slightly salty tongued ad "gal." They didn't want to know from lesbian. So from Lane. Golden to SmithKline it seemed counter-productive for me to "come out."

"The glass closet" is an expression used to describe the whereabouts of a homosexual who believes, usually erroneously, that she/he is "passing" as a heterosexual. For many years, I assumed I was living in a glass closet. It never occurred to me that the people I didn't tell didn't *know.* I believed we were simply colluding to not *speak* of it. In that scenario, being a lesbian could not be a CLM for me. I didn't care what anyone *knew.* I just didn't want that knowledge – or my homosexuality – to impede my career. I wanted to make money, as much as I could, and use it to support women's and lesbian's needs.

As the date of my eagerly-anticipated retirement from SmithKline drew closer, I thought increasingly of coming out. Attitudes in the wider world were changing – not *towards* Queers, but *among* us. Increasingly the question was being asked whether one's staying "safe" in the closet wasn't a betrayal of out (or outed), oppressed Queers. Too, I had made three close women friends at SKF. We had a little reading group that met once a month in each other's homes. (When we met at my home, Carroll went away for the evening. She wasn't thrilled with me, but she respected my need.)

The group functioned more as an old fashioned CR group, with our monthly book getting less and less attention as we grew closer, and our lives became more and more dynamic (at this writing all of us have left SK). I hated lying to those women. They were talking about their lives, and I was inhabiting a fantasy. I got away with it because I was by far the oldest member of the group and there's still a certain respect that people arrogate to an elder. When questions of sex went round the table, they really didn't expect me to answer – after all, by the time you're sixty, you're dead from the waist down anyway, so what the hell difference do your ancient memories make? Given the way brain tissue purportedly sloughs, your memories are probably unreliable. I had children, so my friends let me slide. Nobody ever asked me a question. I assumed it was the glass closet syndrome in operation. We were certainly good enough friends for one of them to have said something. I thought, "They're embarrassed, either they don't want to know or they don't know how to ask." And I didn't know how to help them.

One member of the group frequently said to me, "What I like about you, Alvia, is your honesty." It got to be like a knife in my heart every time she said it. One day, I asked her to be my guest for dinner. At the restaurant, I told her, "I'm a lesbian." She said she was surprised. That was the first time it occurred to me that not everyone knew. When I retired, I told the other members of the group. It was excruciatingly difficult. I found myself apologizing even though in the moment of telling, I knew my emotions were out of sync with what I was saying. I felt guilty. As if I were making a *confession*. It troubled me deeply. I wrote a very bad poem about it, full of anger at all of us.

Retirement felt wonderful. Carroll's a college professor, working often at home, traveling often. Now we could work and travel together. I started to write full time. I thought, "Now I'm going to write all those poems." But in the years of writing poems, at Sarah Lawrence, at SmithKline, on the odd vacation here and there, the poems had grown longer and longer. They were narrative poems – each one a story. In the languid early days of retirement as I began again to write these curiously long, ultimately unsatisfying poems, it struck me. "I'm writing short stories. I'm trying to break the lines, chip away at the words, I'm beyond tight to tense." In late 1993, I gave up and started to write short stories in earnest.

I'd never written *anything* about lesbians (or gay men) in my entire life. In fact, I had been extremely impatient with people expecting me to write about lesbians. I had been eloquent in my denunciations of people who "...cannot write outside of their sexual orientation, for Chrissakes!"

I became a lesbian when I was married and pregnant with my first child. I had wanted to be a lesbian for years, but didn't know how to find "them." I got married because in 1950's America, that was what a middle-class girl did when she graduated college. Nobody ever said, "Don't get married for a while. See if there's something you'd like to do. Find yourself. Express yourself." Quite the opposite. If a girl didn't get married in her early twenties, she was considered a tough commodity to sell – in a buyers market.

So, I got married and I had children and I was a lesbian. I had a few affairs during the '50's and '60's. Darned few because those were not the times, and suburbia was hardly the setting in which other lesbians jumped up to announce, "Oh wow! You're my kinda gal." Not many, anyway. It was the setting in which women jumped up and said, "Is *your* baby toilet-trained?" and, "What diaper service do you use?" I was the first woman in my "circle" to take a job and only because my husband wasn't earning enough to support us. Friends were amazed that he "permitted" me to work. Working eliminated my last opportunity for lesbian love-in-the-afternoon with the few young like-minded mothers who lived in my Chestnut Hill housing development.

Now, years later, when there was no longer any need to hide or live a double life – in private with wonderful women, in public as a divorcee with kids, something was happening to me. I was changing, evolving. She and I were reunited. WE decided our time had come. WE didn't get angry, WE simply took over emotionally. Inside our mind and body, the reunification process was almost as turbulent as East and West Germany's. Rigid behavioral patterns adopted for self-protection had to be unlearned. Attitudes designed to please the hegemonical hierarchy needed to be identified and cast aside. The search for the ME of WE was arduous. Finding and learning to understand, control and use my whole new set of emotions was like going through adolescence all over again. And the process is ongoing.

I didn't know how powerful an impact the changes would have on my writing. Now, I began to understand. I would never be the same. I would never again write by the half-light of the hidden. As soon as the unified me hit the laptop keypad, my writing changed, became deeper, closer to the truths of my experience. The lesbian themes I had scorned and avoided like the plague, plagued me until I owned them as part of the landscape of my life and its imagined retellings.

There are some amusing and some thrilling, and even some chilling, consequences of having all of myself available to me. For example, it's easier for me to rewrite. I can more readily see the emotional holes in the work, and whereas before I was dealing with words, now I see through the words to the emotional lapses where I have not been entirely forthcoming about details that are important to the material but may be threatening to me – or may represent areas I have traditionally (in many senses) repressed.

Less delightful is my growing awareness of the tentacular outreach of repression. In quiet moments I can be overcome by returning sensations heralding memories I've "lost" from childhood onwards. The sound of a lady's handbag snapping shut in the silence of a huge opera house the seconds before the overture saturates the senses has the essence of my mother, can reduce me to muffled sobs.

My brother's dying is the most difficult passage of my life. We talk urgently searching the words to heal our alienated past – our embattled childhood, our estranged adulthood. We have each lied, repressed, run for the nearest exit from the pain of our torturous early years. Now we are tap-dancing through the mine-field of discarded time, indifferent to the demolition's peripheral destructions, if we can just find the way to each other's love.

That's what I'm about now, the business of taking a last look. This time, I can't afford to blind myself to anything. I want to see who we were, how we lived or didn't, loved or couldn't, grew or withered, took and gave, saved, squandered, abandoned, sustained, wounded, tended. I hope I live sentient long enough to reclaim the self I spurned.

Rita Kiefer

Ex-Nun in a Red Mercedes

Nice car I tell my friend as we speed
from the convent the day I am leaving,
my shaved head barely
sprouting stubble, my stuttering hands
not a clue what to do with the seatbelt, one of
the many inventions conjured up to save the body
those 18 years mine was on ice

the nuns concocted less sophisticated, more
moral means, hence more everlasting: a veil,
13 layers of clothing, claw-pronged chains to be worn
at the knee and knotted cords – 33 strokes on Fridays
reminiscent of other brandings – still I am reminded
as the dark red grosgrain belts hum their automatic blessing
over heart, belly and that place *down there*
Ann O'Leary's mother called *our shame* – my mother gave it
no name, my mother never spoke of it at all – yes,
I am reminded of the convent's calculations

something about this particular car, its soft red fur against
        my spine,
reminds me of redemption: no more daily examens, daily
        horariums, daily
accusations, I think, nor monthly chapters of fault and no
        more genuflections,
my knees convinced me to leave

somehow they knew before the mind, they knew the collusion:
mind tricking body, oh, the body,
how far will this sabotage go?

something about this red Mercedes and
my mind that wouldn't have known to leave until
the female blood stopped flowing – I was that in love
with a phantom, that afraid my body would betray me,
that afraid of a man's near flesh, afraid
through some open summer window
I might follow young favorites: *I'll Be Seeing You* or better,
    worse
As Time Goes By, invading the body
as much as *Panis Angelicus*,
maybe more

in this red, red car today speeding
down Cleveland's Euclid, I am improvising
songs for my beautiful body, hymns to
the geometry of bone and flesh   and blood
I will   will   will find again
    again   again

Shadows

for Jerry

We stand at the edge
of the river
clear as our intentions
looking for trout:
voyeurs, not fishers today.

You speak of silver lengths
that flash at you quick and bright
like meteors we watched
from the grass last week
only the blades between us.

I see merely shadows
at the bottom of the bed.
On this mountain pass
my lungs, wild beasts
trapped and struggling in their cage
fight twelve thousand feet
of thin air.

Tonight before our tent
separates us from the stars
we'll light a fire and
my tongue will wash you clean.

I love what the moon does to you.
You stand repeated on the ground.

Switchbacks

Ties

At the old Hawthorne station
my eyes track him on the rails: a double
shining. Inside voices post arrivals, departures and
I remember East Cleveland homecomings, a
familiar trembling on the platform soon to be stage,
my father at center in his unyielding
grey tweeds and I would twirl my pink taffeta,
play pretend-ballerina
afraid he might see through the wish – or
was it a dream – I hid each night
he was gone: just before
the unsteady engine hurls his lean body to the air
I croon: *no more need to please.*
Sooty phoenix, even in sleep
he never left anyone easy.

Trestles

Poor daddy. His father cut in half under an engine. Just
      above
the crotch. Poor daddy. At twelve they found him
spread-eagled near those tracks
wailing to the foreman, *put it back together.*
My father fed on miracles but worked like an agnostic.
At twelve he was messenger for the Erie, his dead father's
      railroad,
left school to support a mother and sisters, but in the end
traded Hoboken, New Jersey tracks for the City

attachés and grey flannel. Nine-hour days then night class
    where
my father spoke a lawyer's line, still his life was set
in numbers, dark commuter stops before sunrise
long legal sheets bulging his briefcase or
filling pockets of the pin-stripes he and mother saved for. Years
later traces through the house, in his oak roll-top
locked to hide the curse of an orderly mind.
Everything turns to numbers, he'd say, if you know how to
    play them.

Signals

Thirty minutes out of Hawthorne
in the glass I am double
against the town of Ridgewood
where ash trees cover his vanishing body.
Before I was born, he dreamed a son.
A sign, he said, but
woke to another daughter.

        Past the dim lawns of
that other New Jersey town of
many losses: a stillborn, four miscarried,
then my father – at forty – held his son
just three days.

The lid on that coffin never closed.

Junctions

The train leans often against the Alleghenies.
I lean into the years
we were apart,
a cancer unraveling my father.

Once he came three thousand miles
west to apologize. Even at eighty his voice was precise:
Mother said you knew... our last chance for
a son... loving your sister more....

It's all right, I said trying to mean it,
and waved his train
the next day headed for Cleveland where
all the early traces lay: my face
absent in the family albums, *Dear Daddy*
notes that begged in unsteady print
signing the dead son's name. Mismatched birthdays
when I thanked and thanked
for mathematical pencils.

Sleeper

From the berth small points of light
burn dim like all stars.
Just a sleep away from home. There is dust
from the midwest plains on my pillow.

    A rocking
        a chatter of wheels. Switch-
backs turn a train
    against itself. And I am deep in dream:
            no blurred windows   no engine
        no bird rising
                just a woman's singed hands
            digging in luminous tracks.

Torn Photo

What were you wearing that day
he snapped the picture?
Half a century ago you tore your face out
of the photo, the only trace: a slim arm
arcing your small daughter
like a covenant.

The baby, left propped on the blanket, scowls
as if even then, she saw a pose
behind the lens: that man
who wanted you to give him a son.

The Egyptian Book of Dreams speaks of
a loss of face. In sleep
I look for the woman you canceled.
For years I could not forgive that tearing
but now I am a woman
it is clearer. We are taught
to veil our faces, to keep them
from our daughters.

Fifty years I rummage for everything
I buried the thin summer you died:
your letters hid in that black steamer trunk,
the velvet evening bag you gave me
for dress-up, a gold compact mirror cracked
in three, tucked in the folds of
an apricot silk you might have worn
as hope for your absent body that day.
And – wherever it is – the other
part of that picture.

Self-Portrait

after Clara Peeters' Still Life of Fish and Cat

Under the gallery's low light I am standing
beside myself at the National Women's Museum
your canvas blazing like a violation
in a room pious with Renaissance forms
and I call back a rage of faces blurred
until now: one by one the dead women coming
down from the walls, clamoring for
what the Dutch Fathers denied you.
Anatomy lessons were improper for women, they said,
and left you still lifes, fruit in lethargic bowls and drowsy fish
instead of their multiple selves in gold-flecked brocade.
Was it your Flemish eye exploding, Clara Peeters, that lent
Rembrandt his opulence like some goddess washing
a whole continent gold?

Now through the door an intruder,
a self-sprouted guide I have avoided three floors,
points out your *Fish and Cat* droning on about technique.
It is clear, he pontificates, the abundance,
a domestic flourish on the table, indeed a chiaroscuro.
But I say to the dead, it isn't clear, is it,
how many carp lean on the bloated one drenched gold
at the center? That green coil, is it an eel
ringing the colander brimmed with the day's catch?
And look – that uneven cat guards a prey
too diminished to name. If the six muted clams sprang
open, it is not clear, is it, what would spill near
those shrimp disoriented on the sideboard?

Oh, all the dead mouths, Clara Peeters!
all the dead gaping!

Since that day I have carried your print, a small still life
in my palm, on the dashboard, through library stacks
        scanning
for more than your name, my blind thumb wearing the dark
mark of ink from pages turned over and over.
Once I found you under your husband and later read
chiaroscuro: an arrangement of light and dark,
also means claire obscure.

In a dream you shout: It is finished! It is finished!
holding your face in your hands, bolting
straight from that canvas. What a tearing, what a congress of
        scales,
membranes no longer clinging, relentless white flesh, a sad
        yellow.
Next morning I wake to my own still life, unread
poems aging on the nightstand. Beside them
a tangle of fur, a slim hint of feathers.

Note: Clara Peeters' painting at The National Museum of Women
in the Arts in Washington, D.C. inspired the founder to open such
a museum.

Second Sacrament

In fourth grade I was confirmed by the bishop who wore
red but blanked the speech (right in the middle) daddy
drilled at home beside his oak roll top muffed *your excellency*
stopped dead after the third *on this solemn occasion* my eyes
tracking sister assumpta who just nodded at the flowers
waiting in the gilt wicker basket I'd been chosen to kneel
(the bishop felt a girl was better sistersaid) and present
to his eminence who smiled as I collapsed the bouquet at
his feet his patron smile shading my face rose the color of
the taffeta mother bought for my second sacrament

I remember his ermine-edged cape pontificating
its velvet down saint philomenas aisle brushing
my chubby calf protruding milk-white from the pew
that trembled I was that disturbed
by the coming of the spirit we'd prepared for all fall
when our turn came I knelt with my partner at the altar
the second tallest girl one step below his crimson slippers
waiting for a blow on the cheek
a sign sisterleosaid we were soldiers of christ
for weeks we placed bets on how hard he would hit us
practiced on each other at recess
but I remember I didn't want the senseless slap
or to be anybody's soldier
I didn't want to be kneeling
sistersaid our confirmation names would shape our lives
spur our fight with satan and *validate* us
mine was mary after jesus mother
who said i am the handmaid of god be it done to me
after my mother the handmaid of
a different lord after the other bible-mary who sat
passive and tranced at the christs feet

I wanted *michaella* as near as a girl could get to
the archangel who drove lucifer
to hell but daddy said it would be *mary*
a dove would settle on each girl on each boy a tongue of fire
sistersaid male names quickened the coming

for all our fear the blow was just a tap
a touch a brush of a palm on the cheek
no sting no mark but now I remember recoiling from
that man's hand the first of a lot that would try
to reshape my face in the name of some holy spirit
and I remember thinking that day an all-seeing eye
split some white cloud far above saint philomenas spires
scouting for boys

I was a girl

Sister Mailee Sequence

Prelude:

I know all about fading. Remember
those petals I tossed from heaven.
They're dim on the edges now. A father
who gave me to God before
I could write my own name,
before my breasts could make the most of blousing.
Think of it – little Therese Martin *fixed* at age three.
Cats and me!   *Dedicated,* they said,
she'll be our little nun, our saint some day.
Therese of Lisieux, chosen by God,
every family needs a chosen.
What a cheap heaven-ticket! but
he always could sniff a bargain,
especially a holy one, my father.

The nuns refused you medicine?
They brought about your death?

It was God's will.

They weren't stopped?

You don't just stop *God.* Besides
I was destined to suffer, make reparation.

Reparation? For what?

Who knows?
They said my sickness was a sign.
The younger we die, the greater the praise!
And I was young, believed in small things.
They dubbed me "Saint of the unspectacular."
At 15 a Carmelite; at 24 a Saint.

A dead saint. Canonized.
Every family wants one.

What do you want, Therese?

What do I want?
I want a new face,
a new fate this time.
This time not a saint.

1. Female Jesuits

I know that if at this moment I had before me a group of twenty
young Germans singing Nazi songs in chorus, a part of my soul
would instantly become Nazi. This is a very great weakness,
but that is how I am.... (Simone Weil)

Soon part of a life will flame from the metal basket
on the side stone porch of the magnolia house. No one will
        find
my words. One burning, then   pffff!
all will be ashes, all
the pages blank.

In my corner blue bedroom, I am saying good-bye
to the dark walnut secretary desk, faithful
hiding place for the secrets since I turned twelve,
six years of diaries and journals,
some scented, some singed at the edges,
thick with accusings, friendships
on trial, reconcilings fragile as flax, pansies,
lilies-of-the-valley bordering my pages.

If we hadn't moved, if I had gone
to the other girls' school at the end of
Belmore Road in East Cleveland, but
daddy wanted the Magnolia Drive house,
destiny pointing six blocks down Liberty Boulevard

to Notre Dame Academy. That first morning
at Freshman Assembly, we shrank in our seats,
248 uniforms, their detachable collars sitting white and stiff
on navy blue gabardine, 248 heads musing as
Sister Ralph said we would be taught by female Jesuits in
the five-story nineteenth-century castle, a fortress of
learning in the mode of Ignatius Loyola.
Years later as Sister Mailee, a *female Jesuit,* I
would quote James Joyce on the possible green rose,
Stephen Daedalus looking for his name
on a geography text flyleaf:
somewhere between the world and the universe
a green wothe botheth.

Good-bye, blue vanity, your glass kidney-shaped top
like the cracked one on daddy's desk when I was five.
No! No! No! I shook at the interrogation
and wondered if he could see inside my head
the way God did my heart, straight down to the lie.
But everyone's a *watcher,* even in sleep.

Flex your muscles Daddy coaxed, then
nicknamed me Pete so I signed notes
with the dead infant's name buried deep
in the family plot, the dead infant
who might have been priest-son
to my Irish daddy. Instead he got a girl
and today that daughter is leaving
the world, the devil, the flesh
to be – next best to priest – a nun.

Dick O. should see her body now,
the body her full mirror had mocked and
those legs he said had *most potential*
climbing stairs, veiled in black lisle
primed for cloister life.
She remembered the night the mirror first talked:
give it to God, that body spells trouble. Or

the morning Mr. Barth tossed her five-year-old body
high in the churchyard air, that pink dress
naughty as a windy umbrella.
She'll get in trouble with those eyes, he said
just before he caught her, and all through Mass she hid them.
Always blaming me for what they do! she thought.

> *Silly you men — so very adept*
> *at wrongly faulting womankind*
> *not seeing you're alone to blame*
> *for faults you plant in woman's mind.*
> (Sor Juana)

2. Elevator Ride to the Cloister

At five I would ask mother, how come
I call me *I*? Everybody else says *she*.

Once more a sad laugh swelling. Like
mother before I was born.
Good-bye world. Never at home on the ground.
The same tug from the bottom, the same start as
ferris wheel rides in Asbury Park summers.

And always the same safe gate,
its accordion metal *Click.* Again, *click*
and the elevator begins its straight climb,
no return-wheel this time. Floor by floor
like Thomas Merton's seven-story mountain or
the seven mansions in the Saint of Avila's *Interior Castle.*
Destination: Cloister.
A sign I'd seen daily as an Academy girl,
its black and white four-cornered seduction:
Cloister. Private. Like private parts
I thought the first time I saw it.
                    Like borderlines,

ultimatums for boyfriends but
I almost changed the rules
on the dim side porch with Dick O.
that night. Almost. Maybe it was
the miraculous medal pinned to my slip
for protection, or the scapular's prickle
just before he tried to cross over to
that place Joan Dorey's mother called
our shame. My mother called it no name.
My mother never spoke it at all.

It will be different when we move.
But mother never wanted the big house.
It was daddy, restless after promotion,
the girls too big for the yellow and red
wallpaper children skipping rope, too old
for the chamber pot in their bedroom,
a regular toilet forbidden, since
daddy is a light sleeper, daddy
still sleeping light in the family plot he planned
even the large chestnut
growing beside him conforms to
the boulder that wouldn't let his body down.

Mother grew quiet in the big magnolia house.
I'm losing my hair, she would say.
Thirteen years after Mr. Barth and daddy,
my diary complained:
I'm not gonna live like mother.
I've decided to marry God.

Trying to drown the foreign sounds
on entrance day: the elevator's metal
scrape, practiced voices down the hall,
the hour bell shrill from the tower.
Outside, a white-veiled novice
fated as my "guardian angel," says it's time
to go up to the cloister and the frosted glass

elevator door slides all the way back
at the fourth floor where the elevator stops
humming – like the ferris wheel almost – and
just before stepping out to the convent world
I smooth my bangs from the reflection in
the brass panel sprouting numbers
but I am not that face, that postulant
all in black, someone else gleams back
from the faint metal. I am dimming.

3. Wings and Fur

At five, my pet canary froze in father's study,
the coldest room in the house.
I got up from scarlet fever and
they'd buried him. Death by freezing.
Even then I knew: we never stop grieving.

When my yellow bird died I turned
my face to the wall. At five I was that bird and

> *lily-of-the-valley, scarlet poppy,*
> *bubble, stone for the pocket, at five pushing through*
> *feather   pistil   stamen   translucent wall*
> *plucking – those days – feathers and petals one by one.*

Grandma showed me my wings sprouting in the mirror.
If they belonged to an angel why were they so black?
Grandma never saw them black, Grandma never
heard the beast, the one with all the voices,
its eyes dark as my black triangle, my black fur.
Why – even though my hair was the color of honey – why
did my triangle stay so black?

Such a cross-breeding, this beast and angel,
such a holy communion.

4. About Mortification

On the fourth day they issued numbers.
Hers was *101*.
She'd heard about absolute zero and
one.

Except for roses or mums or asters
at Benediction or the chaplain's hands sprouting
deep blond hairs or his vestment in the right season,
no color fretted the cloister, but in the middle of
those Nocturnal Adoration nights
before the exposed Host, she'd come quick
from sleep to the chapel, dizzy with roses and ivory
beeswax, to a front pew near the monstrance
exploding gold from the reliquary, its round
glass pyx holding the white wafer.
Nights of blue-white stars flung over Madison-on-the-Lake
that last summer, her bathing suit white, too white,
white as eternity with all its possibilities.
At communion next morning,
the priest's hands, man-hands, elevating
the host. She would practice custody of
the eyes. Since age five
eyes and sex like growths in a Petri dish.

Now she could banish them both with the Rule.
The Rule that shaped each act: how to
fold a towel, place pins in a veil, stack
prayerbooks – all edges turned left – in chapel pews.
Rules for the body too: *the Sisters shall conceal hands
in sleeves to avoid swinging their worldly arms.*
The Rule, at first a foreign language
now her mentor.

Holy Rule, help me expel the devil,
that damned ventriloquist.

She tried mortification: open prongs of
the penance chain, to pinch her flesh
right above the knee. Friday flagellations:
the discipline's knotted cord, 33 strokes
on each arm for each year of the Jesus life.
On feastdays she'd take two fewer olives,
a half piece of cake.

Yet under her postulant cape the irony of
soft, silk blouses flattering her full breasts.
Who'd see them now?
Still she needed to know
if Dick O. drove by in his old Chevy
she would still feel crepe de Chine clinging.

Sister Superior said she was proud so
she shredded her poems, stuffed them
down the incinerator. Her words, burning.
When did the questions stop? That time
in chapel she denied Father Daugherty's stares,
the night she burned her words, or
when the monthly blood stopped coming?
Or was it that Indian summer night in her cell
she prayed to die October third
at age twenty, four years younger than
the Little Flower of Lisieux.

5. Sister Mailee Goes All The Way With Jesus

The Chinese name for Mary: Mailee, so
liquid and lyrical, Mailee. Tomorrow she'd hear
her new name called, and the bishop would
invest her with the white veil of a Bride of Christ.
But tonight they would take her hair,
tonight was the shearing time.

On all four sides of her cell,
white muslin drawn against intruders, this
shedding was private as any first loss, steel blades
poised in Sister Elreda's right hand,
in her left, electric clippers.

Just below the ears or do you want
to go all the way with Jesus?

Her eyes closed to block the electric hum,
she called back other women
who had let themselves be shorn: Catherine,
Teresa of Avila, Francis of Assisi's Claire,
those in camps, shaved out of shame
while she was learning to divide and multiply
and have her first periods. And mother,
stunned when they shaved her
pubic hair before the dead baby, mother
whose raven hair had grown brilliant
brushing her blond child's in singular curls.
Later Mother's quiet grew like
a house emptied of children.
Now the last trace of vanity
scattered, a blond wheel circling her feet.

The dormitory cell   tepid and solitary as death   a hand rubbing
        a bald head   over stubble   an hour ago blond waves
    an hour ago   ravished by the joy of denial   alone now
a slim body   shivering in the stark white   space of a cell.

6. Failing Canonical Year

Not a wrinkle in Father's surplice,
Sister Sacristan directed,
but keep the iron cool.

Canonical Year, a year to perfect the domestic arts,
a year of no study, no books, a year
to contemplate.

She wondered at night, washing scorches
from her dreams, if anyone could tell
through layers and layers of habit the
fruit of her meditation. And Father Confessor's
scent on the other side of the screen as
she listed her sins, was it scorched linen?
Or was *that* the smell of sex?

Small gestures finished her
days in the kitchen, measuring spoons
spinning from her hands,
Make it level, exact! And the spilled flour,
all the burnings. *Don't worry,* Sister Aimard consoled,
we won't leave you alone with the oven,
so they sent her downstairs
to the laundry where her body could whirl in
washers, thrashing white veils, crashing
through foam, in each iridescence, trying
to find those lines she had no time – upstairs – to put
in a notebook. Men write an old story,
the classic rift: Eliot's Prufrock. Joyce.
Augustine. Women know another fracturing, another
split, all the way down the body.

The Infirmary found no cause for the fever, but
she knew her *Thomas à Kempis.*
A gift from Christ Suffering, she thought,
still the flood of familiar voices:
anyone can study or write poems.
Hard work is for real women. A new line
lumined her sleep: *burying brains*
in the garden to see what they sprout.

In the end no one denied it
least of all Sister Mailee.
She had failed canonical year.

7. Retreat

In the notebook next to a muddle about actual grace:
a measure of the degree of disorder… entropy
always increases and available energy diminishes
in a closed system. A shade spills over the facts
when we try to say them, a scrim
between story and teller, they shift form
like negatives blurred by
the right shift of focus.

The thirteen pieces of clothing
I'd worn all those years
                    chemise, pelerine, veil…
tossed off on that final cell night,
a shade over the facts. Eighteen years like dominos collapsing.
Terrifying, the quick face of change.

Prepared to descend, I feel
for the ground-floor button, the elevator up and down
the years, humming names of the women
I'm leaving behind, women who translated me,
who watched my cloistered tower swaying.

Every woman owes her name to another.
I owe mine to many: to Quinnie
who dangled late-afternoon lines of Shakespeare
and quoted Peguy: *my last nickel for white hyacinths, not bread.*
"Dangerous," the novice mistress warned.
Quinnie who knew I harbored poems, and
made me write them

to Sister Marcina of fresh basil and asters
who reminded me I could still *feel* under all that black,

Marcina who sang of *swans on the castle lawn in Oldenburg*
of her young German boyfriends before
the First Great War

to Sister Inez who made her students see Aquinas and
Kierkegaard walking the Flats in downtown Cleveland, and
Sister Borgias who fled her twisted body for the Far East
every Tuesday that last semester…
and took us with her

to Pearl Roderick of the Alhambra
Apartment, its cockroaches larger than
the first joint of a thumb, Pearl of the Hough Avenue
Project, her six-year-old girl, shining at the back door
that first day: *my mama deaf but she a reader.*
Pearl who saw my dark habit, my
colorless skin and still called me *sistuh.*

I owe my name most to Mother
who comes back wearing silk
in rain and lilacs to keep appointments
after death – when I give her
deadlines.

Afterword:

Be it done to me. A favorite phrase with lots of wives and
mothers, daughters meant to be sons. What a woman won't
do for any announcing angel! Promised divine issue, she'll
give everything.

In the end the same nightmares: branding 101 on my bare
back   iced bodies cubed on conveyor belts   a woman
having the same baby over and over, burying it in the garden
once I played a circus part, climbed ropes and ran through
hoops of fire   last time I was a hyena   no one could train
me to laugh.…

Fadings and fates and flowers and female, all the *F* words.
Little ferris wheel friend, what did you know of

fate, when you fled that Magnolia home
like a stunned bird, what did you know of illusion?

It would be easy to read these words and
say you had been betrayed, that
what I have written is not you.
The fact is – in all these years – I have forgotten
your face. Time has confused me.
New diagrams cut the sky. You and I
will say more some day. For now
more blank pages and
these negatives. Blurred.

Shelter

In the kitchen at A Woman's Place
Lucille shakes white flour from her fingers
a bevy of doves in their freedom.
Her words mingle slow as the yeast
she is dissolving at the shelter.
Forty years under his sheets.
Forty years of kneading
bread, manna for a husband and three children.
Last month the beatings began.
A haunted man, she says.

At the shelter Lucille fills jam pots,
shapes noodles thin on the cutting board,
thin as the morning sun stroking her
frayed robe, loaves rising in the oven
bring the women down from sleep
combing their hair carefully.

* * * *

Dear Lucille,

I miss you. You were right. I thought he couldn't follow
me, but a father's hex lives on. *Girls are not good enough,* he'd
say. Now even with a man that thinks I am, I watch our
kitchen shamrocks close against the light, the split-leaf philodendron collapsing to the floor. Lucille, my kitchen's just
one more missed ingredient. One more burning. Outside,
gulls unstitch a quilt against the sky.

* * * *

Lucille left gifts at the shelter:
her smock, a dozen recipes,
for me some stone ground flour,
four ounces of preserves.

* * * *

Rita -

Thank you for your letters. I found my own apartment.
Keep the shamrocks moist not drowned. They need inderect
light. Sounds as if the philodendron wants near the sun.
Here's the recipe for plum jam your husband liked. Take it
easy on yourself. And piss on Daddy.

Your friend,

Lucille

Last Song

I piece the divine fragments into the mandala
Whose centre is the lost creative power.

Kathleen Raine

Just before they cut out her tongue
she cried *I will learn to sign.*
When her fingers laced air
they brought cleavers:
ten spokes, a mandala wailing
red on the cutting board.
At four in the morning she began
whistling a score so original
one of them ordered – his eyes on her
lips – *Bring me a peeler!*

When they got to her heart
it spit in the fire.
At night you can still hear it hum.

Disbelief

He called my last song
overdone, too worked, a bit
hard to believe. The part about
her tongue cut out, her lips shredded
by a peeler.
                              But I saw
the night they brought her home
from the attack, the madman couldn't get enough
of her dear mouth. Was there even a trace of lust?
that pure rage that made him
bite down so hard he didn't know
whose hot rush filled his mouth?
                              When the prosecutor brought
a piece of it in a jar – a swollen pink bladder, no blood
at all – only then did he seem to know
what he'd done.
She was ten.

Dyslexic

for Randi

If they taught me in *Sign*
I could learn, she said. I want words
that won't break into pieces, but as she spoke
above her head a phantom
loomed, the language of startled doves and

I am back at St. Philomena's
Sister Kathleen calling from the other side
of the window where I hung in a tree with
Emily D. – a chaos of letters between us
lined up so nothing could hold
the oak leaves flickering that late April morning
fluttering page after page of
words like old carriage wheels still in motion
after stopping to take us on –

and on and on Sister Kathleen's
voice, guarded as civilized gates,
naming my problem: *an unbridled eye, a lack of attention,*
but around her wimple, drowning her nun-words
dove wings signing a dance
no alphabet held.

Prophecy

It's split all the way
down the middle
he said as I came
out of my mother.
It's
a girl.

In

In the convent we shaved our heads,
> *off at da' earss or you want to go all da' way*
> *wit Jeesuss?* the nun-beautician asked
> the night before I took the veil
and we cut sentences mid-air
when the sacristan rang the bell.
On Fridays knotted cords scourged our arms
and open-pronged chains, above the knee
reminded us of the Passion.

In dreams I often can't remember
I am still pushing, pushing examen beads up and down
on a thin black string hung from the waist
like an abacus. Up for a virtue-act, down for
undarned tears in the habit.

In the first years I could still feel
unrequited love, could still cry until the words
particular friendship loomed like a disease.
Soon all tears stopped.
Any wonder some nights my husband has to hold
my past under the covers.

But look. In telling you all
this, look I'm not lying
tranquil on the couch. I'm crouched
in the middle of the therapy mat.
So here. Let your hand braille
the story still fresh on my face.

Naming It

for the once-a-nun woman

Something in the eyes
of this woman, something deep
in this midnight womb: devil
or holy ghost.

I coax it. Steal charms
from the idols
not drawn easily.

(First I am the Lord thy god
thou shalt not have
strange gods before me.)

Just before sun
my toes fret the water,
stir one more separated

face, one more fractured eye
yet can't tempt it
to surface. Some say
it's in my mind only,

my heart does not agree.
I planned its murder once,
bound the body in serge and

white linen, black veil
for the face. Years later it burst
that coffin; leered.

(Thou shalt not kill.
Thou shalt not and thou shalt
       not).   You

you down there.   Yes, you.
Don't you know these breasts
this hair? I am
waiting for you

to name that woman
to reflect that face long buried.
I am the Judas girl

traitor to that other
who torments me.
This time

I am the Eve girl
who must call the unnamed
certain it will rise. But

forked tongue or wings,
counterfeit or song? Still each night
I cry to the water: Name it
Name it. For now: human.

Afterword

I believe in chaos. Probably all the poems in this book, all the poems I have ever written have sprung from the hunch that chaos is the basis of the creative act. Does this sound right: whatever happens in the interior life of a poet before the poem comes, whatever finally gets down on paper is the result of chaos? At the center of disorder, order is working itself out. Whether I am learning a principle of physics or writing a poem, the discovery that happens doesn't come in a sequential manner. I am fairly certain that eventually, when the whole body of language that I am able to give back to the world is complete, when I've written my last poem, there will be an order evident that I know nothing of now. This faith keeps me writing. I suppose it is not alien to the faith I had growing up as an Irish Catholic girl and, later, as a nun. I simply am seduced by what I can't see.

Most of the doctrines endemic to Catholic belief no longer attract. But one still holds me close, the Mystical Body of Christ, the belief that by living in a certain manner we can connect with others whom we never met and – in some way, through some sort of exchange – we will mutually affect one another's lives. The other night I watched live footage of films taken at the trials of resistors in Germany during the Nazi regime. One film showed a beautiful, dignified, gaunt young man standing before an interrogator who shouted at him, "Why can you not follow Der Fuhrer? What is it you cannot believe?" The young man responded, "I cannot follow Der Fuhrer because what he is doing is evil." The death sentence was immediately pronounced, the man was taken away and then the camera flashed on his widow being interviewed in 1992. That woman closely resembled me.

Adapted from a taped interview.

It occurred to me that the man I saw on the TV screen had been alive on the other side of the ocean when I was a very young child unaware of his story. Still as a little girl I believed that if I gave up a piece of cake or didn't have a second dish of ice cream, I could tap into something that would zip across the sea and connect with someone I never had seen, whose name I would never know, and that I could help him have courage in adversity. I'm not sure how, but I feel that in some mysterious way this belief – now modified – informs the poetry I write, that it also makes me call back ancestors like Emily Dickinson or Anna Akhmatova or W. B. Yeats when I write. Some way.

I never understood the scientific basis for all this until I recently read about the butterfly effect in John Gleick's book, *Chaos*. He tells us that a butterfly, flapping its wings a certain way in Tunis, can change the weather two weeks later in Boston. I read this and thought: my God! what a haunting metaphor. Space doesn't really separate bodies trying to get together, neither does time! A man in Berlin, a young girl in Cleveland…together because of air waves and language. They have exchanged energies. I believe this.

* * * *

As a child I loved to write. In high school, prizes from a few local contests came quickly, but I wasn't a serious writer then. Rather I denied my creative flair. Maybe I thought it wasn't honorable, not the mark of a scholar! And I was distracted by other involvements. I liked to lead, to be out there in front. Most of that leadership had to do with religion. I could have been Student Council President. Instead I chose to be Sodality Prefect, president of the religious organization. I was a bit of a proselytizer in those days, very doctrinaire. Maybe that's why I have so many unanswered questions in my poems now.

Later, after I had entered the convent, I wrote a few poems as an undergraduate in creative writing class. Some of my work was to be published in a small literary journal.

83 | Rita Kiefer

I still remember the night I told the novice mistress; "Miss Quinlivan would like to publish one of my poems and a short story," I said, trying to hide my excitement. She raised her long, bony finger and her left eyebrow and cautioned, "Do not become proud, dear Sister." I was eighteen at the time and didn't write again until forty – until after I had married.

The *Holy Rule* warned the nuns, "never be idle." For me that meant not taking time to do what I really enjoyed: reading and writing. I found suspect anything that gave me pleasure or simply filled my interior life – without practical results. I did write some meditations on the spiritual life. I remember composing one for a particular cook-sister who was very depressed and thinking of leaving the convent. It was all about how she kneaded the dough in order to grow closer to Christ. I now realize that it was incredibly sexual and actually grew from my need to express the longings and desires that I had, none of which was "legitimate." In those years I feared anything that brought comfort or led to success; I cherished sacrifice and suffering. My life as a nun was a continuation of what I had learned at home – a very Irish Catholic home – that as a girl I was to behave and stay in my place and sacrifice for God.

When I left the convent in 1966 my major concern was to resituate myself in the world after having been in the cloister for eighteen years. I had to learn all over again how to be an independent woman, how to choose clothes, how to wear my hair. After a year of doing volunteer work with the Newman Club, the Catholic organization on college campuses, I secured a university teaching position. It was not until 1974, however, that I returned to writing poetry. The first two poems I sent out were accepted immediately by *Descant*. One of them, "Wherever They Are They're Dancing," was written for my mother and father. It was a poem of lovely sounds but built on a lie, a denial of who my parents really were, a poem about their perfect marriage. Shortly after that, *Southern Poetry Review* picked up two more, followed soon by another that appeared in *Concerning Poetry*. I was on a roll. So I thought. Then came the long years of struggling to get one poem a year published. It was very fortunate that I had that initial encouragement to fly with.

* * * *

Gradually my husband and friends began to ask, "Why don't you write about the convent?" My answer, "Oh, that's all in the past!" Could anyone be that naive! When the *Sister Mailee Sequence* finally came, it was an easy labor, it slipped out fast. I loved the first draft. Writing it was pure release. I felt no censors. I didn't care if the nuns I had lived with ever read it. It didn't matter what they would think. I enjoyed forming the words. At first it was a sequence, a set of very structured poems. Next it turned into a long prose-poem, then back to the original format, but with the poems more open-ended. The piece is much freer now. I really trust that work.

With each word, I was unveiling, peeling the scales off my eyes. It wasn't until I wrote about convent life that I actually discovered why I had chosen it. Despite the scars, I wouldn't exchange those eighteen years for any others. They seem now like one great *felix culpa*, a happy fault – isn't that a marvelous term – a kind of oxymoron, a stumbling block in your path that you have to get around. It makes you sharper, somehow more alert. I think it's good for a poet to have such barriers.

If you grow up with the thought that there is heaven/ hell/purgatory, that this world is temporary, your language is less vivid, I think. Even if your beliefs change, the language that comes to you later as you write poetry is limited by the way you looked at the world as a child. I envy poets who have a lush language. I have to push the language to find just the right word. Because I denied the world in my early days, I didn't name the flowers – they weren't named for me. I didn't name the animals – I never had any. Sensory deprivation!

* * * *

Despite my publications and now this book, I always feel behind, not prepared. That feeling comes partly from the fact that I began writing so late in life, partly because nothing was enough for my father. I wasn't the boy he wanted, I could never help realize his dream: to give a priest-son to the world. So I neutered myself by becoming a nun. In that way I wouldn't get into trouble as he predicted. I'm sure he was such a sensual, sexual being himself and he saw himself in me. All his male friends said I was going to "get in trouble with those eyes." I was five years old! I learned early the lesson of being female.

A young woman chooses a life at eighteen, then one day wakes up and knows she must leave it. From that time, her greatest fear is self-deception. She can't name that fear. Now I know those years in the convent I *was* deceiving myself. I wanted spontaneity, instead I chose order and discipline. I wanted to be a maverick, instead I chose conformity. And I pretended that the only love I wanted was divine.

These past years I have learned to honor what it means to be human – to be flawed. I remember my father's saying, when I was growing up, that we had to "overcome our human tendencies." Now all these years later I realize that all I want is to be human.

My mother, who died shortly before I left the convent in 1966, knew I never belonged there. The thought of her impels me to write. She was very poetic. One of eleven children, extremely introverted and shy, she had four miscarriages and a stillbirth, then a little boy who lived three days. After all those depressing experiences she did what she could for me. I am probably trying to get back in touch with her through poetry. And through her with all women especially. In poems I call her back. She had no recognition in her life. I will not live her life. Woman's voice should be heard. I want my poems to be read, partly to say "This is for you, Mother!".

The sad amber glass that I write about was her way of dealing with the pain of being silenced. She wasn't a full-fledged but rather a sad drinker. I know she didn't drink when I was a small child. I remember having fun with her all day. Not robust fun – she was in her forties when I came along – but rather quiet times at the beach and on picnics. In later years I do remember the mouthwash aroma and the day she came down the circular stair in the Magnolia house, my taking that sad amber from her.

At that time the main way woman proved her grace, her ability, her beauty and sex appeal was by having children. But mother had all those failures. She finally gave my father a child and he adored my sister, almost to the point of obsession. The consummate sadness, of course, was that when mother succeeded again, this was her final curse because I was not the boy he desired. In "Torn Photo," I celebrate that fact about my mother and me.

* * * *

I used to think I was one of those children who never had an imaginary playmate, but recently I have remembered how at age six I was to make a retreat – isn't that wonderful, at age six – in preparation for First Communion. We were to keep silence until three o'clock on the day before. I remember leaving the church, walking home up Belmore Road and saying aloud: I don't want this to end. I think what I meant was that I wanted to keep talking to the angel. The angel listened and didn't tell me what to do. The angel was my spirit-friend, my best friend, this wonderful presence that stayed. I think the angel was the poetry part of my language. I have left the practice of Catholicism, but I will never leave the angel.

Leaping ahead these many years later: my husband and I hiked the Grand Canyon over spring break this year. Down the Kaibab trail and up Bright Angel with a two-night stay at Phantom Ranch. We arrived at the bottom about one o'clock the first afternoon. The next day Jerry announced that he was going to take a quick hike to Ribbon Falls, but I was desperate for time to write, to be alone in the Canyon, so I left him and walked along the river in a secluded and shady area. Perhaps it was exhaustion, lowered defenses from the day before, perhaps it was merely my needing the muse, but each time I turned a corner and glanced back, I saw the flash of a white form from the corner of my eye. It might have been white water. White alabaster. A low cloud. Some gossamer flair. The idea of *angel* has shifted since that day on Belmore Road when I was six. Still what remains is the, *Oh, I don't want this to end!*

Somehow all this connects with my poems in this book. I'm always trying to bring what isn't there into being. The urge might be stronger because I've never put out a child. I never wanted one. And I have never looked back and said I wish I had one. But there is an incompleteness I recognize, a trying to bring another me into being – not to nurture, it really isn't that – but to give life to and then send it on its way. Maybe that's why so many of my poems bring people back from the dead. I don't know.

Estelle Leontief

Sellie and Dee: A Friendship

When I was a little girl over sixty years ago, another little
girl named Selena imprinted me. I have not changed much
since then. Nor has Selena.

It began when we were nine and it is as if she had bitten
me with her pretty white teeth leaving indelible marks. I
often wish she had done that instead of inflicting many more
potent, less visible wounds.

I can't recall our first meeting. My family, mother, father
and much younger sister, lived like Gypsies, moving about
every two years in Manhattan as a neighborhood deterio-
rated or our fortunes improved. Pinehurst Avenue, smack up
against the now Cross Bronx Expressway to the George
Washington Bridge, was one of our longest stopping-off
places. Most importantly, it was the street where I met Selena
and where we lived from the time I was eight till my middle
teens; the years when girls make close friendships and eventually have boys hanging around them. Or the girls hang
around waiting for boys. And *they* are more trouble than
they're worth, the undesirable ones always after you and you
eager for the prizes who sometimes pursue just to play the
field. A boy, in any case, when one is fourteen or fifteen is a
collector's item. A notch on a belt.

For a year on Pinehurst Avenue, we lived contentedly
with my mother's family on the east side of the street.
Then one day, when I was nine, I became aware of the two
larger houses on the west side of Pinehurst Avenue. The
two apartment houses on our side were smaller and they
took up only half of the block. The other half consisted
of empty lots where we played ball and baked mickies in
caves of Manhattan schist. Clearly, the west side of the
street was superior, the buildings grander, their entrances
adorned with marble columns. And clearly the band of

girls living in the house at the southwest corner must be superior too.

Perhaps my sudden awareness of these girls came from sitting next to Sellie in the same section of the fourth grade; and liking the way she looked. Perhaps it was because I ran into her at the shul where her strictly orthodox parents and my traditionally orthodox grandparents went. (My own parents belonged to a reform synagogue.) None of the other girls' families in that house, I later discovered, were practicing Jews and one of them was, as we called her, a "non-Jew." Though I never thought one way or the other about Juliette McGee's religion. At any rate, ultimately, I was more or less included in the group, always a bit peripherally. I remained an outsider because of mysterious conditions I somehow failed to fulfill.

I think Sellie and I became "best" friends because, among those girls, we were closest to each other in age. Months count when you are that young and Sellie and I were born five months apart. One other of us, Marjorie, who would have filled this requirement and more with her assertive style and real glamour – she was a full-fledged orphan and her brother was in a prep school – moved into 2 Pinehurst a year or so later.

The girls, there were seven, were exciting and stimulating in their seven different ways: Ada, Juliette, Esther, Ethel, Marjorie, Selena and Selena's older sister, Jean. And though I too became a "girl" (Dee for Dinah), that crown never sat lightly on my head. Perhaps because I arrived late into this established company, I tried too hard to belong. This was not easy even when, having decided to pack up their tents and move again, my parents chose an apartment in the next-door house on the better side of the street. The house was grander, rents were higher, there was a "Persian" rug in the vestibule and a uniformed elevator boy. Still it was No. 12, not No. 2 Pinehurst Avenue where the "girls" lived.

Making it with the girls meant sitting around after school, usually on twin beds in one of their apartments, munching Cheese Tidbits while talking as though one had inside knowledge, originality and/or special perceptiveness. We projected these qualities by matching tales about a cousin who was getting divorced (astounding, then), another relative who was about to marry a non-Jew, a teacher's romantic attachment to another teacher in P. S. 115.... All indiscreet revelations were introduced by the phrase "Strictly Confidential." For our ears alone.

I was getting along fairly well with the girls when some potent ammunition I had almost lost them to me. It was carnal information. This deadly treasure was donated to me by another friend who lived around the block and whose father was president of the synagogue of which Sellie's father was vice-president. Betsy, my informant, who went to a Hebrew school and whom the girls disliked, had visible breasts already at ten. Her family owned a player piano and she and I worked the piano together "playing" the *William Tell Overture* after which I went home to practice the prosaic Two-part Inventions, Czerny, etc. One day, on the piano bench, Betsy told me how the man did it to the woman and I relayed this intriguing information to Sellie.

Almost immediately, though I didn't see the connection then, I sensed a remoteness in my new friends. I tried to rationalize it away; it was my braids (they all had short hair), they were thinner than I – except for short, fat sixteen-year-old Ada whose corpulence as a mother figure was accepted. I later found out that the older girls who all "knew" were protective of Sellie, thought her too young to be initiated (she was five months younger than me!) and had it in for me for corrupting her.

When, so many years after, I discovered what had alienated me, I no longer needed the girls, and moreover, they didn't exist as an entity. But in this sore and innocent epoch, I just worked harder at belonging. I gave up Betsy and the player piano and nagged my mother until she let me have my hair bobbed.

At last, I managed to slip back into the group.

We were all together one day when our conversation got around to preferences, even infatuations within the group. "Strictly confidentially," some of the girls were acknowledging that they had favorites, particularly the younger who had crushes on the older ones. Sellie blushed, wouldn't confess and had to have it teased out of her that her choice was Esther whom she had always admired. I suddenly realized how much I adored Ethel and went to sit near her. Amazing how one can fall in love by willing!

Ethel was dumbfounded but, in fact, she and I were thrilled that she was my idol. Dark-haired Ethel, then fourteen or fifteen, a little aloof, vibrant, very bright and at once flawless in my eyes. Later she went to Smith and married soon after graduating from college. (Her husband was killed in the Lincoln Brigade in Spain.) When she was thirty-two – though I had long lost track of her and learned this from another of the girls – she committed suicide. Ethel Morel.

Ethel "protected" me and I was "in" again, generally speaking. Sellie again whistled signals across the wide alleyway between our houses, we met downstairs and walked to school together as we did before.

We had an outdoor life too. In winter, we belly-whopped on our Flexible Flyers down Snake Hill, which started where Haven Avenue is now, toward the Hudson. (Snow seems to have fallen steadily every winter, all winter *and* no cars!) Or we ice-skated afternoons till it was dark, on the flooded frozen tennis courts at the corner. In spring and fall we played street games, ball, potsy, and jumped rope. We all borrowed books from the same branch library where we often ran into each other and where Sellie's aunt was a librarian. During our bed-sitting sessions we discussed *Silas Marner, Julius Caesar* and other books read at school, most from bowdlerized texts or censored at will by our brainwashed teachers. Sellie and I usually listened while the older girls talked. Increasingly, we added our own ideas and interpretations, vying with each other in order to impress those colossi, our seniors.

For the few of us whose parents observed the Jewish high holidays, Sellie and Jean's place was Jerusalem. All holy days were punctiliously kept in the Bloomberg's clean, vast apartment that was furnished with heavy mission oak, impossible to budge, harder to damage. Mr. and Mrs. Bloomberg reigned over a large real estate empire but kept their everyday costs of living down to a stark minimum. (They were the only people I ever knew who installed a coin telephone in their apartment.) One maid, an adoring Jewish immigrant, did all the housework and cooked the family's uninspired boiled chicken, beef and fish dinners.

During the day, Sellie's parents sat at their dining table extended full length and always laden with business ledgers. This huge table was surrounded by relatives who were accountants, rent collectors, car drivers, etc., all of whom continued in these roles till they were incapacitated by old age or died. (Few Jews left New York City, anyway, until a generation later. It was cold out there and unwelcoming.) At six p.m., the dining room table was cleared, the relatives went home and the table was set for dinner, called supper in our circles.

Since the Jewish holidays were relentlessly kept in this house and because there were two Bloomberg girls – actually four, the others too young to be included in with "the girls" – the rest of us who thought of ourselves as Jews often spent part of each holiday in the Bloomberg apartment. Besides, Mrs. Bloomberg preferred "keeping an eye" on her daughters.

For us, Yom Kippur was a joyous holiday. I started mine by carrying a clove-studded citron to my grandmother in the synagogue. Faint from heat and hunger, she breathed its pungent odor during the service and was revived. Both she and I were dressed in our new winter velvets though, as any Jew will tell you, no matter how late the holy days come, it's always ninety degrees on Yom Kippur. I remember the beads of perspiration on her upper lip.

My mission accomplished, I rushed back to the Bloombergs' where four or five of us sat on the beds talking. Complaining of parents, inspecting and comparing our new best dresses, doing what we always did but *not* eating Tidbits. We were fasting too, half a day, as was judged appropriate for children. Until we were thirteen, (when presumably we would begin our all-day fasts) from dinner at sundown the previous evening, no food or drink had passed our lips. Then, at twelve o'clock sharp, we raced to the kitchen and made ourselves challah sandwiches of tomato and lettuce and Hellman's mayonnaise. The sandwiches were so thick, we could hardly get our mouths around them. I don't remember having been so hungry before or since, nor has anything ever tasted as good as those tomato, lettuce and mayonnaise sandwiches.

Sometimes I was sure I was a bona fide member of the group. But was I? There were differences. For starters, I lived in 12 Pinehurst Avenue. Then our clothes. The girls wore Bramley dresses from Franklin Simon, the kind with those round, white collars. My parents couldn't afford department store clothing because my socialist father was being an unsuccessful, idealistic lawyer while their fathers were rich business men. All of *our* clothes were made by a poor hard-working young French seamstress who cut and fitted everything: school clothes, "good" clothes, even coats. Our mother finished them up on the sewing machine with hand touches afterwards. This made me conspicuous and available for ridicule. Especially when Ethel wasn't around. She did look out for my interests. Sellie, on the other hand, never interceded on my behalf. However, she occasionally made "as if" because she liked giving the impression of good sportsmanship and fair play. It was her *thing.* In time it became my thing too.

I will never forget one gratuitous assault against me when Ethel was away. It was early summer, the dogwood trees were in bloom in Riverside Park and we wandered along the paths perhaps looking for mischief. We found a fountain, drank like mad and took turns pressing our thumbs on the nozzle and squirting water. Suddenly, I was pushed aside and one after another, they directed the spray full force at me. I was wearing a starched, blue cotton dress that, in seconds, was a mass of dark wet splotches. Awful. I probably burst into tears. Worse. But they laughed and kept it up till they were bored. Why not? I didn't budge, paralyzed as I was by misery at the unfairness and incomprehensibility of what was happening. Moreover, when they started for home whispering among themselves, I followed, ignominiously.

In spite of these erratic incidents and sometimes ostracism, my intense, unexplored bond with Ethel continued and my companionship with Sellie developed and grew stronger as we grew older. Was it habit? Was it because Sellie and I were the same age and in the same class while the older girls were entering adult worlds? We did share the same preferences and goals and believed ardently in friendship as a good in itself.

Sellie demanded frankness and I complied. If I wasn't ready with a definite opinion when she asked for it, I often invented one. She wanted to know if I liked a new sweater and, though she invariably looked just right to me, I paused, as if deliberating, then said emphatically (assertiveness was important) that yes, it was a good shade of green for her. Or, with equal affirmation, "That's definitely *not* the color for you!"

For better or worse, we have always been there for each other. But I was more there for her because she threw me over. By then, I was really hooked. And I know that she was too.

Sellie was my model. The frankness, athletic grace, her muscles worked *for* her, her popularity... (if I were more like her would I be as popular?). Even her elusiveness, as she matured and had more to be secretive about, I envied. Though at times I felt cheated by it. For example, I assumed that we confided equally in each other. Years later, I discovered that she had kept important things about her marriage from me when it was exactly these kinds of intimacies I couldn't wait to share with her. Yet I respected her reticence. You could tell Sellie anything and if you asked her not to repeat it, she, for all intents and purposes, forgot it.

I tried to be like her but even persistent emulation doesn't always succeed. I never jumped double-dutch as well as she, wasn't able to ice-skate round and round the rink – she had hockey, I, figure skates. But learn to say arrogantly what I thought, I did.

At this moment, I'm studying a snapshot on my desk: Sellie at fifteen. I see that same girl whenever I meet the older woman excessively wrinkled, wearing thick glasses after eye surgery. Her skin droops and folds under eyes and chin the way her mother's did. This friend, still my "best," has never changed for me. I must tell her that I still find her the same; long, wistful face, thick brown hair now graying, bow-shaped lips that open in a bright, white-toothed smile and a strong body that is slender with small breasts she abhors as she always has her thickish ankles. She's about five-foot five, round-shouldered now (I'm always cautioning her to straighten up – she likes that sort of directive) and her hauteur, that indomitable family pride, adds another inch, at least, to her stature. My own face is considered pretty, my bones are fine, my feet and hands are small. I realize that these are assets and in moments of bitter indignation against her, I glory in them. However, I would have exchanged looks with her anytime, and though I'm more sensible now, more acceptable of myself, Sellie's face and her figure (we called it body) was my criterion of loveliness.

The only advantage I remember having as a child, was a talent for the piano, though I took that for granted then. And do now. My parents could also have been counted as a plus. They had both gone to college and were members of the middle of that upper middle class. The Bloombergs, by contrast, were almost barbaric. Mrs. B., sharp-witted, wary and blunt, nevertheless had imperious poise and digni-ty that came from absolute self-confidence and from her ability to earn lots of money. This wealth (and it was considerable) was to be used to launch her daughters into a more urbane and civilized world. Mr. B. was bouncy, jolly, a bit uncouth and absolutely devoted to his wife. Both parents shouted blasphemies at their children, beat them *and* withheld allowances for various transgressions. We had less spending money but since it was never withheld, it was equivalent to theirs in the long run. My mother never "touched" us and my father hit us very seldom. He had an explosive temper but the worst oath he ever uttered was "darn."

Though I played the piano and was the only "girl" who could carry a tune, this endowment was insignificant. Or simply beside the point. I sensed that being able to hum on pitch was, to them, a sort of amiable deformity rather than the other way around; and since everyone in our family sang, played some instrument and, of course, carried a tune, I considered these humdrum skills. When I won first place, with three other candidates in the city music-memory contest, I was hardly ecstatic. I thought the whole business wasn't worth the paper the notes were written on.

One achievement which should have made me proud and the memory of which pleases me now, so many years later, is playing the Paderewski *Minuet in G* when I was twelve for the general school assembly in the auditorium. This event may have been the epitome of my piano career. It certainly was the last time I performed unhampered by self-consciousness which Sellie helped generate in me by a crusade against any kind of public display.

During summers, Sellie and I were separated. She and her sisters went to a girls' camp in Pennsylvania while, during my early adolescence, our family – grandparents, aunts, uncles – rented houses on Long Island.

I remember one of these summers vividly because, the June before, a prestigious doctor had discovered that I had a heart murmur. This specialist was called Dr. Winter, an appropriately bleak name for a doctor who forbade "all forms of exercise."

Our house that summer was in Patchogue. There were no children of my age in the neighborhood and a plague of poisonous jelly-fish in the Sound put an embargo on even playing in the water. It was a lonely, frustrating summer with one very bright spot.

A bike had been bought for my sister. It was intended not for pleasure but to help her lose weight. No bike for me because I had been warned by Dr. Winter that a patient of his, a nice little boy with a weak heart, had died doing just that: riding a bicycle. My sister, who never even managed to sit upright on hers, gave up trying and that bright red, unused bike seemed to beckon to me from the garage, tempting me day after day. At last I yielded. I wheeled it out secretly every morning, got on, fell off, got on, till suddenly one day, there I was staying on, riding. Mornings when my mother went shopping, or was otherwise too busy to notice me, I maneuvered the bike away from the many-eyed house and raced it through the countryside. Since I fell often while learning, my knees were a mass of abrasions, ugly, gritty and scabby. But I sat above them exhilarated, first two hands, then one, and finally no hands at all, flying over those car-less roads. I still wonder why no one in the family associated my banged-up knees with riding that bike.

Other situations, that summer, worsened. I didn't menstruate as I had dreamed and planned I would. Years behind the older girls, I was months behind Sellie who showed off by magnifying her discomfort and always announcing when she had the curse. For five days she walked clumsily, taking wider steps than normal. And well she might, considering that in the Bloomberg household, you not only made your extremely tough, durable sanitary napkins, you also washed them yourself. The result was a thick, rough bandage that chafed the delicate inner skin of the thighs. Sellie often complained of cramps and stayed home from school the first two days. How I wanted to see blood on my panties! Those cramps! No curse to me, I never worried about *having* my menses, I only felt deprived at not having them.

Sex did come that summer, tangentially. During one long, hot week, our small Boston Bull terrier was mounted by several outsized dogs. The family rushed around shouting every time it happened and tried to yank the dogs apart. At the same time, they ordered my sister and me into the house. We weren't supposed to know but we watched from the windows and saw our little dog and her lovers standing back to back looking positively woe-begone. In the fall of that year, Trixie, our sweet bitch, died of a hard confinement.

Late that fall, I met my first boy friend. I had just returned, one dark wintry afternoon, from the skating rink, had foolishly thawed my feet under a radiator and was dancing around in excruciating pain when there was a phone call for me. It was a boy. He said he had heard about me from Sarah, my very pretty cousin, and wanted to make a date with me. Sanford Jaretsky. A name to conjure with, Sanford the chosen, Jaretsky the given. A name I will never forget.

In order for me to get a glimpse of Sanford, my cousin and I bussed down to a hundred and tenth Street and walked north along Seventh Avenue, one bright Sunday morning. This wide street was a *rambla* for rich upper middle class Jews and Sanford lived in one of the apartment houses on it. When Sarah nudged me, I saw coming toward us a boy of medium height, fair curly hair, unusually light, blue eyes. The stratagem was to pretend to be casual, to look unconcerned. We did this but by the time Sanford had passed us, I was smitten.

Sellie pooh-poohed the whole thing, didn't believe Sanford could be someone either of us would find interesting, *or* that he would ever call again. The miracle occurred. He did call and Sellie was perfectly willing to have a blind date with one of his friends.

Picture the scene: a Saturday afternoon in our small apartment, the library-table-bed where my sister and I slept covered with its Chinese silk strip, books on it neat between

Rodin's *Thinker* bookends, across the room the upright
piano topped with a very large vase sparsely filled with
dusty bittersweet, one couch, two upholstered chairs, one
antique French table near the couch and a bookcase
with the crystal radio on it.

My parents were waiting discreetly, in another room,
to be introduced – a mandatory ceremony throughout my
teens. And Sellie and I were just waiting. When Sanford
arrived, I had the shock of my young life. Seeing him,
I suppose through Sellie's eyes, he seemed insignificant and
unworthy. He was really short and his hair was definitely
kinky. His friend David, who wore thick glasses, was
altogether beyond the pale. Sanford remained shrewdly
silent, the other lad was too shy to say a word. I was the
one who kept things going, chatting as continuously as I
could. I wonder now what I talked about, non-stop, for perhaps half an hour. Then my parents came and went, after
which there was the inevitable pause. Nobody had anything
to say. In the embarrassing silence, Sellie walked over to the
piano, fingered the orange bittersweet berries and said,
"Three skinny branches. They look scared in that big vase."
I was deeply humiliated by this but even more, I imagined
that Sanford's bored, sharp eyes examining the room
and focussing now on the table-bed, pierced right through
the mahogany exterior to the mattress inside. The afternoon
was, at best, not very satisfying and it was obvious that he
knew it was my first date.

It was an uninspired courtship – I found every moment
of it enthralling at the time – during which Sanford tried in
vain, several times, to hypnotize me (this was one of his
stock-in-trade diversions, another being the loaded pistol he
carried and pressed against any willing fool's temple). He
called me his sweetheart but never kissed me. One day,
the following spring, we went to Coney Island. There, to the
tune of *It's Three o'Clock in the Morning*, playing somewhere
in the amusement park, he held my hand, looked into my
eyes with his truly hypnotic ones and solemnly announced

that he had never really loved me. He had tried to fall in love but couldn't.

I had other boy friends from then on and shared this part of my life with my cousin Sarah. It was certainly a more "normal" life than any of the girls enjoyed; just as my musical life was becoming more professional than the older girls' who were by now in college. At fourteen I gave piano lessons for fifty cents an hour to two young women whom my music teacher knew. Good training for the future, my teacher averred. She, my family, maybe even my friends, expected me to teach piano for the rest of my life. They didn't know and I hardly realized how seriously I wanted to become some kind of a writer. Much later, I turned to this deeper and most blissful art of writing fiction and poetry; of making something instead of interpreting another's creation, as I did on the piano.

Then, overnight, everything changed. I became fully adolescent (finally menstruating at fourteen when nobody but my mother cared), and I went to George Washington High School, a long street-car ride away from home.

Early one morning when Sellie and Jean and I were boarding the street car to go to school, a truck plowed into its rear platform. The few of us waiting to mount the steps were scattered like windfall apples. Sellie had already moved inside but her sister Jean, I and a boy neither of us knew, were very near the steps when the crash came.

Jean was badly smashed up. She suffered multiple bone fractures and was hospitalized for more than six months. My injuries, by contrast, seemed trifling: one broken wrist, two teeth impacted into my gums, a six-stitch-slash through my right eyebrow.... My bruised right knee became one thick scab, unbendable for weeks and my head ached steadily all that time.

The boy in the accident was killed....

The worst of the experience was waking up under the truck, being yanked out, stood up and walked, shivering from shock, by well-meaning bystanders the five blocks to my house. There was a reward, however, for this harrowing promenade. I stayed in bed, at home, instead of being rushed off to a hospital for three long months.

On the evening of that same day, I was to have gone to my first "informal." I completely forgot about the dance and when my escort came for me – corsage and all – he stared at me from the bedroom door, and fled. I was a mess, my swollen face almost unrecognizable.

The physical injuries were bad. The psychological traumas, incalculable. When my wounds healed, these commenced with "dress-rehearsals." I found endless excuses for not leaving the house; I woke at night gasping for air and my mother gave me bicarbonate of soda which seemed to regulate my breathing. But these omens were preliminary to more severe anxieties. Whenever, for example, I heard that someone was ill, I developed identical symptoms. My mother, unprotesting, took me, month after month to the doctor who always gave me a clean bill of health. This costly business went on for about three years. There were also ghastly moments when, riding in a bus, I suddenly couldn't breathe. I'd get off, run into the nearest drugstore and be revived by aromatic spirits of ammonia. Or I stood still, unable to draw another breath six blocks away from our house. Then I ran the whole way, panting, so that at least I would die on the doorstep. Away from the apartment, I was never safe. In those years, no one had much information about agoraphobia and not one of my friends suspected what hell I endured every single day of my life. There were positive things that emerged from this catastrophe. Because of my broken right wrist, I developed a fine left-hand piano technique. Then, in those early months of incarceration, I read all the Dostoyevsky novels available in our public library. I also had an opportunity to pose in the nude (daring!) for a young male artist, a cousin of one of "the girls." But the greatest benefit (it was thought to be therapeutic) was to be sent to a summer camp. Naturally, I chose the one where Sellie had gone for three years. It never occurred to me to ask where my parents found enough money to help me overcome my "aberrations" this way.

* * * *

Camp is a happy time for me, in recollection. I've remembered and re-evaluated the experience and think I can be fair to myself and Winonka. Maybe even to Sellie whose twin role as friend and camp mate catapulted us from crisis to crisis.

At fifteen, I was too old for a new camper and too "new" for an old one. Again, I was up against that wall of alienation. Camps, however, are crowded, busy places where you may be lonely but you're never alone. Right off, I had a trivial but important disappointment. My khaki outfit, middies and bloomers bought in Spauldings, from where all sport uniforms came, was of a recently dyed lot, dull tan and not nearly as pretty as the pinkish, warm shade of the original ones. And the girls who wore them looked well-seasoned; a young eager army, well oriented and disciplined. Not one of them was a recruit of my age. They swam the Australian crawl while I pushed out with my side stroke. I could see how amateurish *that* must have looked. I'd never held a tennis racket, volleyball or basketball in my hands.

Curiously enough, my big advantage was being the best friend of a popular girl who excelled in every sport and had just been re-elected captain of one of the two teams; her third time around. Some of Sellie's charisma must have rubbed off on me. People liked me. I was content. For a while. I worked hard at playing games and, as they guaranteed in the brochure, acquired skills. I learned to take a canoe out alone, tip it, turn it upside down and either right it or swim inside it (underneath) back to the dock. I became a good tennis player and rode horseback ineptly but with joy; but I never managed that Australian crawl. More importantly, I knew when, if not why, to groan with my peers or show pleasure if pleasure seemed in order.

Hypochondria, which got me to Winonka in the first

place, slumbered after one gruelling attack. It had caught me off guard, soaking wet in the communal shower room when suddenly, all my skin tightened and began to burn. I *knew* that a vein or artery had burst in my body and I flew out of the shower calling to Jess, the counselor in charge. "I think I'm dying." I must have looked like death because Jess flung a towel around me and half carried me across the quad to the infirmary.

The reason I recall the incident in some detail is that later, the same day, Sellie brought it up for the benefit of our bunk mates. She was not commiserating with me but with "poor Jess," she said, the one "everybody's burdens fell on." We all loved Jess and felt sorry for her. She was wonderfully fair-minded and reliable but she was also twenty-four, plain looking and not even engaged. Now here I was adding to her cares. Sellie made so much of this that I almost felt it would have been better to have died that afternoon in the shower room. Then *I* would have merited some of this sympathy. However, though our bunkies made moos of concern for Jess, they were in a hurry to get some tennis in before flag lowering and hardly stayed to hear Sellie out.

One way I was able to defray some of the camp fees was to play piano for the dancing classes. (We did free-flowing steps in free-flowing, pastel-dyed, cheesecloth veils.) The first dancing counselor I accompanied could have been taken for a handsome, dark, slender boy. Unfortunately, she behaved like one. "Caught" one night at two a.m. beyond a little wood near the lake with a senior camper, she vanished so precipitously, she might never have existed. She was just not there for the next dance group. Mystery of mysteries, there was a new dance counselor, Frances, a very feminine, even voluptuous, red-haired Skidmore College student. Frances was eventually assigned as bunk counselor to our bunk and I got to know her well. She was garrulous and loved gossiping about everyone and everything: college, camp, why she preferred certain girls, what activities she thought asinine and how small-minded the camp director was. We sat for hours, she and I, on the bunk porch steps after taps, Frankie talking and stroking my neck ("It's good for the nerves") till I tingled all over. She *did* keep her job but by then, the atmosphere was charged with sex and all of us tingled.

There was the night I woke to strange goings-on. One of my bunk mates was calling to another, moaning, urging, "Come back. I want you to come back." Electrified, I lay still, listening. The other girl refused. "It makes me shiver too much. I can't. I can't stand trembling like that." "I'll come over to you." Frantic, "No! Don't! I'll put on my flashlight and wake everybody if you do. I can't bear it." Like a litany, the plea, "Come back. Please come back," went on till I fell asleep.

These were girls I thought I knew well. The "importuner," a lively and clever girl was, in fact, one of the girls from our group at home. The other, slight and seemingly frail, had a special kind of appeal that perhaps came from her fragility. You wanted to take care of her. We learned ultimately that beneath her "amiable weakness" lived a competent, tough-minded young woman.

Next morning, that incident might never have happened. No signs of that operatic exchange, though I studied Marge and Westie from time to time. Camp activities had taken over. Both girls were skilled athletes on opposing teams and they were immensely competitive. I think, too, that they were able to survive this crisis and remain friends because Westie had a lot of plain, good common sense.

A boy's summer camp, twenty miles away, provided occasional socializing. Several times each summer, the boys exchanged visits with us. They came, in cheering truckloads, to our Gilbert and Sullivan performances, or for a dance. We were driven decorously in cars to Songedeewin, singing all the way, to watch their plays and dance with them afterwards. I had a "steady" with whom I walked back and forth across our quadrangle and who once, against the rules, took me out in a canoe and kissed me. Sellie was fascinated by a dull, handsome Songedeewin counselor who did not reciprocate her feelings. But boys will be boys and Bims did attempt to kiss her. Sellie told him off. "Who do you think you are!" she said and justified her reaction by telling me that they'd only seen each other twice and that didn't confer kissing status. Nevertheless, she concocted a truly medieval romance, all symbols and signs and secrets, from this two-time encounter. Many years later, she gave Bim's telephone number to a girl called Adele, one of her sudden intense friendships. On a blind date those two met, fell in love and Sellie never spoke to Adele again. (Bims and Adele eventually married.)

Summers at camp, at least on the surface, are clean-cut and clean; all that swimming, the games, inspection of outfits and mopping up the fuzzies under the beds (team points off for any infractions) *and* sportsmanship that could kill with fairness. Never, never did you evince disappointment at losing a point, or even a whole game. With one exception: it was legitimate to commiserate with a fellow team-mate who lost and was sorry she let her team down.

Sellie wanted me for ego boosting, to have someone who belonged to her exclusively. I evidently filled these and other more complex needs. *She* could have preferences and favorites among the campers. I could not. Once, in a play-off of the team tennis matches, I astonished myself by beating one of the opposing team's prize players and easily one of the nicest girls in camp. Teenie (Rowena) was tall, good-looking in the accepted boyish way and quietly thoughtful. She "had everything" but, being a junior, was not eligible for a thorough-going friendship with Sellie, a senior. Furthermore, she was on the *other* team. So, when I defeated her with a freakishly brilliant service I'd developed in four weeks from scratch, Sellie (our captain) was torn between delight at her team's climbing score and annoyed at Teenie's defeat. By me. Rowena took it splendidly, actually leaped over the net to shake my hand. Sellie, visibly in a quandary, first came to congratulate me, then spent an hour wandering back and forth across the quad with Teenie, probably praising her famous back hand. That hurt. Sellie knew just how much.

At supper that night, I didn't let Sellie catch me looking at her. We sat almost opposite each other and while our eyes pirouetted, she was conversing animatedly with her far-side neighbor and I was listening to the girl on my far side. In the typical hubbub of a camp meal, you couldn't hear your vis-a-vis anyway, that's why Sellie and I usually sat together. As long as you were with your age group you could sit near anybody you chose. Seniors sat at tables away from the doors, the younger kids near the doors to make it easier for them to dash ahead from the mess hall to the tennis courts, in that precious free time after supper before evening activities began.

How long that meal lasted! I had plenty of spare time to observe things that hadn't interested me before (and didn't much now). I saw the late summer sun gild the farther wall of the hall; watched it filtered dim by clouds and shine again, but rosier. It seemed to me it lighted another part of the wall than it had earlier in the summer. And of course it did for it had moved during July and a part of August across the sky. When supper was over the head counselor stood up, the signal for that frantic scramble out the doors to the courts. I fell behind and watched Sellie. She was obviously dying to see where I was; what I was up to. But she was too proud to turn around.

I walked out the side door of the mess hall and followed a narrow path inside the woods paralleling the bunks till I reached the senior bunk. It was the last, the one distinguished by being set back and away from the others.

In the time I was alone there, that evening, I could have and still regret not committing the dastardly sin of reading Sellie's diary. (I was also afraid I might be surprised in the act.) How moral we are in some ways and how immoral in others! Sellie and her sister Jean, without any compunction, occasionally charged a dress in a department store, wore it, decided it didn't suit and returned it some weeks later. Then, in a blaze of indignation, if there was any resistance from the store, they berated the salesgirl, the buyer, even the manager if necessary. Their reason was some trumped up flaw in the garment or a supposedly false claim by the poor salesgirl. We "girls" giggled at these shenanigans – all but Ethel who sternly disapproved. This perfidious practice was more or less acceptable in our social class. However, to snitch on anyone, to read a private letter or diary! There was absolutely no condoning such behavior. And I behaved according to the code. I didn't touch Sellie's diary.

We hope and expect that someone will miss us when we don't turn up. They seldom do. I mused on this when I was alone in the cabin. When it got dark, I put my flashlight on and read, first sitting, then lying down on my cot. No one came to look for me and I hadn't put on the bunk light because I wanted to give the impression that I needed privacy. Seniors were permitted a little privacy. A very little.

Suddenly, I woke up. Sellie was shaking me. "Sh!" she cautioned. It was pitch black, very warm and I could hear the orchestra of crickets outside the bunk walls. "Get up and go to bed," Sellie told me, I thought inconsistently. Then I realized I'd fallen asleep in my clothes, that it was late, that Sellie was in her pajamas and that everyone else was fast asleep. "Where's my flash?" This object was more precious than diamonds and almost as precious as a new tennis ball. "Here." She had put it on the shelf above my bed.

I undressed groggily and she went to her cot which was set against the opposite wall so that we slept with our beds meeting, head to head in the same corner. I didn't wash my teeth – it was so quiet and the water gurgled so loudly when it rushed down the drain that the girls would have awakened and raised hell. "Good night, Sellie." I said it tenderly for I was deeply moved by what she had done. She was making amends for the pain she had caused me. I knew just how hard it was for her to do this.

"Come in with me for a minute," she said. "Let's talk."

I crawled under her blanket and immediately felt we had become a pair of magnets irresistibly attracting each other. A whole magnetic field of allure, in fact. The wonder of it, coming together that way! No words, no sounds, not a movement. We adhered. Two bodies meeting and almost merging. We held our breaths and I felt that if I stirred, I would not be able to tell if it were Sellie or I who was moving, and more than this, it seemed that if either of us moved or breathed, the world would shatter and disintegrate into fragments.

How long did we stay like that, not holding, not kissing, just touching in a state of suspended voluptuousness? I have no idea. I only remember that, suddenly, it was overwhelming and that I felt lost and frightened. I drew back and heard her voice asking, "What's the matter?" My answer was instinctive, honest and, I suppose, all wrong. "I'm scared." Then, unsteadily, but very deliberately, I got out of her bed and went back to my own, slipping under the stiff, cold, camp sheets and blankets. "Good night," I whispered. Sellie was silent. I assumed she had fallen asleep. Even the crickets had stopped chirping. I realized why when I heard the incessant spill of rain on the flat roof. For a few minutes, my mind concentrated on that delirious, new experience. An hour before, I had had no idea my body could feel that much, that way. There was no name I could attach to it nor could I make any sense of that dazzling, disturbing sensation.

I slept right through reveille and woke abruptly to see, across the quad, the girls already forming ranks in front of the flag pole. No time to think, or feel or to remember while I rushed into my clothes, combed my hair, grabbed a sweater (one of the rules for morning procedure) and waited at the screen door. What we did, in case we committed the heinous sin of being late for flag raising, was to sneak out and join the campers as they broke ranks and ran for breakfast. You could pull it off if no counselor or the mean, all-seeing director happened to notice. Otherwise, the team lost five points. That morning, I managed. Just.

When I saw Sellie at breakfast, I fell in love for the first time. I had always liked the way she looked, but now she was my beloved, clothed in new flesh, constructed, somehow, of new bones and sinews. I explored her strong face rising from protruding collar bones (which she hated), her high forehead, her nose, large but in proportion to the rest of her face and those perfect, surprisingly small, well-cut lips.

We sat at table and I watched her toying with a piece of bread, her knuckly fingers working at making pellets (another camp proscription). It was her deft fingers that thrilled me most. I studied them, then looked back up at her face. She didn't raise her eyes. Then I realized she had again, for the second time, not saved a place for me next to her. Today of all days. And I sensed we were in for a lot of sturm and drang and that it would hit me hardest because I cared as much about her suffering as about my own.

And so it was. For the three long camp weeks that were left, Sellie communicated with me only in her role as team captain. She was doing her duty, her grim manner implied. I brooded over what had happened between us. In a muddle-headed way, I figured that I had let her down, "physically," as we called it; that she despised me because I was not, in some mysterious way, up to the madness of that night in the dark bunk. Was she?

I felt I'd been quarantined but there were some small compensations. We had so little contact, there were fewer opportunities for Sellie to put me down. In all fairness, it must be understood that I didn't blame all this on Sellie. There was my own lurking paranoia to contend with. My ambivalent admiration and dependence on her. And her dependence on me which was even more ambivalent in the populous camp world where she was a queen.

The days were melancholy, the miseries bizarre. For example, when Sellie ripped open her heel on a rough dock board, I alone couldn't console and soothe her. I, her closest friend, stood by, a pariah, while others rushed to her side. When she won the tennis tournament, made good basketball shots in the finals, etc., I pretended my cheers were for the team. I never congratulated her. The once I did extend my hand, her glacial stare was killing. During the last week at camp, I had an infected finger. It swelled, ached horribly and, under a bandage (which a doctor in the city finally removed), it was turning green. At camp the tip of my finger throbbed so badly, I woke one night, moaning. The bunk light had been switched on and the girls were up asking if they should take me to the infirmary. Sellie feigned sleep.

This infected finger curtailed both pleasures and duties. Missing sports and not being able to accompany the dancers on the piano, I set myself another project: making up team songs, ditties to well-known, catchy tunes. My effort won our team lots of points and got me the "most-original-contribution-to-team-song" award. (No personal acknowledgment from the captain.) Writing those lyrics was diverting. That and riding horseback kept me busy. I had little time to pity myself and I was able to resist asking Sellie why she had banished me. Had I done this, however, everything would have been cleared up and the rest of the summer would have been saved.

On the train going home, I found myself waiting behind Sellie to go to the "Ladies." She went in and I decided to stop her and have a showdown when she came out; to stop her and ask why she had condemned me without, you might say, tribunal or appeal. The door opened. We were so close that she ran into me and I heard my clearest, most courageous voice demand her attention for something "Strictly Confidential," that old magic phrase.

We sat in a vacant double seat and it was as if a tidal wave engulfed us. Revelations rushed forth as rapidly as the rural landscape was rushing into suburban and then city-scape. Sellie told me how awful it was when she realized I was afraid someone would catch us together that night. My mouth fell open and I explained that it was all a dreadful mistake, that she was absolutely wrong. I hadn't thought of anyone but the two of us. It was the experience itself, so disturbing and wonderful and crazy that made me cringe. After a long, straightforward talk, we shook hands firmly and formally. We had come home. The train, too, was entering the city station.

* * * *

Getting back from camp was a let-down. Families, to begin with, show very little interest in those two "wondrous strange" months away from home. Then, our own memories necessarily recede as soon as high school impinges with its day after day monotony.

Sellie and I took the "academic" college preparatory program and did our homework together in my quieter apartment. From time to increasing time, she stayed overnight. Without any complicated maneuvering (I think it was our great longing for each other that made everything fall into place), we were able to convince her "it's-out-of-the-question" mother of the necessity of these visits. Though looking back, it seems we were just plain lucky. It did help that Mrs. Bloomberg approved of my family and that learning takes precedence over everything else among Jews. We had only to say that we were drilling each other for a Latin test or that my mother was coaching us in algebra.... These excuses were sufficient but I knew then that the main reason we got away with it was that neither Sellie's despotic mother nor my morally righteous parents ever could have imagined that two girls in bed together could do anything worse than talk themselves to death and fall asleep.

Late at night, after the family had turned off the crystal radio and gone to sleep (Don't stay up too late!), we worked a while at the dining room table, then opened the old library table – in its own room in a larger apartment by this time – fell into it and, for hours, made passionate, inexpert love.

We were so inexperienced! I wanted to kiss Sellie, she wanted me to touch her breasts, her tummy, her thighs. And she was more dissatisfied than I. She suffered more because while I caressed her, she whimpered, waiting and waiting for what never happened as I went on exploring her body, incompetently. Once, tortured and sick with desire, we decided to call it quits. Weeks of abstinence, then, one day, a letter from her. She wanted to stay over again *but* as friends. "Nothing precarious," she had written. "Every conceivable caution will be *observed.*" My mother found this note and, clearly baffled, wanted to know what in the world Selena was afraid of in our apartment. I said that Sellie was using a few of our much ridiculed school expressions. Needless to say we threw "caution" to the winds and after weeks of not having been together, our lovemaking was even more violent.

Sellie had the stride of a graceful American youth, light, long and swinging from the hips. She still looks well in clothes and perhaps because she's more boyish than womanly, deliberately dresses in softer, more lady-like styles. Her star appearance – how performance conscious most of us are! – was at seventeen in a chartreuse, two-piece party dress with fine, black lace ruching around the neck and lace cuffs that hung over, concealing her rather bony hands. However, her manner was more feminine than masculine in spite of her neat, flat figure. She always smiled flirtatiously in discussions with boys (later, with men) and curiously enough her way with children is slightly coquettish too. Sellie rarely loses her temper in public and has always been, in our comings together, the traditionally passive partner. I led in dancing, for example. Yet, I hardly remember what her body looks like. I of course saw her in bathing suits, bloomers and in the shower room at camp. But in camp we were so often half or all naked, it was never interesting.

Those nights together were spent in total darkness. Our wayward bodies urged us to put out the lights and get into bed immediately. I could feel but not see. Nor do I think I cared to discover her through my eyes and she never displayed her body provocatively, never wore sheer blouses or tight skirts. I can't, even if I wanted to, describe what she was like without clothes. I know that her breasts were small and firm, the kind that last and last because there's simply not enough of them to droop with age. And I knew my mouth on them.

Sellie had an abhorrence for large or unshapely breasts. They disgusted her. This taste was imprinted on me, her own breasts being my ideal. A heavy, formless bosom was almost an abnormality. I remember introducing Sellie to a woman I admired, a wise, warmhearted person. The meeting had been difficult to arrange. Finally, after we did get together, Sellie's first comment on that lovely woman, Theresa Rabinowitz was, "Why doesn't she wear a tighter, better-fitting bra. Ugh."

* * * *

Lovers tire of one another. One gets fed up with the other. Or, simply, loves less. The result, as we used to say, is that one of the lovers is jilted. Sellie jilted me. The erotic, even exotic pleasure that had gripped us for almost a year, ended. But what lingered was the undercurrent of anxiety, the fear that no boy would ever seem as desirable to us as we were to each other. Would this happen? Could it?

In those days, it was unlikely that sixteen-year-old girls had the opportunity to put a boy to such a test. Nor did it occur to me that a date's fumbling goodnight kiss was in the same class as Sellie's embraces. We gave those kisses outside the apartment door for the money that the boy spent on a movie and banana split afterwards. Payments. Sort of.

I remember the last time, a late spring day, when Sellie came over to do homework. My mother who really did help us with math had gone out. We sat by the window facing the brick wall of Sellie's house; the wall with the hall window through which she always whistled to signal. We discussed whether she'd wait till my mother returned that afternoon or whether it might be too late. I suggested she stay for supper, then get the work done and stay over. Almost immediately, with that sixth sense lovers have, I felt that she had changed. Her eyes glazed over, not with hostility but with apathy. No, she didn't want to do that. Why? She just didn't. Not any more. No. Why? No reply until after a few moments when she seemed to have hit upon an excuse. A reason. "You know, you got fatter." I wasn't fat but Sellie was certainly always thinner than I. Nor had that mattered during the nights of our lovemaking. Now, suddenly, it did. And it was obvious that there was nothing I could do or say to induce her to repeal her decision. Even now, I can hardly believe I was killed so swiftly. A guillotine chopped off a head. Mine.

The daytime pattern of our lives didn't change much. Sellie and I went to school together, had intense discussions about books, politics, people; got tickets for theater or concerts when she had money (Mrs. Bloomberg still docked her daughters' allowances as punishment for any infringement of her laws) and we were, as always, inseparable comrades. But not quite.

I had more to do with boys. And once, a few weeks after Sellie let me go, I necked "heavily" with a boy. But it was a one night stand and it ended on a note of absurdity. I couldn't wait to tell Sellie about it, partly because I wanted to assure her that we were no different than other girls, partly to share with her its ludicrousness. But mostly, I wanted to break down the barrier of silence we had erected against our intimacy.

I met Bert at my cousin's house. Sarah's family had moved to Long Island where, on weekends, I would occasionally go to be with her, and meet boys. On this visit, I went to a dance with Bert, a cousin of Sarah's current very serious boy friend. Bert was amiable, bland looking, fair haired and intelligent. (Though I thought him almost preciously well-mannered.) He argued skillfully and I enjoyed sparring. In fact we kept discussing while we danced and

I could see that he was impressed by my "mind." We then drove back to Sarah's in someone's crowded car, Bert with his arm tightly around me. Sarah's boy friend and he were staying overnight and Bert and I were returning together to New York by train the following morning.

The four of us, Sarah, her Jim, Bert and I sat around talking in the living room after the dance. It seemed natural for Jim to turn out the lights, for him to caress Sarah and for Bert to caress me. Perhaps I was hungry for his touch or Bert may have been very adept. Recalling him now, I remember him as one of the least appealing boys I'd ever known and I cannot imagine why he excited me that much. Fully dressed and sprawled uncomfortably over a small armchair, we struggled with each other, groping, grabbing, fighting for and against our bodies for hours. It must have been almost dawn when Sarah whispered that we had better go to bed before it got light and the family woke up.

In the morning, I didn't let Bert get near me. I felt I would burn to a crisp if his hand accidentally touched mine. I even assumed we'd get engaged that day, Bert and I. What else after such rapture with a boy! On the train, when Bert told me, solemnly, that he had something to say to me, I thought, Here it is; he'll either propose, tell me he's already engaged or announce an incurable illness; epilepsy, I decided. He looked so stern, I readied myself for that wounding shock or the proposal of marriage.

He seemed to be leading up to a proposal when something I couldn't have foreseen, intervened. Bert told me he loved and respected me very much but before he could ask for my hand (his words), he wanted me to know something about him. I wondered, more out of curiosity than of love for him, what it could be. Then I heard him say, "I am a practicing Christian Scientist." I can't describe how silly that sounded coming only a few hours after I had almost drowned in passion in his arms. I laughed and then, shamelessly, my laughter turned into a giggling fit.

I disdained, rather ignored, religion but despised Christian Science partly because Jews often used it as a way of "passing." Ready to demolish all the articles of that faith, I challenged Bert on its few obvious inconsistencies. Why did Scientists go to dentists if true belief was all-healing? Would he take his child to a doctor if it suffered from intolerable headaches for weeks? (This had happened recently to a girl at high school who later died of an operable brain tumor while her parents were praying and invoking so-called absent prayer for her recovery.) As we argued, that excruciating desire that I had known a few hours earlier for Bert was becoming muted and even difficult to remember. And I had another reaction, so irrational, so sharp, I can relive it right now. I observed, suddenly, that his thumbs were flat as the handles of table knives – the breakfast kind. They filled me with loathing. I couldn't wait to get away from him, his Science, those thumbs. We parted at Penn Station and he called me immediately; and called and wrote again. I was neither compassionate nor charitable. I was cruel and I knew it. Yet how funny it was; a Christian Scientist! For months I laughed whenever I thought of what happened to me on a train on the Long Island Railroad. The powerful physical craving seemed like a dream. I never felt a trace of desire for Bert again.

* * * *

It is our last year of high school. It is the Monday after the weekend at my cousin's. We are walking to school, Sellie and I, a long walk we're undertaking because it's a fine spring day and our first class is the second period, 10:30 perhaps. We're reluctant walkers who love only active sports, make mild fun of those who hike, climb mountains.... What does a walk do for you anyway? But we're walking just the same for the sheer pleasure of companionship in the sweet smelling New York air of forty years ago. It never occurs to us that this is why other friends take strolls together.

It may have been I who suggested walking. I have something to share with Sellie. Something I hope will bring her, if not joy, then relief. Something we may be able to laugh at, together. I imagine a whole school day when our eyes meet and that irrepressible laughter threatens to break out in the midst of math or Latin or French. For I am going to tell her about Bert. It is essential because it is absurd and because it is proof that I, and by extrapolation Sellie, can find boys attractive in spite of what we have experienced together. I assume I am giving her a gift of life. Our destiny is not to be unusual or grim, our existence not to be confined to a group of girls who never marry and don't ever have children. We are, in simple bourgeois terms, safe.

However, I am cautious and it takes me a long time to get around to the subject. We are more than halfway to school when I introduce it. I tell Sellie that Sarah is as good as engaged; that Jim, though good-looking, is too slick; that Sarah, always the one to be adored, is now the adorer and far too dependent on Jim's love. I worry about her. Sellie wants to know exactly what I find so reprehensible about Jim. I distrust him, for starters. He lies. He told Sarah that he'd been at Princeton and now it appears that he only worked in the town. Sellie is clear-headed and though not particularly tolerant, is resistant to agreeing with any-body right off. Maybe, she hazards, Sarah and her family mis-understand the Princeton allegation. Or again, maybe it's better for Sarah to marry someone already earning a living (Jim is a travelling salesman) than to marry "a college degree." After all, she's only eighteen and being unable to afford college will have to go to a business school. Which makes them more equal. Doesn't it? True, I say. I want, more than ever, to be on Sellie's side this morning. She asks, are they in love? Very much. Well that seems the most important thing, she concludes.

Now I chronicle that weekend, letting her down, you might say, gradually. I speak about Jim's cousin Bert who was with us and about the dance. About staying up late, the four of us, talking. "You know Sellie," I plunge in clumsily, at last, "Bert and I were terribly attracted to each other, physically, I mean. It was wonderful for me to discover that I could feel that way. With a boy."

"Here's the funny part," I begin. But I never get to ridicule Bert's religion or describe his remarkable flat thumbs because Sellie, like a mechanical toy that has been wound up so tight its spring has broken, suddenly stands stock still. Then she looks at me.

When she speaks, I have a vision of the earth stopping in its orbit. There's an eclipse of the sun. An earthquake. Someone is struck by a car before our eyes. An explosion in a building excavation razes the five-story apartment house next to it.... Sellie has said, "How disgusting!"

We are seventeen. Our social life is going to accelerate. She will meet the young man she loves and lives with and marries. I am going to meet scores of young men (at least four or five!) and ultimately will marry a stranger from another land and move away from New York. We write to each other often but neither of us ever mentions our story; our lovely story; the year we loved each other.

* * * *

One summer, Sellie and her husband visit us in the country. I take Sellie for a walk through my favorite wood. It is chanterelle time, the hemlock branches hang low and beneath them the ground is carpeted with golden chanterelles. I pick a few and tell Sellie that they're good mushrooms. "They look pretty," she says, clearly unconcerned with their edibility. I remember that she has never had much interest in food. Besides, I have interrupted her. She was telling me how much she misses not having long conversations with Arturo (her nickname for Arthur, her husband). I sympathize with her. I am always the one who starts the conversations in our house. I throw away the mushrooms and concentrate on what Sellie is saying. "For example, I love being among these trees..." she wants me to learn something about her marriage... "but if when we go to bed I describe the – what did you say the trees were? – the hemlocks and *Evange-*

line where I first read about them, he'll say that he's glad I enjoyed myself and then he'll make love to me. So we never get to speak about trees or poems. But Dee, I'm really happy. I'm not griping." Pause. "If only I loved Arthur as much as he loves me!"

I'm tempted to break our thirty years silence and remind her of how we spoke on and on before and after the voices of our bodies had had their say but I can't decide whether to introduce the subject candidly or craftily. Or at all.

"Tell me about you," Sellie asks suddenly and belligerently as though she regrets revealing imperfections in her marriage. Or is reading my mind.

I tell her one of my "secrets" and wonder if she is deliberately veering away from *us*.

Let it be. Let it be, I tell myself and think of our love as a deep, still ocean where the tides never turn.

When I finish my first book of poetry, there is a poem in it about Sellie and me.

TWO WOMEN

Something to taste
thin blue milk or
barley water.

Store-bright
apple-on-the-stick
or homemade brown.

Lick of chocolate cones
dripping on a dress:
she'd say,

"I'm finished,
give me a lick of
yours."

Prideful pennycandy friends
at each other till
our breasts pointed
and hurt
to be touched.

Immense, married,
we meet again through
head colds and kiss.

O how do you taste
now?

Sellie reads the book and writes that she likes it and is thrilled that I found a publisher, at last. She tells me which poems she prefers and, in some detail, why. Then, like an afterthought, she writes:

O how do you taste now?

We are apart.
We are always together.

Sellie died three years ago.

Afterword

How old is old?

It is 1993 and I am eighty-five years old. A rich age for memories. A rich age for new seeing and new listening. For experiencing the pleasures of works of art once disdained. For example, in my adolescence and early adulthood, I, an accomplished musician, ignored Verdi and barely tolerated Chopin. I even discarded Brahms, Tchaikovsky, Franck and a host of other composers. (But I did welcome the fresh, new works of Stravinsky and Webern.)

I also disdained what I called ecclesiastical paintings, ignorantly and flippantly, designating them as religious paintings. My first trip to the museums of Europe was a bust. I trudged faithfully through the Louvre, the Kaiser Friederick Museum in Berlin and many Italian museums, blindly. Gothic churches were masses of vulgarity and whole cities devoid chiefly of people to speak to.

Writers were in another class. I read almost everything (but realized that Galsworthy was not up to scratch). I read *Swann's Way* as soon as it was translated, *The Waste Land* when it came out, parts of James Joyce's *Ulysses* which I had smuggled into the U.S. on that first European trip, and saw all of Karel Capek's plays. I was impatient with George Eliot, couldn't read Wordsworth, though I adored Keats and Thomas Hardy. (I couldn't have imagined taking on Trollope whom I now devour.)

I won't go on with this typical account of the education of a young, Jewish intellectual New Yorker in the twenties and thirties, only to say that I made up for these and other lacunae with full enjoyment. Still, my heart stops when I think of what I might have missed.

As I said, I was trained professionally as a musician, taught the piano and graduated from a good music school instead of from a good college. However, during all those David Mannes Music School years, I yearned to be writing... something. What it was to be, I had no idea. Then, out of the blue, it came to me. I would write a novel about my late adolescent struggles with agoraphobia, a curse from which I was released, though not without scars, through falling in love. (The description of my accident and the obsessive fears that resulted from it are in the story in this book.) I will only add that writing about this period was another way of coming to terms with a distorted existence. And that the writing itself was a kind of initiation rite into adulthood, as well as the awakening of my creative voice. I worked on "The Oblique Way" for about four years and loved every moment of it.

The novel was provisionally accepted by John Day & Co. through Pearl Buck, wife of Day's president, to whom an agent had sent it. Buck wanted a securely happy ending and some deletions about sex in a remarkably tame, tender love story. Since I was eager to have "The Oblique Way" published, I tampered with it and ruined it. It wasn't published then or ever. In fact, at the time, in my late thirties, I felt so deflated after the collapse of "my brilliant career" that I wrote very little for years. What's more, I was by then a faculty wife, the properly admiring companion of a Harvard God. This was a heavy psychological as well as physical (very little help, a small daughter *and* dinner parties) burden. I had become, without knowing it, an ideal Trollopian model.

There, in what I assumed to be the Athens of America, Harvard University, I was surrounded by people who, though far better educated than I, knew little and wanted to find out less about contemporary writing.* I felt trapped.

Then I met Adrienne Rich who became a close, dear friend. And Denise Levertov, Adrienne's friend. I listened in those years of the early sixties, to these two poets give read-

---

*The one exception was a course, "Proust, Mann and Joyce," given in the English department.

ings and discuss style and form. It was impressive to realize how ready Rich was to change; to open her form more in the manner of Levertov's and to use inner rather than end-line rhymes. If you read Rich's first three books and then go on to *The Will to Change*, you'll find a striking difference. Then read Levertov's *O Taste and See*, for example, to understand how lyrically Levertov uses her lines and some of what Rich learned from her.

Rich encouraged me when I began to write poetry; when I burst into song with my first rather moving poem about a dead thrush. I remember one of the things she told me when my verses teemed with ideas. "Poems are made with words," she said. A reminder that should be etched in the minds of all beginning poets.

Robert Lowell came to Harvard in the sixties and everything changed for me. Poets were in. I went to Lowell's workshops for two years along with poets like Helen Chasin and Jean Valentine. Eventually, two small volumes of my poems were published by the Janus Press: *Razerol* in 1973 and *Whatever Happens* in 1975.

Since there were no prose workshops, no prose writing companions, I read poetry, books about poetry, i.e. William Empson's *The Seven Types of Ambiguity* and I. A. Richard's *Practical Criticism*, and continued to write poems. A few of my friends and I published a poetry journal called *Grist*. *Grist*, four illustrated poetry sheets, was begun in 1975 and ran for three years. Nine of us, ardent, enthusiastic women poets, designed it, had it printed, and distributed it. And of course contributed our work. Many of these women have become professional poets. Miriam Goodman is published by Alice James' Books. Gail Mazur, Carole Oles, Alicia Creus and Alice Ryerson have all done well. And Alice Ryerson went on to open Ragdale, a colony for the arts in Lake Forest, Illinois with the help, originally, of some of her colleagues from *Grist*, that lively, imaginative enterprise.

Of course, in the long years (forty-six of them) I spent as a Harvard wife, I didn't entirely abandon prose. I had been plugging away at a second novel, a stylized, complex work influenced by Virginia Woolf's *The Waves*. (This is the novel that *I* rejected.) In the sixties, I also had a small job as poetry editor for a left-of-center magazine, *Colloquy*, published by the United Church Press. I enjoyed reading dozens of unsolicited manuscripts and was sorry when the magazine, for lack of funds, abolished its poetry department. One of the side benefits of this job was a trip to Castro's Cuba (I accompanied my husband who had been formally invited) where I visited elementary schools and, in spite of my lack of Spanish, interviewed teachers and wrote an article for *Colloquy* on the warm relationship between teachers and their small pupils in these national boarding schools. It was a courageous experiment and I've thought since then that our impoverished urban children would benefit enormously from a similar arrangement.

When the chance came to write about university wives, I jumped at it. *Second Wave*, published in Cambridge in 1972, was one of the first magazines for women, by women. My article on faculty wives, called "Faculty Wife," appeared in the second issue. It gives a grim picture of how the wives of professors live and is a denunciation of the system that still degrades women in many obvious and not so obvious ways. My revelations were personal and so vitriolic that I used an assumed name. (Fat chance that faculty members or their wives, most of whom were blissfully unaware that they are oppressed and discriminated against, knew about the existence of *Second Wave*.)

I love and revere poetry. In spite of this, the conviction grew in me that I would never achieve the purity, elegance and precise expressive imagery that to me is the essence of good poetry. The poets I read, Lowell, Bishop, Rich, Levertov and other splendid ones, persuaded me of my own shortcomings rather than inspiring me to make greater efforts. (Paradoxically, my friendship with Rich and Levertov ultimately added to this feeling of inadequacy.) For this and other reasons, I wrote fewer and fewer poems.

Instead, when I was as old as seventy-five, I began a third attempt in the novel form and also wrote *Genia & Wassily, A Russian-American Memoir* about my husband's interesting family and the indelible effect of that family on me, his wife. This memoir, worked on from the early seventies, was published in 1979. It and the novel I had been writing seemed to unplug a clogged duct in me.

The resulting urge to speak out is perhaps more common to women in their sixties and seventies than they realize and/or take advantage of. Suddenly so much clamors to be allowed to say itself, to be recorded, not to be permitted to disappear. One of the obvious reasons for this surge of fertility in me is that the autobiographical aspects of what I have been writing concern people no longer living: parents, old friends, old loves, an entire milieu of which I am almost the sole survivor.*

Which reminds me of my mother's anxiety when I was working on that first novel, "The Oblique Way." "You're not going to put us in your book, are you?" she asked plaintively.

It also reminds me of a story about Tolstoy who read aloud to friends each night what he'd written during the day. These readings were constantly interrupted by his listeners who recognized themselves as characters in the novels and disliked the way he depicted them. "I'm not like that," they objected. "That's not me at all."

So it might have been with my friend whose lifelong friendship is the subject of the narrative in this book. For years after finishing it, I must have been over seventy then, I held the work to myself not ever hoping to let go of it because I expected, romantically, that since she and I would probably die at the same time, she would never read it and I would never suffer her reaction to it.

---

*I also attribute some of my present productiveness to living again in my native city to which I returned in 1975. New York is redolent, for me, with memories and seemingly endless stories.

Her death has happened.

Now that Sellie has gone from me I have an exhilarating sense of freedom which enables me to write more about people I knew and loved, as well as those I didn't love but begin to understand; to explore the understanding rather than to wallow peevishly in encapsulated experiences and situations. Stranger, more marvelous things have happened. In my contemporary family relationships – grandmother, aunt, mother – generations reverse themselves. No longer grandchild, niece, daughter, I can understand, for example, in writing about my mother, my own daughter's responses to me now. These responses, like reflections in a mirror, are so clear that I keep telling myself, "Now you see how it was when you were twenty, thirty; a wife, a mother and *she* my mother was growing old." Only now, it is as if I am discovering information that only memories can call forth: the keys to the other side of relationships. These turn wisdom on its head and make me feel like F. Scott Fitzgerald's Benjamin Button in the story of that name, who is born an old man and grows younger with the years. My memories reveal upside-down awareness, tidings of lost knowledge. I am living in two worlds at the same time. Two? Many, many worlds.

I have changed the names of the main people in my memoir (including my own) because I wanted to be as forthright as Sellie herself without, however, alerting those who might be offended by our story.

Carrie Allen McCray

Reality

Four years old, and my mother,
with silken cover,
takes my hand and
thick tangled hair
to the Poro lady
a long day in hot-comb
hair-greased rooms
But I return home
with curls, and shake
them now like my
sisters,
And then – rain

Note: *Poro* is the brand name for grease used to
straighten hair.

133 | Carrie Allen McCray

Nobody Wrote a Poem

Nobody wrote a poem
about me
In ugly tones they
called me "Yaller Gal"
How lovely to have been
born black or brown
Pure substance the artist
could put his pen to
Not something in between –
diluted, undefined, unspecific
I search the poets
for words of me
Faint mention in Langston Hughes'
Harlem Sweeties, I think,
yet I'm not sure
So full of "caramel treats,"
"brown sugars" and "plum
tinted blacks," it was
Soft, warm colors
making the poets sing
I, born out of history's
cruel circumstance,
inspired no song
and nobody wrote a poem

I have a poem inside me

I have a poem inside me
that refuses to come out
Someone told me a long time
ago
write a poem about your
husband and your marriage
For two years I've tried
to give birth, poem after
poem shifting in front of
this one, blocking its way out
"I am the writer in the
family," he used to say
controlling my pen as he
did all else
Is there now some
supernatural power he has
over me, holding back this poem
His home was Charleston
where some still believe in
the old "Hag"
Has she silenced my muse
I've been in labor many
times
One aborted, one breech,
one stillborn
I'll try again, I want
to birth this child

Red Balloons

Flapping signs read
Gray's Dixie Carnival
Papa, could I have one of
those red balloons
My sister, innocent at five,
did not know what she
was asking – but Papa did
That wonderful world
of merry-go-round,
red balloons dancing in the hot
southern breeze,
songs of summer in his eyes,
he risked it anyway,
stopped the car, went over
to the carnival gate
Could he just have a red
balloon for his little girl
The words of the carnival
man as hard as his face
"Nigger ain' nuthin here
for you or yourn"
Shaking her blond curls
a little five-year-old
stuck her tongue out
at Papa
Papa stood for a moment
then back to the car
with promises of lots of
red balloons when we get
home

I was eight years old then
but even now, whenever I
hear the sound of carousel,
I see Papa's wintered face
as he watched all the other
fathers
taking their children
through the gate

My Father

I never saw my father in anything but a business suit. As if, after achieving, he could not let go. His hands washed, compulsively, scrubbing away some secret sin? or soot from rough laboring years.

Born of that first generation out of slavery, he worked hard to send himself through school. A brilliant man in a long line of firsts. One of the turn-of-the-century Blacks to finish Michigan Law School. A good man, deacon in the church, superintendent of the Sunday school.

A good father, caring, coming home with big bags filled with bananas, peanut brittle and coconut candy. But I never could run to him and hug him. Those business suits, starched white shirts and clean hands prohibitive to a small child.

A protective father, he watched our development. I, coming late to early signs of womanhood, each month my father would ask "Miss Bussy, have you been unwell?" Always the picture of health – I did not understand. "No, Papa, I'm fine." Embarrassed later when I realized what he meant.

When we were old enough to have company, young men would come to see us in groups. At nine o'clock sharp, my father would come to the top of the stairs and in the same voice used in court that day, call down: "Time for the young men to go to their homes now." The exodus immediate. All of our suitors called him *squire*.

I wanted something different of my father.
Something our mother gave us. She loved working in her
flower garden, would get down in the soft, wet squishy
soil after a rain, make mud pies with us or let us plant her
nasturtiums and phlox. She loved the feel of the earth,
died with some under her fingernails.

I wanted my father, just one time, to take
off that business suit, sit with us like Mama, let the wet soil
roll around in his hands, squish it through his fingers,
get his hands so dirty, he could not get them clean for a long
time. Just once, just once is all I wanted. I would have run
to him.

Strange Patterns

When I was a young child
in Lynchburg, Virginia
I could not ride the
trolley car sitting next
to our white neighbor
But could sit, nestled
close to her
under her grape arbor
swinging my feet
eating her scuppernongs
and drinking tall, cold
glasses of lemonade
she offered us on
hot, dry summer days

When I was a young child
moving to Montclair, New Jersey
I could now ride the
trolley car sitting next
to our white neighbor
but did not dare
cross the bitter line
that separated our house
from hers
and she never offered us
tall, cold glasses of lemonade
on hot, dry summer days

My Grandmother's Leg

A love story and an awakening

She would sit on the long, low porch on Holbrook Street in Danville, Virginia, wait for courting couples to pass, then call out "Come on, come on in, sit in the swing, I have a cool, fresh pitcher of lemonade." That was my Aunt Maggie, a wiry, cheerful, chattery old maid, gathering up her audience for her stories. Her stories always beginning with "before Mama lost her leg" or "after Mama lost her leg" as if her life were divided into two long seasons. I never understood this until the summer of my sixteenth birthday.

As we did every summer, when school was out, we went to Virginia to visit Grandma and Aunt Maggie. The train ride, a happy time, not too memorable the ride from Newark to Washington. But once on the Southern out of Washington, a picnic in motion. A car full of Black folk having their good time, shoe boxes on the racks loaded with fried chicken, pound cake and bananas. A communal people, everyone sharing, singing, laughing. The clickety-clack, clickety-clack of the train like a jazz beat faster, faster, faster. Clickety-clack, clickety-clack, clickety-clack. Taking us "back home."

And back home a round of dinners, parties, picnics and more dinners. As if to celebrate the return of the prodigals. Our trip usually ending with the big Baptist Sunday school picnic. This year everyone went except Aunt Maggie, always at the call of Grandma, and me because I did not feel well.

The house was silent, only an occasional call, "Mag, Mag, come my leg hurts." Aunt Maggie went to take care of her, then came back. "It's always the leg that's gone, bothering Mama. Never woulda lost that leg if we hadn't been in the Jim Crow car and that trunk came hurlin' out the baggage car, long time 'fore they came to see 'bout us in the Jim Crow car. Hospital turned Mama away in the Jim Crow town." I didn't know how to respond so said nothing.

After awhile, Aunt Maggie went to check. "Mama asleep now," she said. "Come on, baby, let's go over into the parlor." No one went in Grandma's parlor except on Sunday, so I knew this was special. We walked into the musty, red velvet room. Aunt Maggie did not open the blinds, went over and turned on the lamp with the rose-colored glass globe. Still dark in there. A sense of mystery. Then Aunt Maggie went over to the table in the corner, took a wooden box, tied with a blue ribbon, out of the drawer. "Here, baby," she said, "my eyes bad, read these for me,'' handing me a stack of letters. The paper so old it was brittle. Strange address on the envelope.

I opened the first one. "Dear Miss Mag," it said, "when I was at the mission tonight I thought of you and wished you were here as my wife like we planned. What a comfort you would be to me and to these poor suffering people of Africa…I know you have your calling there with her. God bless you for it." I read all the letters, each one speaking of his love for her, ending with – "And I remain respectfully yours, the Reverend Authur Moten." I finished the last one with a feeling of being back in a time when I was not. His presence so strong here, the Reverend Authur Moten.

I watched Aunt Maggie take the letters, place them gently in the box, tie it with the blue ribbons, quickly brushing tears from her eyes. Anger welled in me. At sixteen, romance is paramount to all other conditions of life. How could Grandma keep her away from him.

Then I thought of my grandmother who always said about her leg – "That ain' the worse trouble I

knowed. Slavery done took more than a leg from me."
My anger did not belong here, but I didn't know where, so
just left it hanging without a target.

   Summer over. Time to go home. Cousin
Winslow drove us down to the train. Papa got on first, seated
all of us in front of him. The train moved out slowly, then
faster, faster, faster. Clickety-clack, clickety-clack, clickety-
clack. The sound crushing into my skull. I leaned my
head against the window. The vision of Aunt Maggie standing out in the street, alone, waving us goodbye would not
leave me. And it was at that moment I knew.

Thoughts at the Grave Site

October 1935

All I could see
was you in your
red felt hat
walking briskly
out the front door
on the way to
the "fight"
you, who integrated
the living in our
small town
being lowered now
into a segregated
corner of the
graveyard

To my mother, longtime fighter
for equality and justice

Do White People

Do white people say
when there's a crime,
I hope he's not white
I doubt it

The newspaper blares:
"Armed men hold up gas
station, kill attendant"
*Oh! God, please don't let
them be Black*
And we search frantically
to find the signs that
tell us

    William Johnson – *Oh! Lord*
              Name sounds Black
    James Jackson – *Do Jesus,*
             must be

But do white people
Albert Lethington, tall, handsome,
blonde treasurer of Heath Plastics
embezzles $100,000,000 from company
suspected of killing auditor
Do white people worry
that he's white –
I doubt it

Trade-offs

What is this guilt
you're trying to heap
upon me like bales of
cotton
No, life did not take
me into the fields
beside you
But I would gladly
carry your bales,
if you could bear
my griefs

Sixty-some Years

Sixty-some years
His rage beating at
her frail, washtub bent
body
Sixty-some years
Slowly, she rose
Walked over to the casket
Where lay her husband
Like linen for the
white folks, smoothed the
cover over him
Neatly folded those years
Sent them on with him

Back Home

After many years

What happened to this
street of my childhood
once pristine –
Solid, strong houses
brick, wooden, stucco
yellow, white – sun and
cloud colors
wrapping themselves around
us like warm blankets
The old home house gone
now, and with it
all our childhood secrets.
Others boarded up,
weather-bashed, graying,
skin peeling as if
touched by some scourge
Proud homes, they were
built by the first
generation out of slavery
Sitting here, now, like
old men, with empty
dreams.

Recycled Grief

She walked, head bent
small, thin body
clothed in the long
black mourning dress –
sallow, pale skin
creating a ghost
figure
A year she moved
through our house
like the shadow
of the one she
mourned
Eyes red from the
crying
The black period
over
she turned to gray
And wore it now
with only a few
brief tears
Then donned the
purple dress
allowing herself
an occasional smile

To a lady I knew in my childhood

I take my text from –

She walked in dignity down
the long church aisle
This diminutive woman
in a plain red dress
A rough straw sailor hat
complimenting the quiet
darkness of her face
Traces of Africa in
her speech
"Ah cum fum Chawston,"
she said, her voice soft
and light
"Y'all don' remember me.
Two yar ago, I walk in
here, dirty, hungry, homeless
The garbage pail my platter
The sidewalk my pillow
The deacon, whar' he?"
she said, looking over the
congregation, "I don' see
hum here. He give me
food. Church give me money
to get home to Chawston
and found me job."
Then she held up an envelope
"I cum to give back, so
you can give someone else

lying out there on the street
round your corner.
Now, let's all sing 'Reach
out and touch.'"
The song ended.
She walked back down the aisle
like a Nubian queen.

Harvesting

On a visit to Anne Spencer House
Lynchburg, Virginia   October 29, 1990

      Lady of the south winds we came to see you
today, my sister and I, returning to this place we loved
as children. The pungent smell of sweet shrub, in gentle
Virginia winds, says home. Yet on the porch, waiting to enter,
I think of Thomas Wolfe – and wonder.

      The door opens, we walk slowly, tentatively
into – awesome stillness. Unsettled for a moment, pause, as
if awaiting the warmth of your greeting. "My children
from the north winds," you'd say.

      Chauncey, your only boy-child, understands
we need this time – alone, stands back, lets us roam
unaccompanied. We walk around touching the past. Everything the same, everything except the voices. No warm,
soft drawl lingering in the air. No special words for each of
us. The aura of you still here, though, and I want to
whisper your name. My words consumed by penetrating
silence.

      Aun' Tannie, we called you, knew your beauty
as you knew the beauty of a leaf, a rose, a winter's sky. I
see you in long, thick braids, leathery Indian complexion,
wearing those daring Japanese pajamas, in a time of
tight-corseted, Grant Wood women afraid to reveal their
hunger for love, for sex, for free expression, or whatever the
other natural needs of women are.

      But you, you sang of freedom, of love not
stifled by time and gender. Your words, on the wind, found
their way to the birds, the trees, the sky and even the
"wee" spider. They understood their earth sister who spoke
to them of beauty. As Cullen says of Keats, you too, "an
apostle of beauty."

Quietly, we move around – this corner here, your love birds, Dumb, Belle and Stewed Prunes. Stewed Prunes, screwed up in a corner, mad. Dumb and Belle sitting close together on the perch. And who but you would have a crow, Old Black Joe, who could recite a phrase from Keats. And when he did not want to, cried, "I'm cold, I'm cold." Skeptics would say – a childhood fantasy, gone askew. No fantasy this, everyone in town knew Joe. What a place of wonder for a wide-eyed child, summers "back home" from the North.

So late this recognition of those who planted for the harvest, stray seeds, germinating in strange places long after the leaves have fallen. Your words a gift to me from Mama on my fourteenth birthday, Countee Cullen's *Caroling Dusk: An Anthology of Verse by Negro Poets.* I would sit for hours, savoring those words, touching them like precious stones. Yours and other Black poets', speaking to us like no one else had.

So late the recognition of the richness of those childhood moments when you would come to visit. Some of those same poets, whose words I touched, sitting around you in our parlor. We were brought in to meet them. Then Papa, who always feared our "tender" ears would hear something they should not, dismissed us, as he usually did, with a nod of the head. I would stay close by in the dining room listening to the voices of the Harlem Renaissance: Sterling Brown, James Weldon Johnson, Countee Cullen, Langston Hughes. I stand here in the center of you – remembering.

We walk into the sunroom. I see Uncle Ed graciously offering the adults "a little toddy," a glass of something smelling familiarly like a glass of something Papa called his medicinal whiskey. It was here, in this room, we listened to you and Mama laughing and talking about the arrogance and genius of Du Bois, about the beauty of your roses, and about that *full freedom,* a term we heard often not understanding then, you speaking in poetry, Mama, in philosophical phrases. "North is an old narcissus," I heard you say once. Too big a concept for a child – so stored it away. Life revealed the meaning, the same bitter weeds growing in both soils, Mama digging at their roots in the North, you in the South.

Rare friends, you and Mama, free spirits, found the common denominators, loved philosophy, freedom, humor, Du Bois, James Weldon Johnson, Thoreau – and flowers. Defied the tight lady conventions of the time. While most early century women around you, drinking tea and tatting, you and Mama helping to organize the NAACP here and crying out against the hanging tree. Echo of your voices still in the fabric of this room.

We move on upstairs into the room where hangs a painting by our younger sister, Dolly. *Cocktail Party,* she calls it. Everybody drinking scotch and grinning and grinning and drinking scotch. You loved it, said it portrayed the "uppityness of the Black bourgeoisie." You wanted the painting to remind whoever came your way, that "phony-ness never wore a warm cloak."

I look once more at the painting, then walk quickly into the adjoining room, our room when we visited. Sun streams in the window infusing me with the warmth of an earlier time. Bright chintz-covered beds (faded now like an aging beauty). We'd lie here in this field of multi-colored wild flowers straining to hear the words and laughter of adults in the room below.

I walk over to the window overlooking your garden – your garden, your sanctuary. A bird is singing out there. Didn't I see you turn to greet him? Then walk slowly through your roses, pluck the dead leaves? We'll join you there, walk through the rose garden with you.

Chauncey brings the key to your little garden house – *Edankrall.* We walk into a re-creation of the past. Pictures of you, Uncle Ed, your children – Bethel, Alroy, Chauncey, your grandchildren – and over there, Mama. The

walls full of familiar. I stand at your writing desk feeling
like an intruder. Only your Muses, Calliope and Euterpe,
belong here watching over you as you create your poems.

We do not linger, go out by the lily pond,
capture this day for bleaker times. There is a strong sense of
your presence here in your garden. I listen for your words.
Somewhere out there in the south winds. Have gathered
them many times as you gather your roses. Your words about
Browning and the beauty of Virginia, your words to the
"gay little girl of the diving tank," your words to McSweeney
of the Irish Rebellion, your words to a nasturtium, your
words to the "wee" spider about freedom – but most of all –
your words to me.

A sensitive, chubby, rosy-cheeked child with
thick tangled hair. Ugly duckling – some called me. I, the
Poroed, hot-combed one. "Poor lil' thing," they'd say.
"Where'd she get all that bad hair?" But not you. Your greeting for me dispelled the hurt. Always the same. "Here
come Jonathan's winter apples." And by your tone, I knew
they, and I, must be very special.

Piece of Time

I once heard an old Alabama farmer say
"Everybody need a lil' piece a time a they own."

Each morning walking my dog
I find my place in the woods
A special place where I can
crawl inside myself, shed the old
skin from around my fringes
Coco understands, stretches out
quietly at my feet
Allowing me this moment
with other earth creatures

A green lizard there, up early,
sees us and freezes
I want to calm his fears and
say "I'm your earth sister"
He waits, then finds safety in a
nearby tree,
tall Carolina pine that
shimmers in the early morning
sunlight

I listen to my birds
The mockingbird singing his
tee-chow, tee-chow, tee-chow
changing to *chit-e-chow*
as we might change from
Bach to Basie
All sounds are joyous except
the *oo-a-coo-coo-coo* of
the mourning dove

Coco lifts a lazy eye
watching an indecisive butterfly
flutter from yellow jessamine
to wood violet
And an old possum sticks his
head up out of a patch of leaves
"Don't worry, old fella," I say
"I don't eat possum"
Untrusting, he skitters off
into the brush

The clouds speak softly to
me
One the shape of a cotton
cave I want to climb into
I watch them slowly shifting
changing, changing, changing –
infusing me with their gentle spirit
I can go home now
pull out the frying pan
and cook breakfast for my
family

Afterword

I've written practically all my life, it seems to me. But I'm
seriously writing now. I write all the time – I get up writing.
Things are in my head that I need to get up and put
down. I didn't have that before. This is a wonderful period
of my life as a writer. I was seventy-three when this period
started.

I'm seventy-nine now. It's almost as if I'm trying to make
up for lost time. My second husband was a writer, a beautiful
writer, a journalist. Before I married him, I had had one
short story published in John A. Williams' book, *Beyond the
Angry Black* (Cooper Square Publishers, 1966), and that
was all. My husband would always say, "I'm the writer in the
family." And it stopped me. During that period I didn't
write very much – it was almost like writing in the closet.

I kept my poems in a box and in a drawer for a long time.
Toi Derricotte is the first poet who read my poems. My
friend, Annie Laurie Tucker, with whom I exchanged poems
said, "I think you should send Toi some of your poems to
read." (Toi is her niece.) I said, "Oh I don't know. Take them
out of the box and expose myself!" She insisted; she talked
with Toi and Toi called me and said, "I'd like to see your
poems." She took time to do a critique of each one. She said,
"Read Sonia Sanchez for your political poems. Be sure
you read Rita Dove. Have you read so and so?" She was so
helpful.

It was Toi who said, "I want you to send in your works to
Squaw [Valley Community of Writers.]" I guess I was the
most surprised person to get accepted. Squaw was a wonderful experience – it was so open, everybody was so open.
Galway Kinnell and Sharon Olds opened up the closed doors

Adapted from a taped interview.

in my head. I felt like I could say whatever I wanted, whatever was deep down inside.

I also attended the Sandhills Writers Conference, held every year at Augusta College in Augusta, Georgia, where I met Laurence Lieberman, a wonderful critic. He read a poem of his at lunch about a bombed synagogue and a slave market on one of the Caribbean islands. It was striking. I went up to him afterward and said, "You know, I'm writing a poem about my grandmother's face that has to do with the slave market in Charleston." I told him what I was trying to do with it and he was quite interested. He inspired me to finish it.

Wherever I've gone to writers conferences, I've gotten that kind of help and encouragement. But I must say that Squaw was the greatest. When I was looking over my poems to select and send to you, many of them came out of Squaw or after Squaw.

* * * *

Family support has helped me a lot. I had a hard time thinking of myself as a writer. I thought of myself as a social worker and as a teacher. But my family keeps saying to me, "You're a writer." They've been encouraging to me.

You may not believe this, but when I was younger, I was very shy. Even in my high school yearbook, beside my name were the words "Seen – trying not to be." My sisters and I were quite different. Doll was always the bohemian, the really exciting kind of person that your parents and everybody else would say, "Well, you know, that's Doll" – which meant that she had license to do anything. And Rosemary was just sweet. But Carrie had license to do nothing! I felt that there was an expectancy of me to do the right thing all the time. And I'm so sorry I did the right thing too many times. I think I missed out on a lot of things that I could have risked, that might have been a little more exciting. But that is how I was. But in my writing I'm free. Oh yes, I'm real free.

I feel so open about it now. Squaw helped me with it some, but it must have been happening too – that I was becoming more open. And it also may be something of the times – people talk about more things than they used to. Now nobody can shut me up! I don't find any reason to shut down. I feel free to write on any subject now, even subjects I may have had trouble expressing openly before.

Maybe this happens with age. A friend of mine said to me, "You've got seventy-nine years of information packed in there. It'll come out." I guess that's part of it. There is a lot in there – and some of it is just opening up now. I feel a kind of urgency to keep on writing. You never know at any age, but certainly at this age you don't know what's going to happen tomorrow. In a sense that is an advantage because it keeps you going. I write more now, more consistently.

Writing is soothing to me. We all have our problems and instead of the problem weighting me down, I feel that writing eases it sometimes. There are times I wake up in the morning thinking about my son who has psychiatric problems. In the beginning, it consumed my thoughts. My son had his breakdown in 1974 and it's been an up-and-down situation, in and out of veterans' hospitals, sleeping on the streets of New York – I'd learn that after the fact. He was very creative, wrote beautiful, strong poetry and did lovely paintings – he still does lovely paintings. I don't think you ever get over what happens to your child of this nature, but you have to find ways of adjusting to it. I would have been a nervous wreck if I just kept giving in to it. But I found I could make myself move away from it through meditation and through my writing.

* * * *

A day never passes that I won't do some writing. Sometimes it's just revising something that I'm working on, or something will hit me – an old memory, and I'll want to write about that. It may be something that I see in the paper that I respond to. The poem, "I take my text from," came from

something that happened in church. When I looked
around and saw that woman coming down the aisle, I said to
myself, she's from Charleston. And when she got up there,
she said, "I come from Charleston." She just moved
everybody. It was such a wonderful experience for everybody
sitting there. She was with me – I took her home from
church. I kept saying to myself *that* was the text of the day.
This visiting minister didn't even comment on it. He took us
off into something else that I don't even remember. But
that was the text . If our regular minister had been there,
I know he would have incorporated that in whatever text he
had prepared. I was telling my sister about it and I said,
"I'm going to write a poem and I'm going to call it, 'I take
my text from.'" It was just before I went to Squaw and I
wrote it there.

The poem, "I have a poem inside me," – Toi helped me
in writing that. She kept saying, you need to write about your
husband and your marriage. I remember how that poem
came about. I was in Bob Hass's workshop on a Thursday
at Squaw and we were all so tired – Thursday is a low point in
the week of writing. Someone said, "I don't know how I'm
going to write a poem for tomorrow." And I said, "I have
a poem inside me that refuses to come out." And Hass said,
"Write *that* for tomorrow." And next day when I was in
Toi's workshop, I read it and I stopped and said, "Toi, *you*
told me two or three years ago that I had to write about this."
And she said, "It took a long time. Now keep on writing."
And I will.

I also want to write some very positive things about my
second husband, because he was a very strong man. He started the first Black political party, the Progressive Democrats,
back in the 1940's, which became a strong political force.
He had a real fighting newspaper. Everybody says it's a wonder he wasn't lynched because of the kinds of things he
would bring out in the paper. He did spend sixty days on a
chain gang at that time for a trumped-up charge of libel,
although he never used the name of the person in his story.

A white reporter wrote the same story and received no punishment. Everyone knew it was because my husband's political party was becoming too strong. The *New York Times* picked up the story and he became an international *cause célèbre*. But he was unafraid. I want to do some poems about that side of him too – that needs to be written.

I've written about growing up as a Black child in the North and in the South. Frankly there wasn't too much difference except that the South was warmer. Even though we were segregated in the South at that time, we didn't feel the segregation until we were older. As a child, you don't know that you're sitting in the back of the trolley car – your mama takes you to the back and you sit down. The real impact of Jim Crow came to me quite a bit later, when I was sixteen. I write about that in "My Grandmother's Leg."

I wrote about my mother in "At the Grave Site." My sisters and brothers had the same thought in 1935, when we were burying her, we've talked about this – here's Mama who integrated this town and yet here she is buried in the segregated section of the graveyard. It's hard enough to see your mother buried anyway, but to see *her* buried in the segregated section of the graveyard was very difficult.

She integrated the police department. She integrated the high school graduation line – Black students had to walk at the end of the line in Montclair, New Jersey. Mama had been up there many times about that. But when my sister Rosemary was getting ready to graduate, she went up there and she said, "We're not going to have this." This was one of her favorite expressions. She would always say that, whether it was the governor or the principal or the superintendent. She said, "My daughter's name is Rosemary Allen and this year we will have the line in alphabetical order." And sure enough they changed it and her daughter was up there in front.

She never passed, even in restaurants, though she could have. One time Mama was going into a restaurant in Newark and she took my brother Greg with her. Greg was very dark, smooth dark but with very straight hair. They didn't want to serve her unless she would say that Greg was East Indian. She spoke out loud and said, "No, we are Negroes and we're going to eat here as Negroes." She never raised her voice and hollered and yelled, but she would always have things together.

I got so much from my mother, I can see now at seventy-nine, looking back. She was the one who really introduced me to poetry . She bought us *A Child's Garden of Verse* and other little poetry books. And she would buy the poets of the Harlem Renaissance. We would read them and then I had to recite them – we always had to entertain the guests. Since I couldn't dance, I couldn't sing – my brother Bill could sing, my sister Doll could dance, Rose could play *Meditation* on the piano – my mother would have me reciting poetry.

* * * *

My major piece of work now is the story based on the life of my mother. I had thought of it as just the story of my mother. Then I went to a writer's workshop at Duke University and was told I was writing an historical novel. Shook me up a little bit. But when I thought about it, I thought, well – I've *done* all this historical research and my mother's father *was* a Confederate general.

I started writing this in the sixties. I was so angry with my mother's father – I didn't even know him of course. I never even thought of him as my grandfather. All I knew was that he was a Confederate general. I couldn't deal with that. He was always "my mother's father" and it stopped right there.

Since '86 everything has opened up for me in relation to that work. In 1990, when I went to Harrisonburg, Virginia, where my mother was born, the research librarian at James Madison University said to me, "Oh, there's a student here who would be so happy to meet you. He's been trying to find descendants of General Jones."

He called that evening and asked, "What is your connection with General Jones?" I said "I don't know that there's any connection with *this* General Jones." He asked, "What was your mother's mother's name?" I said, "Malinda Rice." He said, "Oh! Will you get upset if I tell you something?" I said "No, I'm searching truth, whatever the truth is." So he said, "I was in the courts the other day and I read that General Jones' second wife divorced him on the grounds of adultery with Malinda Rice." I said "Great!" He said, "What?" I said "Great. That does two things. It confirms for me that this *is* my mother's father." Notice I never said "my grandfather."

And the second thing – as a woman – when I think of all those southern white women who for years just allowed this, and all those young Black girls who were sexually abused – the powerlessness of women in what Mary Chestnut in her diary calls "that monstrous system," a system which continued long after the war – I think it was great that General Jones' second wife divorced him. From the young researcher, Dale Harter, I received a windfall of information on the General's family, going back to 1801 and on Malinda Rice's family, going back to the end of the 1700's. It would have taken me years to find all that. In fact, I had already been searching for years. My sister, Rosemary, travels with me, helps with the research. She has been wonderful through her support and encouragement.

My grandmother was born a slave in 1855 or '56. When she was thirteen, she had to go work as a maid with a Reverend Bowman and his wife who really looked out for her. When one of them died, she went to the Joneses as a maid and then a housekeeper. She was sixteen. General and Mrs. Jones had no children. He always wanted a child and of course his wife did too – she expressed that many times. But because of a long illness, this was not possible. What happened to Malinda happened to so many young Black girls during slavery and after the war.

I've done a great deal of research. I've read books on

Black and white women on the slave plantation and after. I've read all of Mary Chestnut and Black slave narratives to get some sense of what that relationship was. There was a bond between the Black woman and the white woman, and yet underneath there was suspicion and often, certainly, jealousy. Fortunately, General Jones' first wife was a very gentle, kind person. I learned this not from my mother but from my mother's dearest friend, Anne Spencer, a poet we called Aunt Annie. She told me about a porcelain-headed doll that General Jones' first wife had given my mother when she was a small child and a number of other little things that I never would have known, because it was sort of a taboo to even talk about it to your own children. The only thing we knew was that my mother's father was a Confederate general.

But he adored my mother. And she adored him. He taught her how to read. He taught her to learn to love poetry. He took her to many places that he didn't take her brother. It was a little upsetting to me to see that Uncle Billy wasn't treated the same as mother because he was brown – my mother was very fair. He took her into an ice cream parlor or restaurant, some place where Blacks could not go. He didn't hide that this was Malinda's child – most people in the town knew she was. The owner was very fond of my mother and would give her candy and everything. But one time someone in there whispered that this was "a little nigger bastard." My mother's father overheard and went over and knocked the man out.

After I realized what he had done, I had a metamorphosis of feeling about him. He gave land and money for the first Black church there. He gave money to the Black school for ex-slaves and their children. When Malinda died, he had another Black mistress. And he left all of his estate to the second Black mistress.

I'm taking a genealogy course at the Shepherd's Center for Senior Citizens in Columbia, South Carolina – they've done a lot on the Civil War. I wanted to include his Army career, what he did in the war. There was a lot of question about whether he was a coward or a hero; some said he was a coward because his leg was hurt but not too bad. One letter I saw about Civil War generals who lived in that area gave his Army career record and things he had done that were very popular. But it said that after the war he was "a disgrace to himself and to the community." It said he had gotten connected to a Black woman. And it said, "Strike him off the list. And be sure to do it in black, with great big letters: BLACK."

I'm also trying to include what it was like for my mother. You're in neither world really – that is a very difficult position to be in. When I said there was too much anger in me in the sixties, well some of that anger remains. I have a character, Uncle John, in the novel who is still angry at the general. That's Malinda's brother, an ex-slave, a very strong man. I want to keep some of that anger for him. I couldn't just write a sweet syrupy story about the general. I had to have these two sides.

* * * *

I have three pieces that I really want to finish: the story of my mother; a series of stories about the courtyard between two brownstone houses in Brooklyn where I lived for a time – I call it "The Court;" and a poem about Ota Benga. Ota Benga was brought over here in 1904 with five other pygmies. That was a time when scientists were looking for "the missing link." Ota and the others were exhibited at the World's Fair in St. Louis in 1904. Later, he was exhibited in a cage in the Bronx zoo – I can't remember whether it was a baboon or an orangutan's cage. People flocked to see him. Black ministers became incensed. My older brother Hunter's father, who was chairman of the education committee of the National Black Baptist Convention, was contacted to see what to do about Ota.

Ota Benga lived in our home. It's conceivable that my mother taught him whatever English he knew or whatever things within the home you would teach a person. I don't remember much about him except that down at the end of the hall was this nice gentle man. Hunter remembers that he would tell stories about the animals in Africa, he would flap his arms like a bird if he was telling us about a bird, he would act things out.

I had not thought about doing a poem about Ota – I thought of him as part of the story about my mother. But two summers ago at Squaw, I told C. K. Williams that I had started a poem the night before about Ota, but that I didn't have the information – I really needed to do a lot of research. C. K. Williams was very much interested in it and said, "Well Carrie, when you do this, I'd like you to send it to me as you go along. I will do a critique on it and help you with it." I'm just delighted that he made that offer.

In the beginning it was just the joy of writing. Now I would really like to pass it on. I feel that people should know some of these things. I said one time that if a publisher does not pick up the book about my mother, that it's important to leave it even to the family. So I guess I have moved from just the joy of writing and keeping things in a box and in a drawer to really wanting to share some things.

Tema Nason

Short Takes

He had the beachball belly of a Japanese wrestler, heavy thighs, and a rabbi's eyes. Eyes that coupled moral indignation with the consolatory attitude that the coming of the Messiah was regrettably not very likely, at least not in our lifetime. The eyes she'd noticed across dinner at his home, the thighs and belly when they undressed each other afterwards.

He was impatient to make love. She, not really caring for casual sex, was not. But somehow after a little fumbling on the couch, here they were embracing on his rumpled bed. On her part, she supposed it was an acquired indifference along with a physical inertia that simply acquiesced to whatever was already underway. Besides she wanted to please him.

Suddenly though, she was longing for the sweet smell of her childhood, sheets dried on the clothesline still impregnated with sun and wind, the stiffness giving way under your hands as you helped Mom fold them into a neat package. Sheets from the clothes dryer never smelled at all, just like those tomatoes – tomatoids she called them – in the supermarket never tasted like the real thing.

And while he was pumping and moaning, she reflected how different he was from her previous boyfriend, Norwood. Norwood was very quiet when they made love as though he didn't want anyone to hear them. And yet his house was large and empty and no one was ever around. Sometimes she speculated that it was because as a young adolescent, he feared detection when he masturbated. Could be, knowing Norwood. But why did he have to be that way now?

Her thoughts drifted back to Maurice who was still pumping and moaning. She watched his excitement with interest, the way one does when lighting wood in the fireplace – first, that carefully arranged pile of crumpled paper, then twigs for kindling, then seasoned logs, but not the thick ones, and careful not to snap the twigs with the heavier logs placed on top.

Lighting a fire fascinated her always – how the spurt of flame hesitated, then spread along the raw edges of the paper, burned madly for a brief time, then took the plunge and moved upward to the twigs, and then took another deep breath and really caught fire, licking the bark of the logs and then catching within for that steady warmth. Or else died out.

Maurice had peaked, she noticed – long ago she'd given up on herself – and now he was lying quietly on his back, eyelids still fluttering, mouth shaping the first soft sounds of sleep. The ups and downs of his round hard belly were subsiding. He patted her hand goodnight.

She turned on her side. Sometimes it took just starting anew with another carefully laid pile. And yet there were those fires she'd seen that just seemed to catch and burn beautifully, shortly giving off that warm glow and primal incandescence that held the eye and caught the heart.

The heavy drapes imprisoned the night inside. Claustrophobia crawled along her nerve endings. Unsteadily, she got out of bed and felt her way round muffled objects to the large picture window and fumbled for the cord. Finding it wasn't easy, but she did and pulled open the drapes.

The one street light only intensified the darkness beyond. Something F. Scott Fitzgerald had written came back – how dark the heavens are at three in the morning when you can't sleep. He'd said it so beautifully, she wished she could remember, but the words wouldn't come.

After a while, the sky lightened and she watched the birds outside fluttering around the several bird feeders on the patio, some making quite a racket while eating greedily and shoving each other away, others quietly waiting their turn, one in particular off to one side, head cocked, eyes glinting. She continued to watch that one until it gave up and flew away.

A Stranger Here, Myself

It was a mistake. I shouldn't have come downtown today I was thinking when I boarded the crowded bus for home at Howard and Saratoga. Today was Saturday, *the* Saturday, right after the assassination…just before the riots. When the country was still in a state of shock. When you felt you had to do something, but you didn't know what.

Suddenly the bus lurched forward throwing me off balance and I was in a vise, arms pinned to my sides, heavy packages tearing out my arms. Move, I yelled silently, but nobody did. Those faces around me, mostly tired older women with bulging shopping bags from Lexington Market were more openly sullen than usual. And yet you wouldn't have predicted what happened, the angry fires on Gay Street spurting and spreading through east Baltimore that night and the furious looting the next day and the troops, the 4:00 P.M. curfew and all the nightmare rest that followed.

The odd thing is, it's not often that I come downtown to shop any more and rarely by bus, but I had to get out of the house that Saturday. Staying home seemed like doing more of the same. I mean, that's what we do in the suburbs, all hell is breaking loose elsewhere and we stay home and watch it on TV and worry if our maids are going to show up.

That morning when I asked for the car, Sam looks at me like I'm crazy and says, "Why do you want to go downtown today? Today of all days?"

I tell him, "Because there are some things I have to shop for." What can I say, how can I explain what I don't understand myself.

"Can't you put it off for a few days, Eve? Look at the *Sun:* 'NINE KILLED IN D.C. CHICAGO RIOTS'. All hell may break

loose today…right here in staid old Baltimore… Besides the
car's back in the garage for repairs…the transmission went,
this time for good."

Over his shoulder I read

NINE KILLED IN D.C. CHICAGO RIOTS

CONGRESS TO MEET IN EMERGENCY

"I guess so…you're probably right. Hey Sam, read this.
'It's Business As Usual,' the Mayor said, 'All segments of
the city are fine people and there is great rapport. I hope it
can be enhanced.' What a politician! Already he's out and
running for '72."

"That idiot." Anger splotched across his face. "Look, why
don't you stay home today?"

"I can't."

He shrugged his shoulders and went back to the paper.
He cares, but he knows me too well.

I sat there thinking. "How do you think she feels about
us?"

Startled, Sam raises his eyes. "Who?" His thoughts are
still with the Orioles.

"Georgia, of course. I mean with all this anger and hostility coming out, how do you think she feels about us? After
all, we're her employers. Do you think she hates us, or sees
us as her enemies? I mean it's not fair…like we're all lumped
together…the rednecks and us.…"

"How would I know?" Long sigh. He's impatient with
me, that's his way of letting me know, and impatient with the
whole problem. Two lines start at his nose and end at his
chin, two elongated parentheses framing his disapproval.
"How can I begin to put myself in her place?"

I started to clear the dishes from the table and suddenly
I'm so mad I want to smash them.

"*They* killed him!"

"Why are you yelling at me?"

As though he didn't know what's bothering me.

"Ah Eve, you're such a good Jew, you ooze guilt like
other people perspire," he throws in for good measure.

Another long sigh. Then patiently he explains it to me. "I don't have any answers. All I know is I try to treat her like any other human being I know. Anyhow, what's Georgia got to do with you going downtown today? I don't get it. Today of all days?"

How can I explain it to him? Once when my mother had a heart attack in New York, the next day I went out and bought a new bedroom set in Baltimore. Nothing very urgent, but it was a good sale and I was planning to get one anyway, and I told myself, look, what good will it do Mom if I stay home and don't buy that set. Life must go on.... Now I'm not so sure anymore that's what I was trying to prove. There's something I've discovered about doing the prosaic... it denies reality to your fears....

Sam was right, though. I shouldn't have come downtown, and in a red suit. It should have been black, black like the mourning streamers signaling from the passing cars. But I wasn't thinking and only later it hit me after I had left the house and by then it was too late.

That morning a hush lay over Baltimore like a wet dressing. The whole city had red eyes.

And now, all the samelooking streets going by with their faceless row houses and not one happy face, not one child playing hopscotch or jump rope... All of us on the bus patients in an ambulance rushing somewhere... It was so unnaturally quiet... Only the rumble of heavy tires on asphalt and the wheezing of air brakes... And a few teenagers scuffling in the back breaking the numb silence with their taunting laughter....

After a few minutes the crowd shifted slightly and I managed to reach the coin box. A blank. I couldn't remember the fare. It had been raised several times lately and I couldn't remember. Anyhow I offered the driver a dollar bill because I was too embarrassed to ask him outright. That sounds silly, I know, but if you're on a bus loaded with Negroes...I mean, Blacks, there's something almost confessional about admitting Whitey doesn't even know what the bus fare is. I figured when he gives me the change I'll know.

But he shook his head at me. No, like at an errant child. "We're not making change, lady, no more, not since that driver on the Number Ten got held up last week. They killed him for fifty lousy dollars!" Fear and anger speaking. "Didn't you read about it? It was in all the papers. No sir!"

"But what am I supposed to do?" I had forgotten all about it.

His purple lips curled ironically and his eyes shifted meaningfully to the door.

I stood there helplessly, clutching the dollar bill. How much of a stranger can you be in your own town?

Someone nudged my elbow sharply. I swung around not knowing what was coming next. A light-skinned Negress in a good black suit had her leather change purse open, she surprised me. "Here. Here's a quarter."

"Oh, I couldn't do that. It's very nice of you, but really...."

"That's all right." Benignly she smiled and handed me the money.

"No. I couldn't...well, thank you very much...if you'll let me return it. Can I have your name and address, please?" Oh, I was playing the Lady all right.

"Never mind." A little impatiently she added, "Don't bother."

She meant it, too, but I couldn't let it go. "Please let me have your name and address?"

A moment of silence while she studied me, then the smile on her face curdled and she turned away.

That started me thinking about lots of things...the house we didn't buy because the agent, Jack's sister-in-law, tipped us off...you might want to think it over, she confided, you know this is a changing neighborhood...and the private school for Joey this year....

All of a sudden I'm pushed in right behind the driver into a pocket that's trapped all the heat and gas fumes on the bus. Only a few seconds of this and my head started swaying weakly from side to side and everything blurred. Not that please, I remember thinking, the last thing I wanted right then was to pass out on that bus. Instinctively I clutched at the overhead railing and focused on the Black driver whose bullet-shaped head thrust upward from deep between his shoulders as though necks were no longer being used. Near him with her broad back towards me stood a tall Black woman in a faded sweater and the two of them were speaking in that easy going way Black people have with each other, sort of soft and kind. The nausea in my throat was subsiding and their voices came in clearly.

Her rich contralto, "It sure is hot today."

And his deep bass. "Yeah, and it ain't gonna get better tomorrow."

"That's what I hear tell."

That last word *tell* carried special weight, there was no mistaking it.

"What d'ya hear?" he quietly insinuated, bearing down vengefully on a shiny '68 Cadillac.

The whoosh sound of air released, "Nothing much…jes *talk.*"

The rearview mirror reflected his corrugated black forehead and black eyes glaring straight ahead. "Jes…talk," he repeated.

Was he sending her a message, my heart pounded a little faster, or was I getting paranoiac? I was an alien now and maybe that's how aliens feel.

Crouching over the wheel like a captain commanding a large warship, he docked the bus and still more passengers climbed aboard. "Move to the back, folks," he ordered in his deep voice and the tall Black woman almost bumped me. Her large bosom blocked my view and I glanced down at her strong black hands, noticing the pink palms eroded by steel wool and scouring powder. A domestic worker, not like my lady with the quarter. Several buttons, little mother-of-pearl ones, were missing from her sweater and a mono-gram in grand flowing script was badly ripped. The T was missing its crossbar, and only the imprint of the stitching on the L remained. E T L, I made it out. My own initials....

Her face. For a moment, it was just another Black face with a flat nose squashed down at the base, and pink pudgy lips. Then it was Georgia. But a different Georgia. Yet during that split second of recognition I couldn't tell why. How strange, I thought. Now that was really strange.

She was standing there very straight and tall, almost monolithic like an Easter Island figure, black eyes heavy, the weight of them pulling down her face. There was sadness around her mouth, it had all collected in a pool around her pink pudgy lips. Georgia?

We were on opposite sides of the kitchen counter when the radio announced a special news bulletin. When the announcer said the fateful words – Flash! Martin Luther King has just been fatally shot by an unknown assassin as he stood on the balcony of his motel in Nashville! – I got goose pimples all over and I wanted to cry. We both looked up at the same moment so I could see her eyes distinctly and the look in her eyes got to me. They went blank...black blank eyes...as though she were reaching deep, deep inside of herself for something she hadn't needed or perhaps even known was there until that moment when she knew he was gone forever.

And I felt sick and for a minute there, I thought I was going to throw up. But I took a drink of water and it helped. It was *they*, of course.

I'm sorry, Georgia, I said and she said that's all right, just like she always did if the children spoke impolitely to her, not meaning to, it just came out that way in their childish exuberance. And she seemed to understand that they really didn't mean to be impolite, and when I'd say to them, tell Georgia you're sorry, then she'd always say, oh that's all right. And she meant it. But now I didn't know if she meant it and I didn't know what else to say so I left the room.

And Friday...only yesterday...Georgia who always came and went quietly, showed up and smiled Good Morning so that her one gold molar glinted yellow in the morning light. She seemed no different from Thursday or the day before that. I watched her and came to know her face as I had never known it before. One side drooped more than the other. When she smiled, the left side moved but not the right. Yet I had never noticed this before in all the three years she had worked for us. Then I saw the swooping scar near her mouth. It must have been a sharp razor.

I watched her – this tall quiet woman who quietly went about her chores in tennis shoes, white ones, who never talked about herself – as though by measuring her pain I could gauge my own.

But she wouldn't let me read her face, nothing had changed. The more I resented the wall she put up between us, the more I tried to penetrate. That's how I am sometimes....

"What are people saying downtown, Georgia?"

I was fixing myself a salad for lunch. Notice, I told myself, you said people, you didn't even give her a right to her Blackness and say *your* people. All of us are people together, right?

"Nothing really, Mrs. Landsman. Ah jes moved into this new neighborhood and the people haint friendly. Don talk to you. Jes look out the window when they see you comin or goin but don talk to you. Takin it all in, but don talk to you."

"Surely they must feel strongly about King's murder."

"Yes, Ma'm."

"Well, what do they say then?"

"Nothin, Ma'm, jes lak ah tol you."

"Do you think we'll have rioting here in Baltimore?"

Her murky eyes swung out the window spotting a newly arrived robin. "Ah wouldn't know."

I didn't believe her. They must be talking to each other, planning, plotting, spewing out all that bottled-up hate. How could they not? She just won't tell me, I thought, she knows how guilty I feel. She's watching me burn and liking it.

"But how do you feel about it?" I wouldn't let it alone. Slowly she turned from the oven which she was cleaning with some smelly spray cleanser and deliberately wiped her rubber-gloved hands on a paper towel before replying.

"He was a good man. Why would they want to kill him?"

And that's all she would say. Her pale-rimmed glasses shielded her eyes and I wanted to say why don't you clean your glasses, Georgia, they're smudged, and yet when I looked closely, it was only an illusion. They were clean.

Georgia seemed so remote and lost in her own thoughts that about all I could think to say was a formal, "How are you today?" My voice rang out too loudly in that quiet, the quiet of the sickroom, and people turned around to look at us.

She nodded fine, smiled briefly so that her gold molar shone proudly and then casually looked away. What was she thinking? I would have given anything to know. She's got a sweet smile, but I'm never sure what she's saying with it. We were like strangers on that bus, and yet I thought, she's known the ins and outs of our house for three years, how much money we spend on liquor and the nights when Sam and I fight and he goes off to the guest room. She knows the minute she sees that unmade bed. That's more than our close friends know about us and that's what made it such a strange day...out of focus...all the usual connections severed.

But the suffocating heat and fumes and crushing mob... and my aching feet were still real. It was pure agony. I kicked off my shoe. Would you believe it when I finally dragged home from that bus and took off my shoes, one stocking was actually soaked with blood where the metal buckle had gouged into my raw flesh.

Remember the old Georgie Price *New Yorker* cartoon showing a subway guard packing people into a car like sardines and a little old lady says to him, "Gently sir, it's Mother's Day"? Well from nowhere don't ask me why I remembered it and started laughing right there on the bus. I kept on laughing and laughing, people were looking at me and I didn't care. The tears were rolling down my cheeks and I couldn't even reach a tissue in my purse.

Suddenly there was a seat, a woman near me began to collect her belongings. Thank God! If I had ever seen anyone look like a founder of the DAR, it was her. Georgia, I noticed, was also looking at her. Was she sizing her up as a natural enemy? That must have been an important part of survival for the Blacks...white face-reading. There was no expression on her face, she was just quietly watching with that new sad turn of her mouth.

The DAR was taking her goddamn time.

Move, lady, move.

Then as the bus stopped, she seemed to make a last-minute decision and stood up. I lunged for the seat, feeling for my shoe at the same time. It was gone. What a thing to happen!

Frantically, I searched, swinging my right leg around like a compass. Still no shoe.

Desperate now, I bent down hunting all around the filthy feet-clogged floor. Nothing but wads of gum, candy wrappings, cigarette butts and shoes. Everyone's shoes but my own. Already I pictured myself hopping home three long blocks on one foot lugging these damn packages. And the tears had started when a heavy cordovan boot moved just enough and there was my patent kicked under a far seat. I got down on my hands and knees and crawled between all those legs that wouldn't budge – did they think I was a dog or something? – but just kicked back at me viciously. I grabbed the shoe. My heart was pounding double time as I stood up. Hair was hanging every which way over my eyes and clumps were pasted to my forehead with sweat. Just hang on for another minute, I told myself, you'll make it now.

Georgia had grabbed *my* seat.

I tell you I was dumbstruck. Really. My whole body start-ed shaking as though a sudden icy wind had swept through the bus; I couldn't control it. Our eyes met and for the first time in three years, her eyes looked straight into mine, not this way or that way or down at the floor like always before. Those black eyes were sharply clear and seeing. We traded stare for stare like kids vying over who can go longest without blinking. And I lost.

Burning, buzzing inside me, I'm thinking…she grabbed the seat from me! she knew I wanted it…my feet are killing me…I want that seat…can't stand another minute…I WANT THAT SEAT…c'mon Georgia, you'd never pull something like this in the house…maybe she'll offer it to me soon… maybe she just wants it for a short rest and then she'll offer it to me…that would be fair…like you would do with a friend…only goddammit she's not my friend…she's my maid…she'd better remember her place!

It couldn't be, yet I had this frightening feeling that I was talking out loud. The Black woman near me stared at me strangely and I mashed my teeth closed and pushed the hair back. Ten more unbearable blocks. I was counting them the way you watch the sweep hand on the wall clock in the dentist's office when he's drilling. It's funny, the silent bargains you strike with pain…with all of life's outrages. Only thirty seconds more please and then let it be over. But it never is.

Then she offered to hold my packages while I painfully eased on the miserable shoe and I barely managed to nod yes. After all, I tried to tell myself – we had both paid the same fare. But it didn't work.

"Stop pushing me!" I glared at the Black woman standing next to me. If only I could shove her off!

Finally we got there: Panoramic Drive. "Goodbye, Georgia," I called. "See you on Monday."

I managed to collect myself enough to say that much. I even tried to lift the corners of my mouth in a friendly way, but it probably was more of a grimace than a grin. But what's there to smile about, I asked myself as I stumbled down the steps.

Dance Steps

She's waiting. He's twenty-five minutes late by her wrist-
watch when he rings the bell. She presses the buzzer. His
feet climb the long flight of stairs in this brownstone row
house in steady cadence. She swiftly calculates how long
it will take him to reach the top, and just as he approaches
the door, his tread muffled by the muddy green runner,
she always opens it so that he won't have to knock. Is that to
make you feel more welcome, she wonders? It's been two
weeks.

He enters, shyly brushes her slightly rouged cheek, or
her lips sometimes, and smiles wryly, a smile that suggests,
Well, I'm here again, as though a part of him resists coming.
He's a large man, big chested, but there is an emptiness
about his arms – they swing aimlessly as he ambles in, as
though the sawdust had run through a rent in the seam.
Then, as usual, he seats himself in the hard maple chair that
she found at a church auction for two dollars; it came
from their Sunday school, and the writing arm is scratched
and etched by years of students who probably slouched
uncomfortably as he does now. She always selects the armchair opposite him, a folding outdoor chair with wooden
slats and tubular legs and a red pillow that hides a broken
slat. While he has carefully chosen the classroom chair,
she has just as carefully made a choice; she will not start out
by lounging on the studio bed discreetly covered with
a purple batik spread and Marimekko pillows tossed about
with planned abandon. He selects asceticism; she hovers
between degrees of sensuality.

Outside the shrieks of sirens; inside she offers him Bolla.
White or red? She's taken to keeping wine around, several
kinds – though for herself she would not. She's not a solitary
drinker…not yet.

"Well so how are you?" He speaks with the slightest lisp.
"All right."

He dangles his youth before her in this large room with
the three tall bay windows; she has made it her own by covering the walls with good prints and the assorted notes on
white index cards she writes to herself and posts on the bulletin board near her desk:

Give Michael heavy beard.
Mildred wears size 10 ½ shoes, teased hair.
Steiglitz on a 1919 Marin painting: "to paint disorder
under a big order."
WRITE A PROSE THAT'S EXPOSED AND GNARLED LIKE
THE ROOTS OF A CENTURY-OLD OAK — TOUGH, TENACIOUS,
RESILIENT AND INEVITABLE.

Despite his reticent behavior, he is garbed in male
plumage; tight jeans that outline his crotch and buttocks
and have elicited her compliments and caressing hands. In
the warmer weather when they met, he sported an open
shirt, open enough to reveal his hairy chest; on colder days
like today a handsome turtleneck (this one's a Gauguin
purple striped punctiliously in golds) that frames his Slavic
features and curly hair. Once glancing out the window –
he's always fifteen to twenty minutes late, never more or
less – she saw him as he paused outside, reached into his
pocket, and combed his hair. But today he has added a new
note, a beret. Yes, the beret is new.

They talk amiably; he offers a rambling account of a
recent perplexing conversation with an acquaintance of his,
and he pauses between sentences to examine its implica-
tions, then about a book he's reading (Kierkegaard is his
current god). Sometimes about his boss and petty office
politics and his dissatisfactions. Or a rejected manuscript for
her, though she's the more reticent because there are certain subjects she'd rather stay away from – her ex-husband,
her continuing misery, her grown children who present
her with growing problems daily as though cold offerings

on a stainless steel platter were the nexus for their familial connections. No, these are not subjects to discuss with him, she's decided, because they are so painful for her, but even more so, because they would bore him and how can an older woman hope to keep her young lover through sad tales and ennui? She can't afford a bad performance. The play would close.

So she conjures up funny anecdotes, offers her painfully accreted wisdom (if asked), and converses wittily, sagaciously, insightfully about feminist fiction and the diabolics of publishing, and her work – yes, the novel is going well, she says today – another day, she says no the novel is not going well, not at all – these are subjects that will not depress or bore him. The woman writer. Does he speak of her to his business friends – somewhat the way one displays an exotic shawl? A find in a secondhand shop? *By the way, I'm having an affair with a writer...older woman...attractive in a tired way... knows a lot of writers.* He might be a name dropper, though of that she's not certain. They've always been alone together, never going out with friends, his or hers. Somehow they just settled into this pattern.

So far all is proceeding as usual. More wine is offered; he accepts. After enough wine and conversation, he will make some move or gesture that indicates now he's ready. Sometimes he moves from the schoolboy chair casually – as though he really happened to rise to stretch – arching his back in a feline sway – or to examine once again that marvelous woodcut of Emily Dickinson and then happening to sit down on the studio couch. Sometimes he stretches out on the small oriental on the floor, though it's too small for his six feet, slipping off his Danish clogs, or hiking boots, or tasseled loafers, or Italian white and brown shoes with stacked heels. He never says, come here. He never spontaneously reaches out his arms to her, or says, "Hey, you look terrific in that outfit!" though he must realize she's taken special care in dressing and perfuming. She's even begun treating her calloused heels with pumice because he once mentioned liking soft feet, something about a child-hood fetish with his mother.

No, without a word, he will assume position two. Now the next move is always hers: she moves closer so that she's within reaching distance – if he wants to reach her. If he chooses the studio couch, then she pulls her chair closer to it; close enough so that she can place her unslippered feet on the bed. Slowly he will massage them reaching higher and higher up her legs. Or else she lowers herself next to him on the floor (thank God for yoga), though the rug is too small and threadbare to be either roomy or comfortable.

Once she's made it possible for him to reach her without stretching, then their lovemaking begins. Begins and buds and blossoms. They're silent, she because he is. Sometimes he grunts…and she's amused…the writer in her must describe it truthfully…grunts as though…constipated. Other men she's been with yipe or sob or roar with pleasure. But he grunts.

Sounds aside, the lovemaking is marvelous and he knows it and so does she. Last time, afterwards he said to her – it was the only time he ever spoke afterwards – "Thanks, that was a gift."

Was that your farewell gift to me, she wondered? For he went on to tell her he was about to leave the city, taking another job in a small town, west, about four hours away. He had never even mentioned the possibility before. Taken so by surprise, she almost blurted out, perhaps I can drive out and visit you. But she checked herself in time, she realized she had to wait to be asked. It had become a ritualized dance – comic, yes – and such a move would have been out of order, introducing another step. Can you picture Laurel and Hardy changing their routine – Laurel's sly smirk or Hardy bopping him over the head with his bowler? Impossible! The very essence of ritual is that you make no change. That is its hold on one, its magnetism.

So after forty-five minutes of desultory conversation,

she babbling on about Virginia Woolf and her remarkable relationship with Leonard, they're still in first position, though usually by now, they've flowed on to the second. At the moment she's trying also to balance the wineglass on her left palm as she goes on to relate what happened yesterday at the periodontist's. "He's such a business man, he's talking with his broker in between drilling! 'Rinse!' he orders me as he picks up the phone. When he looks in my mouth, I'm sure he sees only money."

He laughs, this time a short polite one, and when she offers him more wine, he gestures, no more. And he never gets up from the schoolboy chair, only shifting uneasily, perching first on one buttock, then the other.

This dance does have its funny moments, she reflects wryly.

He must be keeping an eye on the old pendulum clock on the antique chest (another church bargain) because precisely in an hour he plants his hands on his thighs. "Well, I guess I'd better get going…snow warnings for later y'know…" and his square hand with the short clean fingernails and the fine tufts of hair on the second joint, jabs towards the windows colored by pewter skies as though they were already blurred with white flakes.

"Yes, of course," she replies mechanically. He *is* being sensible. Correctly so. No use taking chances driving into the mountains. From the closet she fetches his blue ski jacket plump with down and the new navy beret, and hands them to him. Once he's snugly buttoned inside, he brushes her cheek, missing her lips, and mumbles, see you soon. She pats his shoulder.

Inside the room, the resonance of silence as she listens to his footsteps on the stairs descending…leaving, leaving her alone. She hears the latch snap as the heavy front door closes.

She rushes to the closet, tears her coat from the hanger, and plunges down the stairs, still struggling with one sleeve, and outside. Bare-armed trees are moving and swaying as the snowstorm whips in with a keening sound. His Mustang is just pulling away from the curb; with his eyes on the rearview mirror, jauntily he waves.

"I hate you!" she shrieks into the wind, her face contorting as her breath is flung back into her throat. "Do you hear me? Do you hear me? You bastard!"

Strands of dark hair caught by the wind wrap around her face like a veil, while playfully he signals with his hand, Goodbye, Goodbye.

Full Moon

It is Thursday again and Rita Kleinman slowly drives through the high curlicued wrought iron gate that guards Shepard-Pratt from the world. Her left hand grips the steering wheel, her right clutches a half-eaten cone. One final lingering bite into the chocolate ice cream, then she flings the rest into the bushes. Next week will be a year, yet it always feels like the first time and she wonders why.

A young woman thin as a scarecrow comes running crookedly towards her across the smooth lawn. "Mommy! Mommy!" her voice catching in the trees.

"I'm so glad to see you!" Leslie breathes hysterically pouncing on Rita. Her daughter's melted-down-to-bone face seems older than eighteen, yet her voice is so high and childlike.

"How are you?" Rita asks, her eyes inspecting her daughter.

"Fine," Leslie answers, her face saying no. Rita hugs and kisses her daughter and hands her the Finesse shampoo and conditioner she asked for. "And I brought you a T-shirt from Harborplace. Like it? I thought the dolphin was cute."

"It's okay. Here, hold it for me."

"Let's visit with the others." She surprises herself. Visiting alone with Leslie, she realizes, has come down to feeding her daughter lines like a straight man and getting 'fine, okay, no, maybe' in return and after ten minutes, there's nothing more to say. So she links her arm with Leslie's and they join the group nearby relaxing on wooden lawn chairs, the old-fashioned green kind repainted bright orange and yellow. Through her dark sunglasses, she studies them, three women and the blonde male attendant. She says hello to Sophie, the depressive with the knobby fingers and thin hair dyed red who smiles back, and Caroline, the young Black woman with the cornrow hairdo who's schizophrenic and looks up only long enough from her Walkman to nod.

Sitting next to Sophie is a new one who's staring at her with frank curiosity. Rita recoils from her direct gaze, yet from behind her sunglasses, she observes her. A striking woman, about thirty-five, she'd say, with the scissored profile of an American Indian, and the straight dark hair that goes with it. Restless, though. The way she keeps crossing and recrossing her legs. What's she here for?

Without a word the woman turns back to the others. "Mommy?"

"Yes?" "Yes, Leslie, you were saying?" she encourages her.

Leslie abandons the sentence and subsides into plucking at her swollen red lip. To Rita, it looks worse. And why aren't they making sure she bathes regularly, shampoos her oily hair? She chews on a hangnail and stares off into space. A year is a long time.

Now these women seem attuned – or else sedated – to the serenity of the late afternoon. The sturdy old trees are sending out that fresh sweet burst of leaves that follow a rainy April. Only the red maple breaks the horizon of green. A leisurely game of croquet would be quite in order, she fancies, with a tea cart waiting on the lawn. Her imagination often orders the complementary details that life has forgotten to supply, though of this she is unaware. She turns her head almost expecting to see wickets and catches only her daughter's clouded eyes clinging to her instead. The Dean at Emerson had called late one night and she flew up to Boston and brought her back. Jerry was out of town – as usual. Leslie was down to eighty-seven pounds, couldn't keep a thing down. Anorexic. Then all the business about getting her admitted here. No beds, a long waiting list…she pushes that time away.

Half-listening to the apathetic conversation, Rita discovers that the new one's name, after all, is really Nedda Goldman and that like herself, the woman grew up in Boro Park, a poor Jewish neighborhood in Brooklyn. And here she was already trying to figure out which tribe Nedda's from. The Lost Ones, of course.

Nedda's throaty contralto, quite audible, pierces her thoughts. "Oh, how I wish I could go back to Cleveland for just a few hours."

"If only I could go back to Cleveland for a few hours," Nedda yearns, all the while trying to calm her trembling left hand with the steadier right one. "I just want to hug and kiss my children and hold them…then I'd come back to this loony bin." She jerks her head towards the long low nineteenth century brick building with its wings extending maternally towards them.

"Loony bin?… Why do you use that term?" Rita's voice stumbles.

"Most people don't. Won't!" Nedda replies emphatically, turning her dark observant eyes from the distant view towards the visitor, "but I do."

"Most people think of it as a hospital," Rita says, keeping her voice bland. She fumbles for a sugarfree mint in her handbag.

"Maybe, I hope so. But a lot of them don't!" Abruptly Nedda turns back towards the west where distant towers of glass and the spires of new high-rises blaze in the setting sun.

"That's the nicest view of Towson I've ever seen," says Paul, the medical aide, who doesn't look more than twenty. Dressed like the patients in jeans and a work shirt, he could be one of them, except that he wears a beeper clipped to his belt. "I grew up a mile from here. Like in the country." His pale apricot skin sprouts the downy fuzz of a teenager who's only shaved a few times. "Now though, it's all part of Baltimore," he adds regretfully.

The patients say nothing.

Those distant buildings seem like a mirage, Rita reflects, recalling a similar sensation driving south on 95 where at a particular rise close to Washington, the gilded and white spires of the Mormon Cathedral appear directly ahead like a

191 | Tema Nason

preview of Disneyland or an ad for *Camelot*. Come to think of it, was the movie with Julie Andrews? Or was she the one in *Peter Pan*?

"If only I could see them for a few hours," Nedda says wistfully.

No one answers. Rita is still mulling about that Mormon edifice – what an anachronism! – but why make the association with this place? Were emotional problems less rampant back then in King Arthur's time? Was there a connection between mental illness and urban sprawl? And violence? Maybe she can find a good course next semester at Goucher.

"I want to see my kids," Nedda shrills.

"How many do you have?" Rita asks, asking only because the others say nothing. Lately she's noticed that her evening courses in the adult education program interest her a lot more than other people's company or even the TV when she returns home to that hollow resonating silence. Funny how then the kitchen sounds draw her in there as though the room has a life of its own – the breathy hum of the old refrigerator, the wall clock's slurred tick, the copper kettle's steamy whistle hazing the cold window...even the unripe tomatoes on the window sill waiting for tomorrow's sun.

"Two," Nedda replies, "ten and twelve – two girls. Now Susie, the older one, she looks after Tish when they get home from school now that I'm here."

"Ah," she replies to convey her sympathy, then returns to her earlier thoughts...which came first, the chicken or the egg? Do cities produce disturbed people – or is it the other way around? Interesting... She reaches for another sugarfree mint.

Nedda is still speaking. "You see, I left here a year ago January – but then I had to come back. 'I'll have you committed,' Jay Dee said." Nedda mimics his browbeating tone. "Fuck him!"

"Oh, you'll get well and then you can go home again," she offers perfunctorily, shifts the mint under her tongue, and considers raising these questions in her Introductory Sociology class tonight. There's something here beneath this deceptive air of a small Ivy League campus she's struggling to understand. Always trying to find answers, she thinks, as though once you could figure things out for yourself, discover the Big Bang theory for life, it would all get easier.

"My ex now – Jay Dee – he's the best orthodontist in Cleveland, I'll say that for him." Nedda says it loyally, reflectively. She props her left foot in a white Nike on her right knee, but the trembling doesn't stop. "But he was a lousy husband!" she bursts out.

"Why?" asks the young medical aide, his face calm.

"Cold!" she spits out. "Damn cold! But, of course, his patients don't know that. They adore him…you have to live with them to know," she adds philosophically.

"That's right." Suddenly Sophie, the older woman, speaks up nervously weaving her arthritic fingers through her dyed red hair. Rita can see that these two understand each other, that when it comes to husbands, Nedda and Sophie believe they know the truth about them.

Hesitantly, Rita asks, "By the way, Leslie, have you heard from your father recently?" Unobtrusively, she reaches into her handbag for the bag of M&M's, pops a few in her mouth pretending she's smothering a yawn.

"No. But I wrote to him two weeks ago," she adds as though trying to defend herself against some unstated charge, "and tried to call him last week. But he wasn't in." Her shoulders crumple.

"He's probably busy. He'll answer you in time," her mother reassures her, careful to keep her own anger out of it. Not paying alimony since he moved to L.A., leaving her with all this.

Speaking of husbands must remind Sophie of something else for she goes on to say, "I wish I could gain some weight back." Her hyperthyroid eyes look down at her emaciated body in white slacks and a skimpy knit shirt and she shakes her head.

"Not me – not another ounce," Nedda says emphatically lighting a thin cigar. "I can't get into any of my clothes." She inhales deeply. "Have you ever seen me in anything but these?" Her proud eyes disapprove of the tight jeans and orange T-shirt on her taut body. Caroline who has been tapping her foot in time to the rock beat in her earphones suddenly stops and nods in agreement. No, this is all she's worn. Then her foot resumes tapping.

I wouldn't mind having her figure, Rita decides, that flat stomach, small waist.

"Now tomorrow – I'm going to wear a shirt without holes!"

"Where are the holes?" Rita asks.

"Here!" Her finger probes a tiny opening in the shoulder seam. Her left foot begins trembling violently and she shifts and recrosses her legs so that the right foot is now propped on the left knee which helps. She starts to play with the strings of a fringed suede pouch, the kind Indian maidens wear in children's book illustrations. "I can't get into any of my clothes. So how am I going to go to the ballet next week?" she demands dramatically cupping her small breasts. "Besides, they never looked the same after nursing. Made 'em sag."

"We have opposite problems...you and I," Sophie concludes. "Now if I could only gain back...you see," she turns to Rita who she wants, it seems, to understand her plight. "I've been on a restricted diet because of this medication they put me on?...but like I said to my doctor 'You try not losing weight, you just try gaining weight when you can't eat sugar or carbohydrates and fats and...'" she interrupts herself to repeat his condescending reply. "'There *are* other foods you can eat.' See what I mean?"

She appeals to them for support. They stare back at her with neutral eyes. She subsides.

"Oh well, now I have a weight problem, too," Rita pitches in, "I go up and down like a yo-yo." Glancing down at her squashy belly and thickening thighs, she winces. Twelve pounds in two months. Yet she can feel the compelling urge for Dunkin' Donuts well up. Probably she'll stop off there on the way back as usual.

"Not like your daughter here. What she lives on...I'll never know." Nedda shakes her head. "Eats like a bird," she adds, "without an appetite." She laughs. "Not much of a talker either. Takes after you? Funny though, she's a beanpole and you're a pumpkin. How long has she been this way?"

Rita shakes her head. This is not the time to discuss her.

"You should have seen her when she spotted your car!" Sophie smiles in remembrance. "I've never seen her move so fast."

"I know. Leslie can certainly move when she wants to," Rita says hearing the sharpness in her voice though it's meant for Nedda. Her daughter seems lost in her own thoughts; only the methodical plucking of her lip goes on. Even when she was little the real Leslie stayed in hiding as though she chose to spend her life behind an invisible curtain. All that therapy never seemed to help.

"Well, as for me, I wish I could gain some back," repeats Sophie. As an afterthought, she tosses out, "My children all have eating problems, too...now my oldest daughter..." Then with a shoving motion of her palm, she throws away the rest of the sentence.

"Imagine! That Winifred on 2B gets dressed up every day. Imagine high heels and makeup ev-e-ry day!" Nedda goes on "acting as though she had someplace special to go to. Not me...not on your life! Not for this place, no way!"

"Maybe it's good for her morale," Rita says wondering why she is placating this fierce squaw. Why get involved in their world?

Nedda twitches her nose in disagreement.

Clearing her throat, timorously, Rita ventures, "I'm going to New York tomorrow." It is a sudden decision, but her voice gathers conviction as she speaks.

Leslie tugs at her lip so fiercely that it cracks and bleeds.

"Will you please not do that while I'm here!" Instantly she regrets her words.

Her daughter's hand drops like a stricken bird into her lap.

"How are you going?" she whimpers.

"By Metroliner." She is surprised by the even sound of her words.

"New York?" chortles Caroline and her enthusiasm sends her beaded cornrows swinging. "New York – that's where I grew up. I was born in Mt. Sinai Hospital – you know where that is?" Her mahogany face with the large dark mole on one cheek laps into folds of pleasure.

"Oh sure," Rita says. "On upper Fifth Avenue."

"Man, I love that New York. Of course, I wouldn't want to live there now. Too expensive. And the crazies on the street. But I love that city. Lived there 'til I was ten." Her pudgy slouching body straightens up and her arms shoot up like a cheerleader's. "But then I lived in the Village for two years. All that corned beef and pastrami…great deli round the corner… Man, I loved it!"

"How old were you then?" Rita asks struck by her sudden animation.

"Fifteen."

"Fifteen?" Sophie exclaims, "With your family?"

"With a Jewish family. I ran away from home."

"Ah," says Sophie as though she's putting two and two together. "No wonder you knew so much about Passover food when we went to that Seder."

"That's right." Caroline says it proudly now that they know she was a New Yorker and that she's lived with a Jewish family. She takes off her earphones and places them in her lap.

"No wonder you understand Jewish expressions." Nedda is smiling now, her hawklike profile relaxing. Her smile makes her face soft and pretty.

Rita pictures her all dressed up in a handsome handknit

sweater and high-heeled black boots striding into the orthodontists' annual convention with Jay Dee and catching everyone's eyes with her arrowy body and sable hair. And those bold eyes. Nedda is definitely a woman who's excited men's lusting glances and she feels a subtle envy.

"Rita," her daughter murmurs, "how long will you be gone?"

"Just for the weekend. I'll be back late Sunday night."

"What are you going to do in New York?"

"Oh – probably see some friends, I really don't know… maybe visit Aunt Lilly." She's just decided to pay scalpers' prices for *Phantom of the Opera*. She also considers calling Jess, though it's been years. Her old college roommate was always more resigned to life's vagaries.

"You'll call me?" her daughter's anxious tearless eyes are imploring .

"Oh sure, I'll give you a ring. As soon as I get back." After all, it'll only be forty-eight hours.

With clumsy fingers she pulls her shawl about her shoulders for the air is cooling rapidly. She can picture pulling into the Double D on York Road, the fresh coffee smell as you enter, the golden trays of fresh doughnuts and crullers arranged at eye level behind the counter…chocolate-frosted, honey-dipped, strawberry creme-filled, jelly… Lovingly, her mind's eye roves, choosing first one, then another.

The aide, Paul, rubs his bare arm and suggests heading back to the hospital where friendly warm lights are shining. All together the five women stand up and start across the lawn.

"Let's take the road back. I'm exhausted from climbing up and down these slopes," Sophie complains to Rita. "I'm too old for keeping up with these young ones."

Silently, they comply and plod along. The moon, a circle of diaphanous white, is outlined on the dark radiant blue – as though pasted on by a child, she thinks. A pigeon coos in the stillness.

"Tonight I turn into a werewolf," Nedda remarks, her eyes on the lambent moon.

Her words soak into the silence. Walking alongside her, Sophie's eyes dilate, and she darts a worried look at Nedda. Caroline catches up with the aide who's just ahead. Leslie sidles closer to her mother.

Nedda smiles slyly. "Full moon."

Everyone sharply inhales the scented twilight air. Involuntarily Rita's hands stray to her neck and her eyes gravitate to the enigmatic sphere hanging above the shadowy trees glowing with secrets. *That woman's impossible!* No wonder she's back here again. "Vaguely I do remember something… if there are male werewolves, there *must* be females, too," she snaps and wraps the shawl more tightly about her neck.

The group is silent, preoccupied. Nedda frowns and looks away into the trees. Something somewhere inside Rita is rising like a wind borne on strong currents.

As they near the hospital, Rita says, "Guess I'll say goodbye now."

"Can't you come up for just a few minutes?" Leslie pleads. Her long ragged fingernails clutch at her mother's sleeve.

"Visiting hours are over," says Paul.

Reaching across the short distance that separates them, Rita embraces her daughter, leans over to kiss her goodbye. Her daughter's body stiffens as she averts her face and allows Rita's kiss to land on her cheek. Rita's feet feel stuck in mud. She pictures the bright lit, steamy, fragrant inside of Dunkin' Donuts. Yes, she'll get the jelly-filled cruller. And maybe something else, too. A chocolate-frosted doughnut. Her pulse quickens.

Her daughter closes her deepset blue eyes. "My father loves me more than anyone. I know that," she says softly as though speaking to herself. "And I love him more than anyone."

Suddenly the image of a werewolf drunk with rage erupts before Rita's eyes. She sees that werewolf so concisely, so three-dimensionally, staring at her, yellow teeth bared, spittle dripping, his sulfurous eyes lighting up the dark. Transfixed, heart pumping, her mind reels on…secrets invoked…

Her conjuring eyes fasten on her daughter. Those skeletal arms. The mouth like a bloodied begonia. Will it be like this forever? The two of them tied into a knot? She wants to howl, a wild unearthly howl that will hang on in the air forever.

"Will she ever get better?" bursts out of her in a voice you use to talk to a God who's not listening. "I can't stand it… I can't stand it…anymore…coming here…like this… *How about me?*" Shaking with a mother's crazy urgent anger at her own helplessness to fix it all, she bites down hard on her knuckle, needing that hard unyielding bone under her teeth. Harder, harder, she bites until she's weeping, weeping with a child's high piercing cry, but coming out strangled, as though at birth she'd received instructions never to cry. Why Rita Kleinman, she thinks, this is so unlike you, and yet she can't stop.

Leslie's hand tears fiercely at her raw lips. "Don't cry, Mommy," she pleads. "Please, please." The frozen child's face dissolves at the sight of her stricken mother. She reaches out to stroke her mother's arm, stops, uncertain what to do next. Sophie passes Rita a clean tissue. Caroline kicks at the grass. Paul stands still, his teenager's face puckered. Only Nedda moves swiftly swooping to pluck a dandelion at her feet which she solemnly hands to Rita as though she were a novitiate in a religious ceremony.

Still crying Rita removes her sunglasses and eyes the spiky tenacious weed. The yellow petals will turn into gray furls, she thinks, as kids we used to puff at them and chant… loves me…loves me not…loves me…loves me not…loves…

Thus they all stand motionless silently ringed around her, enclosing her, their faces grave, their eyes protective.

Slowly her shoulders stop heaving, her hiccups subside, and she meets Leslie's eyes head-on.

Afterword

I think it's very important that older women don't buy into any of the stereotypes that are being handed around. I made up my mind in 1978 when my husband died, that stereotypes and statistics don't apply to me, that I'm an individual and I would try to live my life the way I wanted to rather than prematurely accept that certain things were already beyond me because I was too old. That's worked very well for me – my first published novel at sixty-nine.

I am always pushing myself for the truth, to go behind and behind what seems to be, not to mistake appearances for the reality. Along the way, I decided that while I admire a number of writers who are great stylists, for me writing is an attempt to push for the truth and not to obfuscate. I made that commitment to myself. I would not let any piece of work leave my hands until I felt it had the truth – my truth – in it.

I felt that very strongly in writing *Ethel, (Ethel: The Fictional Autobiography of Ethel Rosenberg*, Delacorte Press, 1990), that I was searching for the truth in it. Our whole society today has been desensitized to violence of all kinds, whether it's physical or verbal. There is silence about abuse. There's a lot of fiction that's very good and very skillful, entertaining, interesting, but it doesn't move you. I want my work to move people, to touch them where they live, to connect with them. When people say to me, "I read *Ethel* and I was crying," I feel I've accomplished something as a writer, to reawaken those emotions for them of a sense of injustice and of moral complicity that we practice that isn't recognized.

* * * *

Adapted from a taped interview.

A Stranger Here, Myself was written under circumstances that filled in gaps for me. At the time riots were going on in Baltimore, my husband and I and family were on a sabbatical in Rome. I was reading about curfews and looting in what I knew was a very sedate city and one where the whites congratulated themselves that they had a very good relationship with the Blacks. I was trying to visualize what it was like to have a curfew, and how it would have affected me, or women I knew, living in suburbia as we were.

When we came back several months later, I found myself asking friends what was it like. And the responses were, "Well, you know, really it wasn't the way you read about it in the paper. We watched it on television." And one friend said, "I had a dinner party planned for Saturday night and I was worried whether my maid would show up."

Previously, I had had a related personal experience. We, like others in our neighborhood, had a Black maid. I had run into her once downtown and for a moment didn't recognize her because she was not in uniform. We were on a bus and spoke briefly. We had what I considered a good relationship. As I was sitting there I thought, well suppose there was only one seat, what would happen? We're being so friendly, but what is the real relationship. I thought I would like to write a story about it. But it hadn't jelled.

When I came back after the riots, I decided, now *there* is a dramatic setting. This will really put it in the right perspective. And that's when I was able to pull the story together. I wrote it trying to come to grips with what my real feelings were, as a white person, as a person who had quote "the power," who thought of myself as a liberal. And yet what were my deepest feelings about it? In that sense I think I was taking a risk.

* * * *

Full Moon took me ten to twelve years to write. That story was risky for me, too. It started out realistically with a visit I had paid my daughter who is schizophrenic and was in the hospital, very much like the one I describe – it had a very Ivy League feeling to it, a sense of unreality because everything was so green and plush and orderly. I was taking in the conversation of the women whom we happened to sit down with. And it stayed with me. I wrote it down and didn't know what to make of it, but it kept plaguing me. I kept trying to understand what it was saying. I realized how often women talk about food when they're feeling deprived, and that my own relationship with my daughter was so nonverbal.

When I finished it, I was in the process of trying to organize a writers' group. At the first meeting, I read this story. Two of the women jumped on the mother, that she was a very unloving person – why wasn't she paying more attention to her daughter? I was terribly upset because I *knew*, that's not what the problem was. I couldn't sleep that night. I have found at times that the criticism that upsets me the most is exactly what I have to look at. If a critical comment doesn't hit the mark, I can dismiss it. But this bothered me – maybe because it was around the issue of motherlove and the ambivalent feelings with which we have so much trouble in relation to our children. The more I thought about it, I realized that I hadn't done my job as a writer because it was not my intention to show the mother as unloving, but simply how much pain she was in and covering up and denying it to herself.

So I started to work on the story again. I started to "beef up" the opening paragraphs, to slip in phrases that would indicate there is caring, but also there's pain that is being denied. I kept returning to that story. It would reach a certain point and I would think, I'm finished. Someone in my writers' group said to me, "You're obsessed with that story. Why don't you finish it?" But I still didn't know what had to be said. And finally the last few sentences, where the mother bursts out and says, "How about me?" and looks her daughter straight in the eye – when that wrote itself, I knew that was it!

What is even more interesting to me is that the novel I'm working on now, which is the outgrowth of dealing with the conflict between being a mother and a person – how much do you commit to your own life and how much have you already committed to others – didn't really get going until I finished *Full Moon*. I wanted to write the novel, but in some unfathomable way I wasn't released to do it. I couldn't get it off the ground until I had that final last sentence. Then I knew I was ready. It's an amazing thing, isn't it, when these experiences are happening to you. You're being led.

* * * *

I started with the view, based on my own mother's, that the children came first. Before I had children, I had worked, I had professional skills and I felt good about myself. When I had children in the fifties, suddenly I saw myself being measured by what I now consider as a very unrealistic standard – "How good are you as a mother?" It was as though you had been handed a ball of clay which you then had the power to shape – and if it came out misshapen, you were flawed as a mother. The first piece I ever wrote, this was about 1956, was called "Mother Talks Back." I was absolutely fed up with reading all these experts and their stupid advice.

I realized I was trying to measure up to some kind of ideal mother that was impossible. I've seen so many women caught up in the same trap, of feeling the responsibility was all theirs, the blame was all theirs. I see it with young women today – not only feeling they're responsible, but also very conflicted between what they want for themselves, how much they can ask for themselves and how much they have to give to the children. I'm not sure there's an answer.

I have a quote from a short story by Isaac Babel called *The Rabbi*.

> All is mortal; only the mother is destined to immortality. And when the mother is no longer among the living, she leaves a memory which no one yet has

dared to sully. The memory of the mother nourishes in us a compassion that is like the ocean. And the measureless ocean feeds the rivers that dissect the universe.

Large order? I want to scrutinize this honestly in my work.

I don't think there are many women of my generation born in the twenties or early thirties writing their stories. So I want to get mine down. These have been very important years for women both publicly and privately. And our stories must not be lost. The role of the mother is so sanctified in our society, and yet demeaned in another way. You're so easily at fault. You're either a saint or a sinner. For a writer to honestly talk about the ambivalent feelings – the frustration, anger, hostility that come up at times, all the negative feelings that I think women are afraid of tackling – as well as the abiding love and deep attachment and concern – all this, it's loaded and a cultural taboo. And I believe it is a subject that has to be tackled. Otherwise we'll never know the mother's voice. You can't have a real dialogue unless both mother/daughter, mother/children/husband can talk to each other honestly.

It's become important to me, through personal changes, to attempt it. Some of it, for myself, comes out of greater clarity as a feminist – not feeling I have to co-opt with prevailing cultural roles. But I think it's a very scary one, because certainly it can offend one's children. I mean it's accepted that a daughter can write critically about her mother but the reverse is definitely not true.

I've gone through a lot of difficult personal experiences, painful growth, and I've come to believe that none of us should sell ourselves short. Whether I'm a mother, a daughter, whatever, no relationship should demand of me that I sell myself short. I think it's dangerous for women to do that. You pay a price. And no society should be built on certain people paying a price so that others can prosper. That's not a healthy world.

There was a period when one of my daughters and I

were estranged (but no longer). The morning of her birthday, about five in the morning, I awoke and sat down with a yellow pad and pen and started to write a letter to my daughter. For about three months I got up every morning like an alarm clock had sounded and wrote for two hours about whatever was in my head. I never stopped to reread what I had written. I must have written a hundred-fifty, a hundred-eighty pages in longhand. I'd never done that before. And then it was as though I'd gotten it all down. It was only much later that I reread it – it was the mother trying to explain to her daughter what had happened in her own life. In writing this current novel, I have used some excerpts. In this letter she's trying to explain herself to her daughter who feels as though she's been lost between an older brother and a younger sister who is mentally sick.

You see you've never been with me, Claudia, when I go to visit her. See with my own eyes what's happened to her, how much she's changed, physically and otherwise, her mouth, the tics and twitches that wrack her body, her voice a child's. It tears me apart. And the pain. And that ferocious desire to change her back to our sweet gentle innocent-faced Deenie. Remember how soft her hands were? To make it all better, like a mother should. And I can't. I can't, and oh, how that hurts. My own lack of omnipotence, that I was raised to believe mothers have. My mother assured me she had it and I completely believed her, oh yes, I did. So I believed that when my time came around as a mother, I would have it too. And I waited and waited for it to happen. That one day it would be there in me like a legacy handed down in the family from mother to daughter. And someplace within, there's still that longing for that unfulfilled promise. My mother's to me and mine, I suppose, to myself. And then there's mine to you, given early on – that I had

those magical powers to protect and keep all of you
safe forever. When I still believed in them. When I
still believed my mother. Which is what you hold
against me, I know. You promised! I hear you saying,
you promised. You feel betrayed. And I, I am caught
between the two of you, unrelenting women that
you are. You have it, you have it, she keeps whispering from the grave and I hear you echoing her
words. And then I truly believe that in your eyes,
and therefore mine, so closely are we linked, I do
have it, that power. And I'm just not willing to
use it, to save our Deenie. Why? Why don't I want to
save her, I ask myself, for at times like these I really
believe I have the power. Go there, be by her side,
that would do it, her whispers say. And her whispers
echo in your silence. Let Deenie know you will
always be hers, that you will always be by her side,
for she can't manage without you. And that way she
will get well. The madness will leave her. And yet
I've learned that madness doesn't heed a mother's
prayers. How can I silence these unsilent voices?

We don't have it, but our children are telling us, we want
you to have it and therefore you must have it. There's this
child wanting to feel you are all-powerful, you can, you
have the power, you're withholding it. And that's the greatest
betrayal, really. That's why daughters end up feeling so
betrayed by their mothers. That's what the real anger is
about, isn't it, that's the real betrayal.

I think we're probably the first generation, at least here,
separated from our mothers enough so we are looking at
it and not just living it. We have the perspective, the freedom, the education to do this. We need to tell our stories.
It's a way of freeing ourselves up, not to carry forth this
bondage. And I really see with my own children, now,
when I made these demarcations, how it has really helped
them to seek their own answers. But until we do that,
we're not setting them free.

I probably always wanted to be a writer, but growing up in the Depression, I thought I had to be practical. And it also seemed like a very awesome undertaking. I always thought in terms of "the great writers" and saw them like Jesus Christ, born with some kind of aura. I never could see them as just people.

I started writing after my third child was born. I felt, because of this whole mother myth and trying so hard to be a mother in those days, that someplace I was getting lost, who I was, whatever I was. And so I started writing. I didn't think of myself as a fiction writer – in those days to be a fiction writer, that was awesome – but I started thinking in terms of doing non-fiction, writing articles.

I wrote some articles. Several of them were on scientific subjects. One was a long article about an outstanding scientist who had discovered Vitamin B and was co-discoverer of vitamin D. The *Johns Hopkins Magazine* devoted a whole issue to that article which was picked up by Voice of America and translated into Russian and Polish. I did some articles for the *Baltimore Sun,* also some book reviews and then I admitted to myself that I wanted to do fiction.

I wrote a novel in the sixties, which was about the scientific community – I knew it quite well. I had an agent – in that way I've always been fortunate – but the novel wasn't placed. Had I known then what I know now, I would have pushed harder. At the end of the sixties, I had a chance to write for national magazines as a non-fiction writer, doing free-lance articles, and decided no, I really want to focus on fiction. I was indeed fortunate because my husband was very encouraging. Once when I was offered a job as a magazine editor and would have taken it because I was discouraged, he said, "No, you write. I think you have something. Write – I'll be your patron." He was great!

I wrote a second novel. I took a risk – I wrote a novel within a novel within a novel. Editors balked at the structure of it. They were saying, this isn't the novel for us, but she's talented, we'd like to see the next novel. And then my husband got sick. I kept writing, but obviously I couldn't focus on my work.

In 1977, I had a collection of short stories, *A Stranger Here, Myself,* published shortly before my husband died. It was the first time people read my work. I was really a closet writer – it was not what you were supposed to be doing in Baltimore in the early sixties.

That helped, getting a book published. And then I was accepted at the Bunting Institute as a visiting writer. That's when the idea for writing *Ethel* came to me. My growing sense of myself as a writer, the response of others to my work, fortified me. I gave it my all. I felt it was very important to get the facts straight since it was a controversial novel about a controversial case. I spent seven years researching and writing it.

I had an agent, someone who was very committed to it. There were at least six or eight editors who loved it, but it wasn't accepted for publication. But I had toughened during this process. I said to myself, somebody is going to give in and it ain't goina be me. And I think that made the difference. I say to other writers that you have to believe in your own work more than anybody else. If you give it your all, you have to be prepared to gamble on it. And if you believe in it, you will find a way. I had said to myself, I will self-publish, but this novel is going to get published. You have to feel that way, have that much commitment. If you're shaky, it may not work. It's something women writers have to learn. Men are more resolute and can accept *no*, and just go past it. Women tend to take *no* as a measure of their worth. And they shouldn't. I feel very strongly about this.

I always felt that rejections basically said I wasn't good enough so it was incumbent on me to get better. I wanted to get better, I always do. That, to me, is tacitly understood. But something was operating here that was not any longer based on quality. And then I began to realize it was political.

This was 1987 and Reagan was in office and this was a novel that was sympathetic to the Rosenbergs. My agent finally agreed.

I went to England for a month and a friend urged me to look up a British agent she knew. My New York agent was agreeable. This woman said to me, we Europeans will have no problem with your novel, please send it to me. And she sold it to the third publisher who saw it, Collins, which now is Harper Collins, and from then on, everything worked. They bought global rights, sold it to Delacorte for the American rights, distributed it throughout the Commonwealth. A very good Dutch publisher, Meuleuhoff, bought it and translated it. What thrilled me the most was the catalogue they sent me – on facing pages, here was Philip Roth and here was Tema Nason. That felt great.

It did something for me. It's as though I can truly say I'm a novelist. And that does give you a certain fortification.

It isn't that I won't be nervous when this new one is finished and it's out. And I know if any of the book reviews are critical, it will bother me. But it was a very important step to be finally published as a novelist. It would have been very hard for me to write another novel if *Ethel* had not been accepted.

Anneliese Wagner

God's Scout

We will get rid of the Jews, Hitler says
and my parents hear him. They can
hope it will blow over. Or send me off
on a Kindertransport and make a suicide pact.
Or emigrate. It is the last thing my father
wants: leave his land, house, mother, the only
work he knows. And yet we wait years and years

for a godsend at the mail box, for
affidavits, for God to direct an angel
to scout the world
across any sea on any continent for
one person to vouch for us. Deadly mushrooms
float in our soup. A warning comes. Hiding
in a nearby village, we listen for boots
on the stairs. Sweat runs lively
under armpits and the chamber
pot tops full.

Next day, in a charade of casual shoppers
sauntering down the road home, we greet
neighbors as if nothing happened. Nothing
did, this time. *They came for you,* one says
to my father swinging the pole of his rake
to show what clubs in human hands
had meant to do.

Saturday

As if tears are rain I wash
my face this morning. As if God is
my uncle, I sit on His knee. Saturday morning
on the steps of the synagogue
I was the right height for my father's
blessing, his two hands on my head sure
roofs for the coming week. Saturday afternoon

from home through stucco walls
of houses my mother, like God, saw
everything, saw me playing alone
on the path along the Neckar, my red ball
rolling into the reeds, me running
after it.

     Look at your muddy shoes.
Pity you didn't drown. My mother tore
from my hands the wildflowers I'd picked
for her. She hit me hard
across my ear. I can't hear myself
or God cry. Rain is the river of God's tears.

Instrument

Mothers the world over
mean well. Mine says
she does as she slaps me
across the cheek, jiggle-
jawing my teeth. I am

within reach
after her arms knead bread,
churn butter, scrub
yards of floors, haul acres
of potatoes, lug deep baskets
of wet linen to the line
at the foot of the garden.

No carpet beater whacks
like her steel palm, no
splay-rod fingers leave
welts like hers, her hand
the same instrument
that all my first life

feeds me soup, cools
my fever-brow, bandages clean
gauze on bloody knees,
grasps my hand when no other
reaches to save me
from the truck headed for
the depot and the train.

Salt

Someday I will learn to love
the ocean, jump waves, dive
and chase a seaward ball, laugh while
sputtering brine. Plopped from its
lap, salt-blinded, I will sit
and hear its gruff lullaby.
Someday
     I will love the ocean, its
rightful child, delivered across
high seas by the *Columbus*, registry
Nord Deutsche Lloyd, during a slaughter
of raw wind and sea, foghorn unending.
My mother says: *You look Aryan,*
a charm too weak to spell
her and daddy too. She prays
out loud that first
night on the Channel.

In the salon above our heads
Brownshirts sing: *When Jewish blood*
spurts from the knife....
Jump or pushed, three Jews would make
a tasty snack for sharks. In terror
of blows and the brig
my father strokes
nervous knuckles on his hand.
Beneath us the ocean
rolls its loopdeloops while we
sit on our bunks as gongs
announce dinner and breakfast,
the bureau wedged against the door.
In Southampton, the Brownshirts

in civvies descend
the gangplank, soccer balls
in nets slung like
carbines. We sail on
without them, climb to the top
cold rail, released
into savage wind: eight
chancy days to walk
the German deck waiting
for sun on the fog-wrapped
roistering North Atlantic.

The Dizzy Girl

She struggles to picture
how the earth was made
if God didn't, how a mountain
happens, asks the librarian
for diagrams, sits at the window
looking into night for a blueprint
of the firmament, strains
with naked eye to see Saturn,
believes that if she thinks
hard enough, reads enough books,
watches, say, a blazing fire
correctly, how flames in
desperate ascent reach
for something high, grasp up
hand over hand a rope of air,
how underneath sticks
disappear, burn down
give heat, in their end
a beginning, she'll
know.

In the kitchen her mother, hands
sticky in dumpling dough, dips
in water, rolls an answer:
The stork brought you.
No storks in America, it says so
in *LIFE*. Medical texts
explain babies and Goldwyn's lions
roar love. The girl, a walking
menagerie of facts, trots out
her animals, earns 'A's. Somewhere
there must be a true house
of God, without her parents' scorn

for the rabbi. She likes the rabbi
but scorns God, dead
for her, killed by Hitler. Her head
lies dizzy on the pillow
until the radio's Fibber McGee
opens his closet for the whole country
to laugh at clanking junk
falling out, the cacophony like rocks
of an avalanche clattering
down the mountains of America.

Greenhorn

When I read about the old-time
rich at their Adirondack "camps" I think
of maids lugging chamber pots, men
skinning deer, guides scaling
trout, women stoking stoves to cook
seven course breakfasts, and remember
my first job, age thirteen, waiting
on table in fancy Rockaway for
Mrs. Epstein and her sister Edna,
the two taking four meals a day under
a crystal chandelier, heat
trapped by draped windows, droplets
beading their upper lips. *More pie,*
Mrs. Epstein said. *Serve coffee*
on the right. In the pantry
I detoured around the butler's
pistoning pelvis until my free hour
between lunch and tea: barefoot
walk on the beach, giant waves
crashing. From a silver platter
balanced on one hand, I served
roast beef, pudding and potatoes,
smiled, asked, *More gravy, Ma'am?*
Mrs. Epstein didn't ask for
working papers, said she likes
greenhorns: *They work hard.*
Summer's end she gave me
one hundred dollars and her old
lizard handbag from Ecuador,
a baby lizard pasted on it.

A Direction in Life

Copper-green mold creeps
up the iron strong-box stuffed
with musty college papers
creased down the middle: stout-
stringed bales of stories, poems,
essays on Yeats' plays and

Existentialism, a few stupid jokes
on restaurant napkins, snapshot
of a very young woman smiling,
waving, going off to buy
red shoes. Who does she take me for?
Blind fan? Fairy godmother? Archivist?

Who does she take me for, looking,
she notes, for a direction in life?
Where does rolling nylon stockings
down her legs, not yet nineteen
in bed in a fleabag hotel
with Gary, the Texan, take her?

Where do a sheaf of love poems
from a guy named Jerry point to? He's off
logging in the Rockies, "finding material"
while she works in a luncheonette:
four crazed pinball machines
tilting, the register jangling,

calls for BLT's lots of mayo and
a blow job on the side, honey; her
salary entered in a ruled notebook,
tips itemized. Neatly stacked, a hoard
of story plots and typing ribbon for
their shared writers' cabin-to-be

at the shore. And here're Jerry's
parting words on a postcard: "Cabin
out of the question. My nerves
shot. As last favor, please date
Andy, my Jersey friend. He's deaf."
Yes, a picture of Andy, a winsome

suitor from Jersey, clearly generous
and not mute in his five page
marriage proposal: *Good enough*
for Jerry is good enough for me.
Let's hope she sent sweet regrets
to Weehawken saying she vows to live

alone by the sea, write savage plays
and poems to wow the world. That minx,
who does she take me for, anyway?

Widow

When I think of you I picture
a cobblestone street, the half-
timbered house dim, no chairs,
no tables, no pictures, the doors
swinging on hinges, the key dropped
through the trapdoor
of the cellar floor, clinking
from rock to rock, flipping
down to the furnace of the world.

There you sit weeping. Husband
David burned up by fever, three
children under five, my mother
at your breast. Thirty-five
years the shutters bang until
roof ripped off, you flee
east, then west on the last
plane out of Prague

to the Bronx. Evenings, in
the room we share, while
your lilac-scented cat's pelt
unjinxes your rheumatic shoulder
we open the album of portraits:
David's handlebar moustache finer
than the Kaiser's; you, a waltzing
duchess, Roman-beaked in profile
glide out of the arms of barons
and hussars to spin lightfooted
past midnight toward David, lips
pursing, trembling that long year
for his first kiss. I sing: Praise,
praise for the duchess and the dance.

Requiem for Oma Berta

It's not the absence of your lavender
scent, your voice not calling my name
in German, it's not that all there is
is the official record: resident
of Heinsheim, widow
of Abraham, mother of Isaak.

It's not that they took you
on one hour's notice from the house
you came to as a bride
fifty-five years before, took you
to France, the Pyrenees, took house,
goods, the family acres, took
Fredericke, your daughter, but left
for constant replay the scene at
the station: her handkerchief waving
in slow flutter, her smile
pasted on for Inge and Siegfried as
they leaned from the train window
calling, *Auf Wiedersehen, Mutti.*

It's not that you shivered in Gurs
in the damp air of the camp
that first chill October; it's not, old
hip bone breaking, you lost the bribed
rescue to Switzerland;

it's not that you're frozen into one photo
figure, your hair center-parted, pinned
in a bun, wearing your blue polka-dot apron
over a long black dress; not that you have
no grave. Oma, for me

you are terrible. For years I forgot
to think of your 1,390 days in the mud-floor
barracks for 60 women, daily cabbage leaf
floating in foul water, bread too hard
for false teeth, nor your 1,390 nights under
one frayed blanket, bugs devouring you.
Oma, others dying or killing themselves,
what kept you alive after they loaded you
into a cattle truck in the last of France's

331 convoys, 77 in 1944, 32 in July,
one month short of eighty years old?
For three days jammed into the cattle
train to Auschwitz,
imploring God to let you die, did He?

It's not that
on the third of August I light
no candle, no candle in memory of
Berta Kahn Ottenheimer. Say no prayer.

It's that, Oma, behind our house
in the latticed gazebo covered and cooled
by grape leaves, the lemonade you poured
from the gray and blue pitcher
for our garden thirst
flowed over the beading glass
into the small hollow of the white saucer.

A Visit to the Old Émigré Doctor

Flashing eyes, skin the color of linen.
    From the bivouac of his nursing
        home bed he speaks

of courage, war, of ancient Greeks dear
    to him as his own sisters.
        In '45, on hearing Auschwitz

killed them, he went to bed, prophesied
    cancer. Ever hopeful, he waits
        through years of bed sores,

the sheet flecked red. Fingers, once feathers
    on fevered brows, scurry
        across a map of the ancient

world to the day's battle. To a charmed
    claque of nurses, doctors and
        visiting cousins wrung

pity-free, he signals late news
    of Alexander, exultant in shared
        triumph, his hand in fierce

salute on the white ramparts of skull.
    Victor, he says, *invincible*
        warrior of the field.

Alchemy

Endingen, near Freiburg

1. Trial, 1470

The Prosecutor:
Confess you butcher Christian children
for their blood, bleach it
not as sun whitens linen
but as alchemists draw gold
from lead. Confess, speak truth.
Give the formula, equipment, method
of manufacture or the flames
of hell will consume you.

First Defendant:
May it please the Court, Excellencies,
to hear our story. We slaughter
only prescribed meat, not *trefh*...

The Prosecutor:
Stick to the matter. You stand accused
not cannibals, but sorcerers who rob
more than red from blood, plunder
– as you do our coffers – innocents'
purity of soul to inspirit wafers
essential to your rituals.

Second Defendant:
May it please the Court, Excellencies,
it is Christians who say
the Lord lives in bread
held on the tongue.

Third Defendant:
May it please the Court, Excellencies,

the children are dead, yes,
but not by our hands.

Judge:
What? Here are their bones. We hold
our children dear. Dare you say
they perished at the hands
of Christians?

Light the stake!

2. *Endingen Church, 1967*

Tourist:
Where are the bones?

Sexton:
What bones?

Tourist:
The childrens' bones. The guidebook says
a reliquary in the altar
contains the Christian childrens' bones.

Sexton:
They've been removed. A few months ago.
A fuss, a big fuss over nothing. Almost
500 years in the altar. People came
from all over, like yourself.

Tourist:
A shame. Why were they taken away? What
harm did they do?

Sexton:
None. The Jews are gone. History
can't be changed. All said
and done, our bones could have been left
to us.

(Whispers into the ear of the tourist):
I've fooled them.

Tourist:
How?

Sexton:
I was told to burn the bones. Instead,
I buried them.

Tourist:
What alchemy!

Sexton:
What do you mean?

Tourist:
Save them, cherish them. History
can and does change. In time
they'll turn to gold.

Return to Heinsheim:
Ancestral House

From my first bedroom Ehrenberg glitters
gray-white in the sun, central in my child's eye
when I woke: the ruined tower a castle
rising from pines to the sky.
And our synagogue, a post-war autobody shop
now gutted, padlocked, flickers in cream sunlight.
Village synagogue and ancient keep
hold vigil for natives passing this or that year.

Helge shows me my old garden. Carrots
and asters she plants. The strawberry patch
we raided as children. In the parlor
drinking homemade currant liqueur
at 10 A.M. on a washday morning, I hold
her brother's picture, the visored cap's
swastika burning my thumb. Wehrmacht
officer, dead at thirty. Stalingrad.

In the room our eyes follow a Monarch
trapped this side of the window. *Skipping
cabbages, two little girls in dirndls run
chasing butterflies; play house: you be Mamma,
I'm Papa; trade silver necklaces, your cross
my star.* The Monarch finds a crack of air.

Passing the church, the soccer field, we walk
to the ragged edge where the village
ends, to outlying gardens, Helge's summer hut
under a cherry tree. *From the bowl of a child's
hands, small fingers choose cherry twins, loop
earrings over ears.* Helge reaches, picks
a triplet. Centuries of summer
live in the fruit. She gives it to me.

German-Hebrew Prayer Books

To throw them away
is sacrilege. You can't sell
or give them away. They're
obsolete: *machsors,* set
in Gothic German, Hebrew
en face, pages tan, covers
worn by fervent hands
at the corners, e.g. my mother's
machsor blemished with prayer stains.
Red: thanks for the season's
first strawberry; coffee: tremors
for a brother shipped
abroad. Green: worm
dead in first love's
last bouquet. A mocha-cream smudge
from the lakeside honeymoon.
Purple: pressed violets
for the May child's birth. The prayer
to curb rancor covered with coal
prints left from buckets
lugged morning
and evening from shed
to black stove.

In secret she packs one bag
for her, me and my doll, calls:
Adieu, buys one adult, one child
to a town on a map.
The fourth week her mother sends
advice on marriage and fare
back to sooty buckets, to
boiling pails, to the washtub
in the drafty shed. We stay

231 | Anneliese Wagner

away all of March, most of April
until my father – tipped off by
her own mother! – finds us.
You ran to him calling, Papa, Papa,
so happy, so loud the whole town's
shutters sprang open, my mother says
years later. *What could I do,*
keep you from him? I opened my machsor.

Village Games

1. Only Child

Please God, a sister.
A brother, like Hans-Lota.

Mother says the stork
will come. *Put sugar
on the windowsill.*
She sews

a sailor dress.
Soon I'll put it on
and run off to sea.

2. Playing Dolls

Hans-Lota, my boy doll
in peach-colored knit leggings,
cap, sweater to match
is bedded in his carriage when
my best friend, eating bread
and mustard, skips into
the courtyard to play.
I'm the papa. I navigate the buggy
across the cobbles past
chicks and grandma's
pirate goose. She's the mamma,
shakes and spanks Hans-Lota,
says, *He's a rotten kid.*
Bare-bottomed, dropped
in chicken shit, celluloid head
dented, cap torn off

Hans-Lota doesn't cry; his arm
dangles, the white-rubber thread
so stretched it won't
snap back. No matter
how much she begs
to stay until lunch, I say
no and hold my baby
against my chest, his mouth
pressing my rib until it's drained.

3. Peas

Deep in my first forest a hush weaves
tall trees into tangles until past

the Gypsy camp pine needles
become the road and I've foxed them

out of another stolen child. Famished,
knees bruised, my leaf-lined basket

of wild strawberries on the blue cloth

in the kitchen, I find my grandmother,
her lap a basin for

peas to shell. I count how many
in a pod family, roly-poly grannies

and slivery kids, before the boiling
water leaps and drags them down.

Leather Apples

Brown fuzz skin. Dribble of spicy
juice on the tongue. In one tug
a handful of tart September
pungency conjures up cider in jugs
stored all winter in the root cellar,
at every meal the pitcher's aroma.

Looking across the fields
and treetops, up towards
the ramparts of what was
a walled town with spires, words
well in the throat, taste like
gnarled, tough-hided apples,
my down-home German dialect
mangled and specific
as creature speech, slow
as country time. Nothing better
for laying curse
or speaking love.

Mouth and tongue scoured,
replenished with vocabulary fresh
as green walnuts, my first language
returns in snatches of song
about the miller: *Traveling is
the miller's joy....*

There was no miller, no mill, no
redress from *verbotens,* no place
to go no place to hide, only an hour
that last stolen afternoon
when my young mother
sang as we strolled through the forest.
From America, this is what I come for:

melodies, to draw their loved
lying words in my mother's firm
soprano from the orchard
of leather apples with all their
murderous music.

Brown Shirt

Walking the pine-needle path along the icy road I passed a tree with a big iron nail jutting from the trunk. I hung my mind on it and told myself, All is not lost, you still have your heart and soul. So I kept going until I came to a cottage at the end of the street. It looked like the house I was born in. I decided to knock. The woman said I couldn't be the girl who used to live there, that girl grew up to be a movie star. So I knocked on the door of a neighbor. No, he barked, he doesn't want a vacuum cleaner and slammed the door but the third person, an old man in a faded brown shirt said, Stand in the light. Sure enough, he recognized the scar on my forehead. So you came back to where it all happened, he said. Yes, I said, I want to hear you tell about old times. It used to be safe, the old man said, to walk in the forest.

Bunker

During the war a bunker
meant a dugout for anti-
aircraft guns like those
in pastures along the Neckar

meant a hole in the forest
floor under a camouflage
of seedlings and sheets
of moss for Jews
to hide in. For the one

who shoots
or the one who flees, a roofed
trench gives asylum, the blue
privacy of a grotto, float
of a single boat.

Dig a hole, take a blanket
and a good-size pot, disguise
the entry and leave
no forwarding address, then wait

as in the grave for nerves
to lie down, the dark to grow
thin as gauze, the door
to dreams to unlatch and
for a time

be a bear in its lair,
roll in the humus of living.

Afterword

The poems in *Murderous Music* are different from my other poems, more autobiographical, more narrative in style. As I was writing them I realized that material I had previously suppressed – my experiences as a Jewish refugee from Nazi Germany – was not only difficult to use in poems but also important.

My memory of my early life is practically non-existent. I don't remember anything at all except a vague map of the village where I was born: I know my house was over here, the castle ruin over there. But I have no memory, no visual memory of people I knew or what happened on this or that day. Nothing. Everything is wiped out until about age thirteen.

The facts in the poems are from stories my mother or other people told me, not from first-hand experience. Take "Requiem for Oma Berta," for instance. I knew that my grandmother had been in a camp in France, Gurs, and that when the camp was dissolved, she disappeared. It wasn't until I went to the Leo Baeck Institute to do some research some forty years later that, glancing through lists of names, I found my grandmother had been recorded as killed in Auschwitz. She was a very old lady and I'm convinced she died on the way there. She couldn't have lasted three days without food and water in one of those crowded cars. The records show what her name was, where she was born, where she had lived, the names of her husband and children, where she died, but I have to imagine the rest. Obviously, she couldn't have told me these things; if I had been with her I would no longer be here.

The image at the end of "Requiem" is a mystery to me. I can't explain it. I tried the poem without the image and it wasn't right. I remember that as I was writing the poem all

Adapted from a taped interview.

the lines somehow zeroed down to her and me and I saw the "beading glass." I know it didn't happen; it's not a memory. I'm making it up. I guess it's a metaphor for precious mutual moments I've forgotten. We lived in the same house for the first eight years of my life and she was my constant companion. I have a picture of the gazebo. When I think of her I think only of her suffering. Writing poems has given me the license to make certain things up.

And writing is an uncovering; it brings to light what was meant to be lost. For example, in the prose poem, "Brown Shirt," it took me a long time, months and months, to realize that what I was writing about was my early experience. Only later, by the color of the man's shirt, did I even get a slight indication of what it was: not a real memory, some kind of *ur*-memory. I wrote that poem at MacDowell where the walk to my studio led through a bit of forest. One morning a first line came to me. I started to free-associate. I wasn't looking for meaning. I wrote five versions one after the other. This one I worked on after I came home. It took me a long time to find out it was a quest, a going back, an effort to preserve something.

Take "Bunker." There aren't many positive things to say about a bunker but at the end of the poem there's an upbeat moment. The phrase is as it came to me: *the humus of living.* I must have gone back to the idea of earth, of land we owned in Germany. For many centuries Jews weren't allowed to own land, not until about two hundred years before my time. Our "land," with all its connotations, meant a great deal to my parents and grandmother. Eventually, in the States, my parents bought a house and my father had a garden. I guess my mind jumped to *humus,* the earth, the garden, something very hopeful for me.

I didn't realize for a long time how traumatic my experiences must have been to make me forget everything. We came to America with fifty dollars for the three of us. We moved in with my uncle and aunt into a tiny apartment in the east Bronx. My parents had a terribly hard time trying to find jobs.

They had no skills, didn't know the language. They were afraid. My parents saw huge headlines, a front page blow-up of a Nazi rally in Madison Square Garden held by Father Coughlin for 22,000 people. His clerical collar didn't help. They thought the war was coming any minute. And they didn't know where their mothers were – both my parents' mothers were in danger at the time – or where their siblings or other relatives were, what camp they were in. Anxiety, I think now, turned my mind to the present and fixed it there.

It wasn't until much later that I believed I had the right to think back to the life we had before we left Germany. My mother told me many stories. She always marvelled, as I still do, that we survived. Most people didn't. Why did so and so die and not me? Anne Frank was born one month after me in Frankfurt, about one hundred miles away. Her name was also Anneliese. How come I survived? Perhaps, since I survived, I ought to make it worthwhile.

* * * *

When I left Germany in 1937 I had had one year of school, which amounted to learning the alphabet. English is my second language. I once heard Richard Howard say that the language you speak in your first seven years is the language in which you write later on. I've never had the impulse to write in German, but it's a big factor in my poems. I like to speak German, particularly my old dialect, a sort of hills-of-Kentucky kind of speech, inventive and vigorous. There's a way of intimating a lot with innuendoes, with old sayings. And it's very musical. That music is definitely a part of the way I write.

I loved school, I loved learning. Take "The Dizzy Girl." It was important to know things. I learned about procreation from *Life* magazine. At some point a great landslide of information must have happened in my mind. I loved to read. My mother and father always joked about looking for me and finally finding me with my "nose in a book." Reading was my lifeline. It's what brought me to me. There was no history of learning in my family. My father traded cows, my mother scrubbed, made butter, baked bread.

And I was good in school. In fact I got a prize when I graduated from high school, a big fat treasury of poems edited by Carl van Doren. In calligraphy the citation read "For the Best Foreign Student." I was very chagrined to be considered a foreign student. I wanted to be an American. My parents were very proud that I spoke English so well and always encouraged me to correct their English. When we first came, it was a great liability to be German. Don't speak German in the streetcar, my aunt said. German clothes, German style of cooking, German songs, all suppressed. I took the cue. I forgot everything. We were lucky: we made it and that's it, close the door.

For a long time there was an unspoken prohibition against talking about the Holocaust among our relatives and friends. It was all so painful, so morbid. In the fifties people were making up for what they lost in the war, in the sixties other things were happening. For decades I didn't talk about my life as a refugee. For a long time I didn't write about it.

When I went to college people would talk about their childhood, about things like summer camp: *When I went to summer camp I did this and this. Didn't you?* Summer camp! It took me a long time to say, *I didn't go to summer camp.* When I read "Greenhorn" to an audience recently, I asked how many people had heard the term "greenhorn" before. A few older people did. It was used in a kind of affectionate yet pejorative way when I was young. We were self-conscious about being immigrants. When my mother got a job in the garment district her co-workers made fun of her German-accented English. My father suffered job discrimination, sometimes from native Jews. As you can see in "Greenhorn," I was very aware of class.

* * * *

For a long time I didn't permit myself to write. I read a great deal, wasted a lot of time sitting around and drinking coffee, smoking cigarettes. I watched a lot of TV. My husband and I were very devoted parents. We were for the most part secular Jews, not members of a synagogue. Nevertheless, I wanted my children to learn service to the community; I became a Brownie leader, a Girl Scout leader; our troop pasted Easter seals on envelopes for the lung association.

And I felt great responsibility for my parents' welfare. My mother frequently reminded me: Honor thy father and mother. I worked alongside them when they bought a store. I learned to sell. Even after I married, if they called to say they needed me, I jumped in the car and went to their aid.

I lived an ordinary life. And I was very unsatisfied. One time another young mother and I decided we'd write a play together. We sat down and wrote for a few nights after the children were in bed but didn't follow to where the writing was taking us. It wouldn't have occurred to me to take a playwriting course. It wasn't part of my job. Sometimes, instead of watching TV, I'd commit some thoughts to a notebook. I still have a pile of them, untouched in my basement for ages. I did the kind of thing would-be writers do who are not writers. They think that just because their emotions are powerful, they have intrinsic worth and deserve to be recorded.

For a long time, without realizing it, I went to the library and came home with books written by women. Adrienne Rich's books were very important to me. After I earned a master's degree in writing from Sarah Lawrence, I started to teach classes with titles like: "Images of Women in Fiction." I remember I was scared to read *The Feminist Mystique*. Some years later when I got around to *The Second Sex*, it had a blow-on-the-head effect on me. Many women fought a personal battle at that time. It was a long time before I could say I was a feminist out loud.

Then one day, in London, where my husband was director of Sarah Lawrence's summer school, Jane Cooper, who had come to teach poetry, asked if I would teach her class. "How could you ask me to do that?" I asked her. "I don't know how." Just from talking to me, she thought I could do it.

I often think that two people have had a cataclysmic impact on my life. One was Hitler and one was Jane Cooper. My mother used to say that Hitler's intent to kill me was, perversely, my good luck. Thanks to him I didn't have to throw my life away as a village drudge. The second person who had a life or death influence on me is Jane Cooper. She thought I was worthwhile. She believed I could write and teach.

While writing, I realized part of it would have to be about the girl who escaped from Germany. I can't afford not to write about it. It's very important for me to read and write about the Holocaust, to make sure people don't forget. Often I read about individuals who didn't make it, but who made it clear that what happened must be remembered. I believe I owe it to them.

I want to say how I came to the phrase, "Murderous Music." My mother had a very lovely voice. When she sang, which was seldom, it was songs she learned as a young woman in Swabia. Her lute was part of our baggage when we arrived in the States. It hung on the wall for a few years. Then, when singing seemed incongruous to her life as a cleaning woman and "salesgirl," it disappeared. When she moved to Florida, already quite old, I'd visit her and she'd sing old songs again. We'd listen to German records. The music brought back the good parts of my life, which I had denied along with the bad parts. However, music never brought back my elusive memory.

The murder part, of course, is hindsight. The music had undertones of peril all along, but German Jews preferred to ignore it. Once in a while at a movie, when the director wants to allude to Nazi Germany, a snatch of the Horst Wessel song is played. I quote it in "Salt": *When Jewish blood spurts from the knife.* I always begin to cry. Even if I'm in a perfectly good mood and the movie is good, that bit triggers tears. I don't remember hearing the song when I was a child, but I must have heard it. There were loudspeakers strung on poles all over the village. It must have been very frightening music for a young child.

Sondra Zeidenstein

Late Afternoon Woman
at the Pond

for Tilla

Late afternoon woman
lowers herself smoothly
into the pond
or slices
with her thinnest edge
the water's skin
of silver and shadow.
She has come sweated,
instep smudged with humus,
for coolness, yes,
in slow deliberate reaches,
but also for the silty
flavor staining her tongue,
silky weed threading
her thigh. Suspended,
her eyes eyed
by hovering dragonflies,
she trails slight ripples
at her shoulders, toes.
Water parted by her body
longs to join again – water
bracelets sleeve her wrists
and ankles. She wants
what the water wants.
In the center of the pond
she breathes evenly,
wears it – the whole dark
taffeta edged in hemlock
spread around her –
like a gown.

Siren

Amazing, I thought of myself as brave then.
I kept my back straight, shoulders squared.
I held my head high.
Of course my jaws were clenched
and the muscles of my cheeks
knotted like a squirrel's.
My eyes glanced down, hooded,
if anyone spoke my name.
My fingers were always at each other
grubbing flaps of cuticle loose enough
to get my teeth into.
At night I pulled Mother's
starched bleached ironed tucked sheets
tight over my mouth. And of course
I never went near the narrow mouth
of the storm drain. I'd seen runaway balls,
my favorite pink-chocolate rubber,
slow down, come to a stop – almost,
then lose their will
to the slope of the pavement,
its dark, cracked underlip.
At the reservoir I edged back
from the steep slope down to gray water,
without foothold, useless
to try to scramble back up
if some thing had whispered for me
through the scrolls of the wrought iron railing,
some thing close by, in my own house even,
with Mother downstairs.
Once I answered.

When the mouth of the air raid siren opened
in the blacked out night,
before I could take myself in hand, a scream
ripped from my sleep, long shrill ribbon flung
high above the spiral of the siren
singing alarm out over quiet, depressed houses.

On Learning, Years Later,
That My Father Had a Mistress

Who she was
    is no surprise.
        I remember
plump fingertips,
    red, red nails,
        how she said
darn it and *aw heck*
    like Mother
        when she chipped
her new polish,
    how she stirred her spit
        in a sooty palette,
how her tears
    rolled clots of soot
        down her lashes
when he made her cry.
        I remember how the clocks
        on her stockings
lengthened her ankles,
    how she'd tongue
        her finger to a ladder
climbing silk, how
    she counted dollars
        with a licked fingertip.
Har, she called him,
    like Mother. Twice
        he sent me with her
on vacation. We'd curl
    on our beds
        and she'd teach me

to oil my cuticles, leave
    a little moon uncovered.
        The boss's daughter,
she'd laugh in the faces
    of sailors who flirted.
        But I'll never, ever know
if she tended him skillfully
    as she tended her eyebrows,
        pencil-tip thin
over the absolutely bald
    bulging of her eyebone,
        if Daddy was quick,
if she minded the mussing –
    I can't fire her,
        I imagine he said,
if Mother threw the dishes
    one by one
        or swept them
in one motion off the shelf.

Getting It Right

I was the little girl
who could not breathe
in second place.
I was always the first –
narrow, pared down
my starched sash pulled too tight
the part in my wispy hair
carved with a tooth
of my mother's sharp comb –
to shoot my hand up
so high, so fast
it pulled me out of my chair
to wave it back and forth
to get the teacher's eye
up and up
as if I were waving
to the Pilgrims:
Plymouth Rock. 1620.
I loved the getting it right:
the eyes of the teacher
on my eyes, a smile
unwrinkling her lips
the swift unqualified nod
like a check mark
the silence for a moment in the room
as if I'd settled something
comforting as the chair edge
fitting the groove behind my knees.
Gold stars. *A*'s. Check marks
marching down the page.
Good's. *Excellent*'s
slanted across the top

with exclamations.
I didn't show them
to anyone else, or tell.
I'd skim them in one quick glance
like pirates' gold
more precious than my name
in my mother's mouth.

Outdoor Shower

We cram the narrow wooden stall,
unpeel our Speedos,
we three sisters
who as little girls
were naked only to mother.
I don't know which shoulder
I've lathered, whose knee
is whose, if I've even done
my ankles. The gummy slips of soap
are spangled with midges.
Yet twice a day we rush in,
fold into each other's
hollows, arrange ourselves
around the showerhead
like streamers – we
whose childhood baths were lonesome,
the shut door sealing us in
one at a time,
mother's thick fingers
scrubbing each one's clavicle,
knobby spine, scraping
each one's gray scum
down the drain,
sending each one turbaned,
flanneled, a little moist
into the chill:
tell Myrna/tell Janice
she's next.
Myrna, her nipples
smooth as peony,
arcs sideways to a knee,
Jan boasts her chest

into the coarse hot drops,
I linger in the chilly corner
half soaped, peeking.
I don't want to miss
the new pink scar
below the belly button,
the spider vein
purpling a tanned thigh.

Storm Pattern, Miami

Twice a year outside their door,
under the small brass *mezuzah*
holding its tiny white folded blessing,
I hold my breath.
I want to fly out of there
before Mother opens the door,
arms flushed red, face half turned back
to the living room.
My father, dazed, walks toward me
slowly as if leaning into a tempest.
The air, wild and trapped,
whistles with it, the old story:
how my sister whips them up like dust devils –
bursting from her room an hour ago, say,
as my plane touches down on the tarmac,
flaunting lifeless hair, withering skin,
veins in her always frightened eyes,
or announcing, *I don't want any*
when they call her to breakfast,
or coughing, *hack, hack, hack*
until she can't catch her breath.
And then it begins: my mother hissing,
Do something with yourself!
my father wrenched from his calculated calm,
the whip of his anger snapping,
my sister sobbing, fisted, stomping,
Everyone else but me has someone, has a life.
I slip through their distracted arms,
dive for a corner of the yellow-flowered couch,
lash myself into it, probe with thumb nail
the tenderness of my writing callus,
swallow my shining life.

Mother's Milk

Her last act of mothering at night
was to tip the burnt and silvery tin of syrup
above the glass of cold white milk
and wait
while a slow tongue of chocolate
slid from the puncture
gathered its weight at the rim
and plunged
a dark snake shimmering
into the blank white round
as if a channel had opened for it –
rising then as a disc of darkness
a quarter inch
and *clack clatter clack,* her spoon
furious against glass
milk spinning down the handle
in a whirlpool, she whips it
until the rich stuff
stubborn as pond muck
thins, mists, pink tint at first
then lavender, deepening.
I take it eagerly
draw it down
past Shirley Temple's curls
and smiling teeth. No kiss
or touch or tucking in
but my tongue is coated with sweet.
In the morning, a hollow ache
sudden as a puncture, then
I enter my dress, flowery and crisp

Mother ties a pretty sash around my waist
draws the blue and yellow hairbow
through my hair.
I never tell her it pinches.

Now Daughter

Now daughter, when we sit across from each other,
necks thrust forward, talking about your work,
how you midwife babies into the world
and you skim with two fingers
your soft dry lips as you talk,
I remember how I stroked your cheek,
its fine red veins,
as you sucked the nipple of your bottle.
(I didn't want to feed you from my breasts,
though once out of some belated longing
I forced my nipple between your lips
and you spit it sourly.)
God! how long you would take sucking
with half-interested puckers.
An hour for three ounces.
You didn't have an appetite
for spending your days in my silent
other-mindedness
when I wasn't fitting you into a pink nylon snowsuit,
tucking you deep in the shadow of a carriage,
putting you down in playpen, high chair, sandbox.
I think you wanted to hold me there, make me
not just test the pale, sweet formula
on my thin wrist, not just needle the nipple hole
wide enough for your faint drawing,
but look from the blue and white dance of television
to the small pink birth stains
darkening between your eyebrows.
I wanted to sleep, burrow into darkness.
I gave you morning nap, afternoon nap, put you to sleep
at six. My dog – russet at the corner of my eye –

let faint interest be enough, but you made me
watch your clear eyes doze up under your lids,
touch your cheek, tickle the small fat sole
of your foot, flick it with thumb and middle finger
until your body startled
and your lazy mouth remembered.
You set yourself against my darkness,
spun me like a thread from my knotted spirit, you held me
to the world.

After Reading *Hole in the World*
by Richard Rhodes

After I scarfed all two hundred and fifty pages –
his mother's suicide, stepmother's dumb cruelty, his growing
    up –
in one starved, bug-eyed gulp,
I hugged its hard bulk against my breast bone
where for weeks now I have ached
as if a brace, a bandage, a Dr. Scholl's moleskin pad
had been peeled.

She wouldn't let him take a bath – he stank with grime.
She wouldn't let him pee at night – his sphincters cramped.
She fed him weeks' old beans while she sat mopping steak
    grease.
She beat him with a studded belt.

I envy him.
Mother cut lamb for me in mouth size bites.
She punctured tins of sweet Carnation milk for my cereal.
She put me to sleep with chocolate.
She sat me in the tub, her square knees
wormy with the imprint of chenille and
scrubbed the stubborn skin below my hair line.
She twirled her finger in my ear.

I envy him.
I cannot dredge up one slap,
one threat that would explain the digging
at my breastbone
I spent my childhood covering.

No evidence except this rim of bone burning
as if it were her tub
scrubbed blue white with Bon Ami,
vast glaring absence,
not one pubic hair curled on the porcelain,
no telltale weave of skin cells and soap scum
clutters the drain.

After I heard the news

and called the children
and got our flights
confirmed and packed dark clothes
an appetite came over me.

Wollensky's Grill. You
would have hated it.
Confidences flung
at the top of the voice.

Easy laughter. Flippant
waiters. And the prices!
Even I had trouble.
But oh boy, Dad

with you dead I suddenly
felt hungry. Juicy New York
strip. Arugula. Imported
beer on tap. My senses

pummeled. Then all at once
mid-spittle, the whole scene
dims. A sullen little
spirit whisks my forehead

just between the eyes. *Not now
Dad,* I manage and the din
resumes. I raise my Tuborg
to the rumpus. *Later*

will be time enough.

Last Rites, Miami

1

He lies in an unlined box.
They have taken his glasses,
tinted his skin, shaved stubble from ruts

in his slack flesh, his yellow
knit shirt is open at the neck.
We ride behind him a long way

out of the city, huddle
under a canopy – it is not raining.
The slot, sharp-cornered, lines up

in the rectangle of grass the way
he placed a stamp, edge cleanly
separated, on an envelope.

The dapper rabbi slices our black ribbons,
chants the magnitude of God. A cup
of sand is passed. We sprinkle it.

Two Haitian men unwind the winch. The box
sways a little in the onshore breeze,
enters without nicking.

2

Back from the burial,
Mother leaves the door ajar.

They come on walkers,
canes, in wheelchairs,

they tell their stories:

My husband. Ten days
in intensive. The children
slept on cots outside.

My son — at thirty-nine. Why,
I begged the rabbi.

Yours was a blessing,
not like mine.

Slowly, Mother begins:

Oatmeal for breakfast,
the way he liked it.
I heard a thump.

He was still warm, curled —
she makes a cradle
of her chunky fingers —
like a baby sleeping.

3
White sun. Endless flat. Growling
flight path overhead. We stand
bewildered on the grass, zoyzia
daggery and coarse,
not like a lawn up north.
                    Xeroxed map
provided by the cemetarian, we track
Mt. Sinai section, Mt. Tabor,
then sixteen paces from the path
his plot, the temporary nameplate
overgrown.
            I should have brought
scissors, Mother says.
                    Sweat pearls
her forehead. *I wanted aboveground,*
my brother has one, what do you call it —
a crypt?

Mother, come out of the sun.
He didn't say 'I'm dying' or anything.
Another jumbo levels out and rumbles north.
He won't like the racket.
                    Mother!
She flaps her fingers at the grass –
hello and goodbye – the way she shrugs
a daughter's two-day visit.

4
Our mothers, all of them blond and curly
sit by the pool in flowering latex

sandals stretched
to the spread of their bones:

*Milly broke her hip
falling in the lobby.*

*Sadie couldn't climb
out of her tub all day.*

A sun-stained woman –
at ninety-one the queen –

starts from her drowse.
Selma's days are numbered,

she pronounces. Gold heads
turn. She dozes.

*Dinner I put a book
in my hand, put the food*

*in somehow,
I don't even know.*

The queen wriggles forward,
tries once, twice

Give me time, rises,
stumbles toward the elevator

holding the wall,
stops a moment leaning,

all eyes on her.

Achille Lauro

I refused to read about it
but this morning in the tub
helpless to turn off television
I heard how they shot
one old man in a wheelchair
and dumped him into the sea
I saw the wife
platinum like my mother

Which of you are Jews, they asked

I don't want to leave my house
my russet dog
the red fox I saw dash
across the highway
into the golden field
the flaming maple

but when they hold the gun
at my forehead
the turquoise sky
promising Jerusalem
(they made them sit without hats
platinum heads in the sun)

may I remember how
the red fox slides into gold
how geese in the port of Dragor
where Danes launched
their Jews to safety
chew the grass with a constant
chip chip chip

may I despair
that I have not mourned
the Palestinian child
dark with wild curls in the rubble

only the Jew, only the old Jew
at the ship rail

The Fault

for Laura and Susan

These two women, lovers,
mothers of newborn
Julian
split the earth
along its fault:

those who trust
that love
surely
as the rush
of milk
will nourish;

and those who'd
narrow
to the sanctioned
jet of semen
who would be allowed
to bear a child.

These two women lovers
drive a canyon
deep as Susan

witching her love
when labor slows
in the terrible night

with tales
of how the moon
draws down the tides
draws down;

wide as Laura
on her hands and knees
opening.

These two women
draw the line

firm as the memory
of curls
in Laura's sweated hair

unambiguous
as Julian's crimson cry

sure as the fit
of lips to nipple.

Let skeptics
rear back
in discomfort.

The blessed
hold up a flower
and smile.

My love...

I am always startled
after the dark passage –
muck rich swamp or silty rapids –
to arrive in our narrow room
sunlight blazing
around the window sash
to see your eyes
vivid as summer
almost Ionian
and your cheeks –
sunrise or an August peach –
the pink life
of your loved face
looking at mine.
How long and slow
its flowering
like the hard, unpromising
bud of a peony
this love, candid
as the skin
of your cheek
most delicate parchment
I curve in my palm
or graze
with the backs
of my fingers.
How we smile and smile
as if moored!
How my thumb
wanders to touch – there
just there
around your eyes

the elaborately
fleshed-in socket
intricate as old smocking
as silk bouclé
with its random knots
and ravels –
our fine expendable lining.

The One Dream
(A Spell)

Over this longmarried pair sprinkle nepenthe.
Let them forget for an hour on Sunday
    Afghanistan, Palestinian camps, child's face
    crumpling under a threat.
Clear the airwaves honeycombed with sorrow.

Let the sun flash through maple flowers tasseled
    like earrings, through smallpaned windows,
    touch their peach duvet, peach flannel sheets.

Let karmas of cramped children, stunting parents
    give room.
Shut the sad brain, let them be skin only.
Draw a circle around their cherrywood bed for this hour.

Let the peach glow of the cave burnish away
    their imperfections.
Let their eyes be slits, discriminating.
Let hands soften, hips unknot, backs let go
    old compressions.
Let failure spice their soft bellies, their tinder
    take fire.

Let them not be young betraying each other, oh not young.

Let them touch each other's eyes smiling.
Let words move sweetly in their saliva.
Let her breasts be richly complicated.
Let his penis rise wise and humble.
Let him seek her in his fingertips.
Let her moisten a tangy nectar.
Let them be careless, slippery, forgiving.

Let their cries enter brooks rushing the gorge,
        ring in the calls of Canada geese,
        red-eyed vireo, raccoon.
Let that saferoom spread its held heat into the world.
And let them naked, entwined, sleep,
        dreaming like Vishnu
        the one dream.

                              for George

Afterword

I started writing when I was forty-eight. The outpouring of creative energy released by hard work in psychotherapy was steady and blissful. I rushed to my writing with joy. By the age of fifty, I knew that poetry was my genre. My first teachers, Honor Moore and Joan Larkin, nurtured me and gave me ideology. The poems of Sharon Olds gave me hope. I have been writing poems for almost ten years, hardly stopping for breath until now when, restless, ready to move on, but not sure of my direction, I want to collect what I have done so far.

Gathering my poems into a collection has given me a chance to see what my imagination looks like. So many mouths, fingers, tongues, cheeks, veins, nipples, thighs! So much skin! So many reds, pinks, purples. So many poems about mother, father, sisters, daughter, and then mother and mother again. Not without pain, I see that the vein of poetic inspiration these ten years has been narrow. My muse has ignored my intellectual life as student, teacher, critic and editor, my years of travel, my years of living deeply in other cultures. My muse is not interested in ideas. For a moment I am dismayed. Oh, is this all – after so many years of work!

And then I remind myself that my journey as a late blossoming poet is out of suffocating silence. I was potently stripped of expressive life in infancy. The possibility of making language my own, of making shape and song, has come to me very late. In these ten years of finding voice and form, of learning craft, my real struggle, I think, has been to fight off the voices in my head that want me not to say anything. Or if I must, to say it nicely.

The voices are strong. They say, *How can you be writing this kind of poem at sixty. Anger is bad for you. Especially anger against Mother. Grow up. Anyway, it's been done. And it's not lovable. Or*

literary. The voices are menacing. One of my earliest attempts
at a poem begins:

> Cold woman
> my familiar
> my demon
> comes at blood's ebb
> mocking:
> > *Ridiculous!*
> > *Your life, your words!*
> > same old litany
> > *Too many years*
> > *of silence*
> > *ever to dance*
> > *so old*
> > *no matter how mauve*
> > *and gauze*
> > *your dress.*
> > *Give up.*
> > *Give up.*

I have had to fight my self every inch of the way for my
existence as a poet. I cannot bear to part with Mother,
destructive though she has been. Nor can I bear to fulfill her
curse that I be silent. Therapy has brought the conflict to
consciousness. For me, therapy has been like going down
into a collapsed mine, through a landscape of dread and
loss, to rescue the separateness of my own breath, the truth
of my own eyesight. My poems are not therapy, though,
by saying what I don't yet know I know, they light my way to
the surface.

So I am not surprised that my muse is obsessed with
warped relationship. She is right. Where, if not in my poems,
should I move against the threat to my creative life. This is
my last chance. These poems are my voice hauling me out of
silence.

* * * *

In narrowing my collection of poems to a representative core, I let go, with only a few regrets, early poems that were bold but not fully realized, new poems whose faults I knew I couldn't yet see, favorite poems whose subject matter was outside the evolving scope of the collection, my "pretty" poems, melodic and boring. But one poem that clearly belongs in this collection I didn't even consider publishing. I was afraid its appearance would make me feel uncomfortable with three or four of the people I hold most dear. It is a love poem – to my husband. I have written other love poems to him and never thought twice about publishing them. But this one comes out of my separateness in marriage, not my union. It reveals secrets.

I survived infancy and childhood by secrecy, especially by keeping the truth of my terrible deprivation from my own heart. I lived my experiences as if they were discrete, as if each took place in a sealed, windowless compartment. The connection, the integration of experiences was missing. For the rest of my life, I will be blasting open passageways, letting in air and sunlight.

The poem I am not willing to publish now came to me easily, unexpectedly, riding its energy like a skilled surfer. I wrote it at Squaw Valley Writer's Workshop. It is not a poem I was likely to have written at home under the shadow of my censors. Participants at Squaw write a poem a day. This poem came on day five when my unconscious had no time to swing its barricades into place. I like the form, the music, the voice – the poem rings true to me. I wish I didn't feel I had to hold it back. But I would mind much, much more not having written it.

I want to open to the secret places more boldly. To write anything. I can decide later what I will publish. I don't want to swallow my words because a censor stands guard over my unconscious, the way Mother stands at the bedroom door in all my sex dreams, her lips pressed in disapproval, her arms folded over her breasts.

The problem is that I don't know what my fears are, what

my secrets are. I only know that the thrust of my language toward honesty is hemmed in on every side. I have to find ways to support myself in subverting my negative voices.

I know I need time and place, the support of critic friends who want me to be bold. I need to keep from revising the "objectionable" out of my poems. I need to be my own diagnostician. Read Schuyler, I advise myself, for the way he brings his "dailiness" into poems. Read Carver for his shocking honesty about his children. Read them all for words I'd never dare to write: *In my vagina, I am always beautiful,* in Elaine Terranova's poem *Second Marriage. I stopped trying not to have his* [my father's] *bad breath,* in Sharon Olds' poem *Fate.* Read any poem of Olds for words I won't push myself far enough to say. Read again and again poems by gay and lesbian writers, by feminist writers, for their urgency, by Marilyn Hacker and other formalists for their outrageousness.

I do not need now another workshop where criticism and craft are the focus. In the last ten years, I've attended six such workshops. I've received useful criticism and learned by criticizing the work of others how to help my own poems. But too often I've had to take home a scribbled-over poem, holding it gingerly by the corner of the page as if it had been slimed, and put it away for months until I can look at it again.

I'm not sure any group is appropriate for me right now. For more than five years I belonged to a wonderful support group with a shared ideology – a commitment to emotional honesty. Now I belong to a group that combines criticism and support. We are a dozen women, most of us middle-aged, some beginners, some accomplished poets. Our meetings are marked by talent, intelligence, open-mindedness and an unusual depth of grace. Unfortunately, I have come to want the approval of the group – another kind of hemming in. I feel myself influenced in my selection of words and in what I leave out, by what I imagine they will like. I am afraid to have their gentle voices in my head.

What seems most right for me now is the experience of

279 | Sondra Zeidenstein

Squaw Valley Writer's Workshop – the experience of creation, not criticism, as Galway Kinnell has described the program. I have gone to the workshop for three summers. At Squaw Valley, participants are challenged to be shameless, to write without inhibition. We are reminded that a poet is someone who wants to share her most private soul. We write a poem a day for seven days. There is no time to worry even if the reception to our work is indifferent. No time, in my case, to indulge the negativity that rushes in like thunder when I've opened to language.

The first two summers, the experience was mouth-drying (not only from altitude) and nerve-wracking. I didn't sleep. I lost three pounds. My resistance was palpable, like gristle, like a clenched muscle. *I won't. I won't.* But I need that next poem. The third summer I learned to trust my unconscious, to rise early for that morning's poem, to release what was brimming, to let the rest of the day, mysteriously joyful, fill me for the next morning. I experienced for the first time what it feels like to allow no-one's voice, not my own negativity or anyone else's criticism or indifference, to curb or bridle me. For the first time in my life, I was unafraid of my own voice. I need to hold on to the memory of that experience in my daily work.

Above all I need to remember what I, feeling timid and circumscribed, call boldness. I need to push on through the image, through sensory detail, relentlessly, until I get to the nakedness which is always new. I respond to all sorts of poems, to all magic in the music of language. I am in love with poems. But my soul, my core, responds to the deepest, most courageous openings of another soul. That someone would say *that*, name *that*. Then I am touched. Then I am not alone. Then I experience what I crave above all else – profound connection. I know this is what I want to do in my poems. This is my challenge in my sixties.

Also available from Chicory Blue Press

A Wider Giving: Women Writing after a Long Silence, edited by Sondra Zeidenstein. "A masterly achievement." – May Sarton.

Memoir, poems by Honor Moore. "It is not only beautiful work, it is brave." – Carolyn Forché.

Heart of the Flower: Poems for the Sensuous Gardener, edited by Sondra Zeidenstein. "This is an anthology of pure delight." – Gerald Stern.

....

Order from:

Chicory Blue Press, Inc.
795 East Street North
Goshen,CT 06756
(860) 491-2271

Please send me the following books:

_____ copies of *The Crimson Edge* at $16.95

_____ copies of *Heart of the Flower* at $13.95

_____ copies of *Memoir* at $11.95

_____ copies of *A Wider Giving* at $14.95

Name _____

Address _____

_____

Connecticut residents, please add sales tax.

Shipping: Add $1.75 for the first book and $.50 for each additional book. Or $2.50 per book for Air Mail.